COLD JUSTICE SERIES
Coming soon: *Cold Light of Day* (Book #3)
Cold Pursuit (Book #2)
A Cold Dark Place (Book #1)

THE BARKLEY SOUND SERIES
Dark Waters
Dangerous Waters

STAND-ALONE TITLES
The Killing Game
Edge of Survival
Storm Warning
Sea of Suspicion

'HER' ROMANTIC SUSPENSE SERIES
Her Last Chance
Her Sanctuary

For Jean Anderson.
Who never stopped asking for this story.
Best mother-in-law ever.

Chapter One

Her footsteps rapped loudly against Bleecker Street's bustling sidewalk, her swirling black coat creating an illusion of sophistication that usually amused her. But not right now. Josephine Maxwell kept her head down and her stride firm, only the white-knuckled grip on the handle of her art portfolio betraying her inner apprehension.

Her eyes scanned the street. Fear prickled her skin and crawled up her spine. Fear was weakness. She'd learned that before she'd hit double digits.

Stealing a short, hard breath, she figured she should be used to it by now.

The usual Friday night cocktail of locals and tourists milled about in every direction, all intent on devouring the vibrant Greenwich Village scene. Trees lined the avenues, the base of their trunks dressed up in fancy metal grills. The smell of freshly baked bread wafted warm and fragrant on the chill fall breeze. Lights began to glow as the sun started to fade behind Jersey.

And *still* fear stalked her.

Nothing stood out from any other day except the subtle sensation of being hunted. Danger flickered through her and her heart gave a stutter. She ignored it, pressed down the tendrils of panic and kept on walking—nearly home. Nearly safe.

On the patio of a little Italian restaurant, a swarthy dark-haired man in an expensive business suit stared at her with hunger in his eyes. Never breaking eye contact, he tipped back a bottle of beer and took a long swallow. The action brought a childhood memory sharply into focus and a fine shudder ran through her bones. Uber-confident, the guy raised an eyebrow and curled his tongue suggestively around the top of the bottle. Her stomach somersaulted. For one split-second he reminded her of Andrew DeLattio, but thankfully that murdering asshole was dead.

She didn't flip the guy off. The old Josie would have, but nowadays the concrete backbone she'd constructed over the years had started to disintegrate, leaving her less sure of herself, less bold.

She looked away. What the hell was wrong with men anyway?

The memory of one tall, good-looking federal agent flashed through her mind, but she shut it down, determined to forget the biggest mistake of her life. She didn't have time for self-pity or regrets. Life was a struggle for survival, so why waste energy with delusions or fantasies of what-might-have-been?

She kept walking. The odor of wet tarmac, exhaust fumes and damp fallen leaves mingled with hot spicy foods from nearby restaurants. Her stomach rumbled, reminding her she'd skipped lunch. But the need to get home, to escape this irrational fear overrode even basic hunger. Her footsteps quickened and the urge to bolt hit her with every instinct she possessed. She walked faster. Turning the corner to her Grove Street apartment, she watched a piece of litter keeping pace with her boots before being swept ahead on a stronger gust of wind. Fighting the breeze, she shifted her unwieldy portfolio to her other hand. It was heavy, but at least the contents had gotten her another commission.

Dusk was starting to take hold. Sinister shadows hovered between parked cars. Dying leaves rustled as they fell from spindly branches. Finally she was home. A siren went off in the distance as she groped in her coat pocket for the key to the main door of the apartment building. She slid a furtive glance around, saw nothing to justify this uneasy sensation of being watched.

When am I going to stop looking over my shoulder?

Biting back a curse, she shoved her key into the lock and pushed open the heavy black door, wrestling the massive case through the narrow gap.

The lights were off.

A drop of perspiration rolled down her temple. Her hands shook as she turned on the lights and she breathed out a massive sigh of relief when illumination flooded the stairwell. Stepping across the threshold, she closed the door and bent to open her mailbox on the bottom row. A brush of sound was all the warning she had before someone grabbed her around the neck.

She dropped her portfolio. Mail scattered as her attacker swung her off her feet and whirled her around. Adrenaline surged through her bloodstream, sending her pulse skyrocketing. Her fingers dug into cloth and flesh, and she somehow managed to gather enough purchase to stop her weight from snapping her own neck. Her legs smashed into the balustrade, shooting pain through her limbs.

Crying out, she gulped a breath as he dumped

her to the floor. Her vision blurred. She lay there in shock. Then survival instinct kicked in. She rolled, scrambling away from the whistle of steel that grazed her ear as the knife hit the mosaic tiles with a sharp crack. On hands and knees she snatched up her portfolio, twisted, falling onto her back, using it as a shield from that sharp hunter's blade. They stared at each other, frozen.

She recognized him.

Recognized the sharp intent in those lifeless silver disks.

Oh, God.

Sickness stirred in her stomach as she stared up at him, helpless. She'd always known he'd come back. *Always known.* The constricted muscles of her throat choked the breath she so desperately needed as they watched each other in silence. Predator versus weak, pathetic, useless prey.

Dressed in black, a balaclava covering his features, he crouched beside her, a dark faceless monster. Ice-gray eyes stared from thin slits, reflecting the gleam of the knife he carried in his left hand. He wore surgical gloves that made his flesh look waxy as a corpse. Blood smeared the latex.

Whose blood?

Moving slowly, as if he knew he'd won, the monster lifted the portfolio from her shaky grasp and laid it carefully against the wall beneath the mailboxes. She couldn't move; just lay there petrified as memories bombarded her.

The predator tilted his head, considering her as if she were already cut and bleeding. He clenched the handle of the knife, strong fingers squeezing the weapon possessively. For all her big mouth and fighting pride she could not move. Because he'd *created* her all those years ago. He'd created her and now he was back to destroy her.

Without hurry he flicked open the buttons on her coat. Lifted her sweater up and over her breasts and terror welded her to the spot. He cut the material of her bra with a jerk of his wrist.

Nausea threatened, but she forced it back. Cold air flicked over her skin. *I can't survive this twice.* The memory of pain crawled over her body like hives. She told her limbs to work, to move, but they wouldn't obey.

Is this what I've been waiting for? For him to come back and finish the job? She flinched as his finger traced a faded scar.

What did he think of his ancient handiwork?

He lifted the knife. She watched as he trailed its razor edge along a furrow of shiny, white scar tissue. From her hipbone, up across her stomach, slowly, over her ribs, *bump, bump, bump.* She held her breath. The flat edge of the knife stroked her nipple, and horror, not desire, had it puckering.

His mouth was hidden by the mask but Josie knew he was smiling. Tears formed. Bile burned the lining of her throat. Their eyes locked and she clenched her fists in frustrated rage as he turned the knife upright and let the weight bear down into her chest. Blood pearled. Pain burst along her nerves with excruciating clarity.

Sucking in a gasp, she braced herself. "You promised if I didn't make a sound you wouldn't kill me." Her voice was ragged, air stroking her vocal chords with the sensitivity of barbed wire.

Time suspended between them like a big fat spider on a whisper of silk. The light in his eyes darkened. "You just made a sound."

She whacked the flat of her hand as hard as she could against his ear and grabbed at his knife-hand, pushing it away from her body. She sank her teeth into his wrist, narrowly avoiding getting a knife in the face. His pulse beat solidly against her lips as she clamped her jaws together until she tasted blood. She didn't let go.

Her other hand clawed at his eye, her legs finally working as they scrambled for purchase on the slick tile. His body fell against her hip, his breath hot and violent against her cheek. Gouging her sharp fingernails into his eye socket, she scratched at the smooth hard shell of his eyeball. Blood filled her mouth, the taste of him bitter and repugnant on her tongue. Her stomach twisted but she didn't ease up. If she did, he would kill her.

With a furious roar, he fell back. Scrambling to her feet, Josie grabbed her portfolio from against the wall and held it in front of her again as a last desperate defense. The predator rubbed his hand over eyes that glowed with malevolence.

In her nightmares he was immortal, unstoppable. In reality, he was just another fucking asshole who liked to hurt people. And God help her, right now he wanted to hurt her.

***

Aesthetically, the 17th Century Dutch painting with its fake *De Hooch* signature left Special Agent in Charge Marshall Hayes colder than a witch's tit, but even so his chest tightened and his heart rate stepped up a gear. It was only 7:30 PM but the place was packed for the grand opening of yet another trendy New York art gallery. The party atmosphere and chattering crowd faded as he took a closer look. Someone jostled his elbow, someone else brushed his ass. He ignored everything except the painting.

It had been stolen a month before the infamous Isabella Stewart Gardner Museum robbery and the two might be linked. The theft had been kept under wraps because the owner didn't want to look like a moron for hanging artwork worth a fortune on his lounge wall with nothing but an aging German shepherd for security. It wasn't even listed on the National Stolen Art File or Interpol.

So maybe after so many years the thieves had figured the painting was finally safe to fence. Or maybe the thief died and the painting had passed into the hands of a legitimate collector. Marsh didn't know, but it was his business to find out.

Anticipation tingled over his skin. The suckers who'd opened this gallery had probably been taken for a lot of money. Unless they were involved...

Music beat through the air with the low throb of sex. Cameras exploded in the background like emergency flares. Marsh looked across the room. Gloria Faraday, one of the owners, was air-kissing some woman wearing thin silk on a cold New York night. He vaguely recognized the new arrival from billboards. Some cat-walk model who'd been outed in the tabloids for drug addiction and had just got out of rehab.

His mind wandered to another woman with a waif-like figure, big blue eyes and a *Titanic* attitude problem. He forced the image away. He was working, dammit.

A nipple peeked out of the model's halter-top, a quick flash of scandal sure to make tomorrow's gossip pages. With carefully staged embarrassment, she slipped the silk back in place and moved away from the cameras. Maybe sensing his gaze, she tilted her head and met his eyes. He didn't smile, but didn't look away either. She swept him with a look that switched to interested in a heartbeat.

Marsh turned away, irritated with his own lack of interest in an undeniably attractive woman. And okay, it wasn't a lack of interest in beautiful women that bothered him, more his obsession with one particular female. His teeth locked as he pushed Josephine out of his mind and reminded himself once again he was on the job—kind of.

The owners, Philip and Gloria Faraday, were British nationals, recently moved from Paris. He didn't know much about them—yet. Not even if they were husband and wife, siblings or a couple of hustlers looking for fresh marks in the Big Apple.

Gloria looked early forties, but it was hard to tell exactly in the era of cosmetic age reduction. She wore thick makeup and a garish print blouse that clashed and repelled the eye. Philip looked younger, dressed down in designer jeans and a long-sleeved gray tee. He sported a salt-and-pepper crew cut and dark glasses even though it was dark outside. Pretentious ass.

Philip slipped through a discreetly hidden door, probably a storage area or maybe where they kept the cash register in a place too up-market for price tags.

The Faradays owned galleries in London, Paris, Barcelona, Nairobi, Sydney & Tokyo, and now it seemed they'd decided to head west. Total Mastery NY was a nicely put together concept. Old masters mixed with contemporary artwork to update the classic look. Crusty old portraits hung above funky metallic vases, exquisitely carved side-tables complimenting the paintings and ceramics. A classy place. Persuading the clientele you really could buy good taste.

Marsh caught Steve Dancer's eye through the crowd. He nodded to his tech who returned the look with a familiar light of excitement in his eyes. *Game on.*

"What do you think of it?" The woman at his side stood on tiptoe and raised her voice over the noise of the crowd.

Damn. He'd forgotten about her.

Lynn Richards was beautiful, charming and well-bred—apparently all the ingredients for a perfect wife. And sexually she did as much for him as the portrait. Her mother had told him that the girl was eager to attend the opening and she knew he was going, so would he take her? Lynn provided good cover so he'd agreed, but she seemed to think they were on a date which made him feel like a goddamn pedophile. He did not date children.

She dug her nails harder into his bicep and he winced. He twisted slightly, loosening the girl's talons without making it obvious. But she clung.

He smiled but it was grim at the edges; hell, he felt grim at the edges. "What do *you* think?" he countered, willing the girl to get an opinion of her own and stop trying to please other people. Why else would she be out with a man old enough to be her father? Although, damned if he knew what it said about a man in his position that he'd ended up manipulated by his own mother. Just thinking about it made his jaw clench in frustration.

If his elder brother had made it out of the

Middle East alive no one would give a damn whether or not Marsh got married and produced an heir to the family fortune. But Robert had died in the Iraqi desert and a giant piece of Marsh's heart had died alongside him on the battlefield. His parents had been shattered.

Marsh's suggestion to leave everything to the dog-pound hadn't gone over well. He loved his mother. There was nothing he wouldn't do for her, except get married to some debutante. How in God's name did he explain that being drugged, handcuffed to a bed and having sex with a woman who hated his guts had been the best experience of his life? One that had altered him forever and made every other encounter pale into insignificance?

A tortured laugh escaped unbidden.

He straightened the cuffs of his tailored jacket and exhaled until his diaphragm collided with his stomach. He was tired of fighting about it.

"I like it." Lynn flashed him a hesitant smile.

He jumped. Crap. He'd forgotten about her again and she was so damn polite she made his head ache.

"But I'm not really into art." Lynn clung to his arm like a limpet-mine.

Looking into her innocent young eyes, Marsh struggled not to feel like an annoyed parent. *Christ.* "Then why did you want to attend tonight?"

A flash of guilt and annoyance moved across her features. Dammit, he could almost see their mothers clacking like hens as they plotted his matrimonial downfall. *How do I get into this shit?*

His jacket gaped and her startled gaze flew to his holster, carefully concealed beneath the dark wool.

Exasperated, he put his hands on her shoulders, held her gaze. "Lynn, you *know* I'm with the FBI, right?"

Eyes as wide as cue balls, she nodded, and he wanted to ask what the hell she was doing with a man she didn't know, who she couldn't possibly have anything in common with and who obviously scared the crap out of her?

She was a teenager, so what was his excuse?

Sighing with resignation, he looked for Dancer through the thickening crowd and told himself he wasn't searching for another face, another blonde...just because he was in New York City. Dancer was propping up a wall, soaking up sparkling champagne within a ring of women all vying for his attention.

Women. Not children.

Lynn followed his gaze and her eyes lit on Special Agent Dancer with a flicker of interest. Maybe Marsh should introduce them and she could fall head-over-heels in love with his agent, they could get married and have babies.

The idea brought an unexpected pang of envy curling through his gut. Not for Lynn. For someone else. He squashed the thoughts.

He caught Dancer's gaze and jerked his head toward the back room. *Watch Philip Faraday.* With stolen property on the premises no artwork was leaving this building until provenance was proven for each and every piece. They'd decide later whether the Faradays faced criminal charges for handling and trying to sell stolen goods.

Marsh looked around the gathered celebrities and reporters and braced himself for a general explosion of hysteria. The situation had goatfuck written all over it. Unfortunately his undercover people hadn't been able to wrangle an early viewing and he hadn't wanted to tip the Faradays' hand by telling them the FBI wanted to go over their inventory prior to tonight's big opening.

"Well, well. If it isn't Marshall Hayes." A low hearty rumble called out behind him. "You still chasing bad guys?"

Marsh recognized the voice before he turned to face the newcomer. *Just when you thought it couldn't get any worse...*

"Brook." He schooled his features into flat lines of polite indifference. "I heard you were back in the country."

Brook Duvall was the former United States Ambassador to Australia and a newly elected senator with an eye on the next presidential campaign. The prematurely gray-haired politician practiced his perfect smile, but Marsh recognized the shrewd gleam in his eyes.

They'd trained together at the US Naval Academy nearly two decades before. Duvall had been in his final year when Marsh was a sophomore. He'd been a political animal even back then, unashamedly using his contacts and influence to cushion his term in the Navy and launch his career using any leverage he could find.

Marsh had been guarded about his family connections until Duvall had outed him during a training exercise along the intracoastal. Marsh had worked his balls off to gain the respect of the men under his command and had to redouble the effort once they'd found out he had a five-star Army general for a father.

They shook hands, the senator's still cold from

being outside and Marsh suddenly let go of his tension. His grudge was a little too insubstantial to hold on to after all these years.

"This is my wife, Pru." Duvall drew forward a beautifully put together twin-set and pearls lady. A pale looking aide hovered behind them, wringing his hands and holding his cell phone like a cherished baby.

"Nice to meet you, ma'am." Marsh took Pru Duvall's hand and introduced Lynn to them both, not missing the obvious leer of appreciation lighting the politician's gaze or the way his fingers lingered on Lynn's that fraction too long.

Pru smiled and took Lynn's hand, sliced a look at Marsh that clearly said he should know better than to date a girl too young to drink liquor. "I believe I went to school with your mother, Lynn." *Ouch.*

For the hell of it, Marsh slipped his arm lightly around Lynn's shoulders and watched the frost build on the face of a potential future First Lady. His smile was all teeth. Hers was all lipstick.

But when Lynn melted into him like chocolate on a warm day a pang of regret shot through his conscience.

"You still with the FBI, Marshall?" Brook eyed Lynn's cleavage, which Marsh hadn't noticed until that moment. Right now the swell of her breast was pressed up against his shoulder holster, chafing his skin and interfering with access to his weapon.

If Josephine Maxwell knew she'd turned him into a eunuch she'd laugh her freaking ass off.

"Are you *boys* doing anything to track down this serial killer attacking women in Manhattan?" Pru's voice was sharp, striking him from a different angle.

"I'm sure the *boys* are doing everything they can to apprehend the killer, Mrs. Duvall." Marsh produced his diplomatic smile. "I'm Special Agent in Charge of the Forgeries and Fine Arts Division. We track stolen artwork."

"Sounds dangerous." Pru Duvall snorted derisively.

"Art fraud can be a cover for mobsters and terrorist money laundering schemes." Marsh resisted reciting his arrest record and military career.

Brook leaned closer and asked in a rough whisper, "So what are you doing *here,* Marshall?"

Marsh smelled enough bourbon on the senator's breath to ignite flames and rocked back on his heels. The aide tapped Brook on the shoulder and pointed to a nearby photographer who patiently cradled his camera. Brook and Pru posed for a photograph insisting Lynn and Marsh join them for the shot. Then, instead of moving away and working the room, Brook turned back to him and lowered his voice conspiratorially. "Is this place a front for the mob?" The laugh was hearty and cordial and drew peoples' attention to their intimate little group.

"Not that I'm aware of." *Yet.* Marsh wished to hell he'd come alone. Or forced his way in early, before the gallery opened. But he'd had nothing to go on except an unsubstantiated rumor from an unreliable source. Rumors were a given in the art world. Who'd have thought it might lead to the biggest break they'd had in a decade?

He let go of Lynn, ashamed of himself for giving her the wrong idea. His attention focused on Gloria Faraday who, with a satisfied smile, was tottering her way through the crowd toward his painting. The painting that might be a possible Vermeer worth millions; the painting stolen from Admiral Chambers, an old friend of his father's, back in nineteen-ninety.

She reached up to pin a tiny gold heart on the plaque, but Marsh caught her wrist before she got there. The superfine bones shifted within his grasp.

"Sorry, ma'am. You can't sell this picture."

"I *beg* your pardon?" Judging from the volume, Gloria's outrage was genuine.

Marsh displayed his shield.

"Special Agent in Charge Hayes with the FBI. This painting is believed to be stolen." Suddenly, Steve Dancer was beside him, herding people away.

"If I need to," Marsh continued in a quiet voice, "I'll get a warrant to remove the painting, but if you cooperate—"

"Whaaat!" Gloria shrieked. The blood drained from her face as she looked around the staring faces of the elite crowd and wobbled slightly in her designer heels.

"Have a seat." Dancer maneuvered the woman into a nearby chair before she passed out.

Lynn edged away from Marsh, her cheeks flushing bright scarlet, clearly embarrassed to be associated with a public scene. That should put paid to any attempt at a second date.

Pru put her arm around the girl's shoulders and patted her gently. "We'll take you home, dear." She raised a razor-thin brow at Marsh, her smile glinting with victory. "Looks like your brave FBI agent will be busy for the next little while."

One side of Marsh's lips quirked with irritated amusement. Sparring with Pru Duvall was better than dealing with a naïve teenager and a hell of a lot preferable to dealing with Gloria Faraday who was now crying loudly, make-up tracking down her pasty cheeks.

Prudence leaned close to his ear, perfume thick and cloying, her gaze resting on Gloria's ashen face.

"Better watch out, Special Agent in Charge Hayes. She looks dangerous." Then she was gone, shepherding Lynn out of a side door.

Chapter Two

"This way, sir."

An agent he'd never met before led him and Dancer through the businesslike reception area on the twenty-third floor of the federal building, toward an unused conference room in the FBI's Manhattan headquarters.

Marsh handled the painting cautiously, mindful of the priceless nature of the work and all the excited bodies buzzing around him like bees in an overheated hive. They'd packed it in acid-free paper and bubble-wrap. With laser induced fluorescence the forensics experts might get lucky and find a usable recent fingerprint or trace evidence, but latent prints didn't last long and chances were the thieves weren't that stupid. Until they could arrange safe transport to the crime lab, the painting needed to be stored somewhere secure. He didn't think it got more secure than the heart of FBI headquarters.

Lights blazed. The grinding noise of a fax machine shrieked through the air and resonated through his ears. A tiny portion of his brain wondered what was going down, but the rest was focused on where this investigation might lead. This was the biggest potential break they'd had on the Isabella Stewart Gardner Museum robbery in years.

Gloria Faraday had dissolved into a hysterical mess, but Philip had turned the fiasco into a media stunt and sworn to help the authorities in any way he could to capture the thieves who threatened legitimate business.

Marsh and Dancer had photographed every piece exhibited at the gallery and requested inventories from Total Mastery Galleries worldwide. More agents would descend tomorrow to go through the books and determine provenance for every item the gallery showed. Marsh didn't know if the Faradays were innocent or guilty, but with a little manipulation they might lead him to information he'd been hunting for years.

Focused on the job, he flicked an uninterested glance across the bullpen. Enlarged photographs were pinned to one wall. Pictures of mutilated women.

He stopped dead.

Dancer bumped into his back as Marsh turned toward the images. His heart drilled a hole in the wall of his chest.

It wasn't the brutality of the pictures that rocked his world. It was the pattern of the wounds.

A group of agents huddled over a desk, gesturing toward the photographs and punctuating sentences with sharp jabs and sour expressions. One agent looked up, a flare of recognition zipping through his eyes before he walked over to where Marsh and Dancer stood gawping like a couple of schoolgirls.

The agent stuck out his hand, raised his voice over the goddamned fax machine that still screeched through the air. "Agent Cole, sir. I took some of your undercover courses in Quantico."

The young agent followed Marsh's gaze to the photographs, planted his hands on his hips. "This sick sonofabitch got another one down in the Village earlier tonight. We've got some guys from

BAU consulting and we're trying to link the last two victims."

Marsh nodded, but his throat was full of coarse sand and his heartbeat dampened to a mute thud that barely kept him upright. "Where?"

"Sir?"

"Where. In the Village?" He forced the question out over the background noise because, God help him, Marsh was praying with everything in him that he was wrong.

Agent Cole stuffed his hands in his pant pockets. "Grove Street. Scene's a mess."

The world crashed and Marsh stumbled slightly.

"You all right, boss?" Dancer murmured, holding him upright with an iron grip on the back of his thousand-dollar jacket.

No. He jerked his head. *Not all right.* He hadn't been all right since the day he'd walked away from Josephine Maxwell in a cow pasture in Montana. Right now he doubted he'd ever be okay again.

Forcing his legs to work, Marsh shoved the 17th Century Dutch masterpiece into Dancer's arms and turned back the way he'd come.

Josephine lived on Grove Street.

Josephine had scar tissue that matched those mutilated women.

Faster and faster he moved. Legs pumping even though he felt like he was wading through zero gravity. Panic stabbed as the noise and bustle of the office exploded through his senses and he broke into a run to the elevator. Ignoring the alarmed glances, he thrust the doors apart and slid inside the metal tomb and rested his head against cold steel. Heard his heart racing through his ears as if it were being broadcast over a loudspeaker. Sweat beaded his brow and scored a line down the side of his face. He loosened his tie, jerked open the top button of his shirt.

Why did I leave her alone? Why didn't I protect her?

Because she didn't want you. She never wanted you.

It shouldn't have made any difference.

Somehow he was in his car with no memory of having got there, peeling out onto the street. Traffic wasn't heavy on the Avenue of the Americas. Yellow cabs mostly. He wove in and out of the steady stream and jumped a red light.

Sweat filmed his body and made his starched white shirt stick to the skin across his shoulders. He blasted fresh air into the suffocating interior of the BMW, the draft scouring his face, helping him regain a little control.

Pictures flashed inside his brain. Sliced flesh. Pooled blood. He tried to put the images of death and silky, matted hair out of his mind, but it was impossible. Perspiration dampened the palms of his hands and made the grip on the steering wheel slippery. He wiped them on his thighs. Nausea coiled in his stomach, but Marsh seized it and clamped down hard on the panic—let his training take over. Blowing lights and breaking speed limits, he pulled onto Grove Street in record time.

A beat cop tried to bar his way, but Marsh flashed his badge and was waved through. Parking behind a squad car, he got out, slamming the door behind him, the noise echoing off tightly packed buildings like a gunshot.

When the echoes faded it seemed unnaturally quiet. The hiss of traffic far away. The rustle of slender branches nothing but a gentle crackle on a cold wind. Marsh focused on the black door one hundred yards up the street. It stood wide open. Lights from the foyer flooded down the three stone steps and metal railings threw skeletal shadows across the sidewalk. Crime scene tape sealed off the area. Police officers kept a subdued crowd of reporters and spectators at a distance.

Josephine's house.

Atheist or not, he started praying.

He held his badge high, pushed through the onlookers, and dipped under the tape past a green-looking rookie. They exchanged a silent look and Marsh nodded, climbing the three steps, his heart vibrating in his chest. He braced himself. He was a professional. Everything was under control. A gurney with a body on it was pushed out the door, the wheels squeaking.

Josephine...

He reeled and averted his eyes. The woman he loved was dead because he'd been too stupid to realize she was in danger. Too cowardly to risk rejection. He took a deep breath as the gurney rattled inelegantly down the steps and was lifted into a waiting wagon. He grabbed the railings, not knowing how to walk or even if his legs worked anymore. Grief wanted to shove him to his knees and make him howl. The woman he loved had been murdered and he'd never get the chance to make things right. Why hadn't he tracked her down? He hadn't stopped thinking about her for months, why the hell hadn't he at least called?

"Who're you?"

Marsh looked up into the sharp eyes of an NYPD detective and reminded himself this was a murder investigation. He wanted to know what the hell evidence they had and how close they were to nailing this sick fuck.

Marsh took a handkerchief out of his top pocket and wiped his brow. "FBI." He fumbled for his shield and hoped to hell it didn't show that inside he was dying.

"Another one? Jesus-H." The balding detective stood back to let him through, rubbing at his moustache. "At least we got a lead this time."

A lead? "You working this case?"

The detective flicked a glance over his sweat-drenched appearance as if deciding whether or not to trust him. Whatever he saw must have worked.

"I worked the first two vics. Ran it through ViCAP, got hits in D.C. and New Mexico." He glanced over to the gathering crowd as if mentally tallying faces. "The feds took over and then Interpol got involved. We figure this perp has been active for more than a decade. *The Blade Hunter*, the press calls him." The cop gave a derisive snort and his moustache quivered as an Evidence Response Team dusted for fingerprints in the hallway behind him. "Sick bastard. Cutting up blondes all over the world."

Marsh pressed down hard on the bridge of his nose, swallowed the bile that formed as he envisioned photographs of Josephine's dead body pinned beside those of the other women.

"You're not on this case, are you?" A suspicious note entered the detective's tone.

Marsh's phone vibrated on his hip. Grateful for the momentary respite in answering the cop's question, he held up his hand in apology. He pulled it out, found a text message from Dancer asking him what the hell was going on.

"SAC Marshall Hayes? To what do we owe the pleasure, sir?"

Marsh glanced up from his cell phone. A tall wiry Supervisory Special Agent from the Behavioral Analysis Unit in Quantico reached over the local detective's shoulder to shake Marsh's hand. Lifting his gaze further, Marsh connected with the cobalt eyes of the woman who haunted his dreams.

Josephine.

His world spun. He gripped the doorjamb tighter, fingernails cracking the smooth black lacquer paintwork. His breath rasped in his throat as the world leveled and relief burst loose inside his chest.

Alive. She was alive.

Beautiful.

Dressed in black jeans and a black sweater with a drab army jacket thrown over her shoulders, her skin appeared almost translucent under the fluorescent light. Fear and vulnerability tightened her expression, but she hid it by narrowing her gaze. Her lips curled in their usual scathing manner.

He didn't care. She was alive—and apart from looking a little shaken up, she seemed as pissed as the last time he'd seen her. She'd pulled her silver-blonde hair back into a ponytail. Her deceptively delicate features were set in a heart-shaped face that disguised a vicious tongue and a mean temper. For the last six months he hadn't been able to get her out of his mind.

Why her? It didn't matter why. He'd thought she was dead and it had reduced his life to meaningless ashes.

Marsh wiped the sweat out of his eyes and remembered the SSA's name. Agent Nicholl. He was a damn good agent.

His heart settled back into a normal sinus rhythm and he took a deep breath absorbing the fact that she was not dead, not bleeding, not hurt. A huge rush of relief swamped him and suddenly it didn't matter that they didn't even like one another. Because, despite all the differences between them, despite their complicated unconventional dealings, she was alive and he wasn't ever letting her go again.

***

Josie curled her fingers into fists and stared down at the face of the one man she'd hoped to avoid for the rest of her life. Make that *two* men she'd hoped to avoid—both of whom had showed up tonight. She glared at Marsh, wishing she was anywhere but here. Wishing she was a better person, a normal person.

Last time she'd seen him, she'd acted like a brat and told him she couldn't stand him. He'd helped rescue her from a hostage situation, and had feigned ignorance to protect her best friend Elizabeth Ward from being arrested. Instead of thanking him, she'd been a bitch. And she'd spent every day since regretting her actions.

Butterflies the size of vultures took flight in her stomach. Marshall Hayes looked as slick as ever, but thinner, the lines around his mouth cut sharper, deeper. His hazel eyes pinned her and for a moment the relief she saw there staggered her. But then the cold hard mask of law enforcement slammed down over his features and he blanked his expression until she wasn't sure of anything anymore, except someone had tried to kill her.

She swayed slightly, her tongue welded to the roof of her mouth. She couldn't swallow. Panic began to build and she started to tremble. She'd tried to lock her reactions up inside, needed to survive the police interview so she could get the hell out of NYC. It wouldn't be the first time she'd gone on the lam.

"I came to see Ms. Maxwell." Marsh was speaking to the tall fed, Special Agent Dickwad, though his eyes never left hers. The second fed, the cute one whose name she'd already forgotten, hovered on the stairs beside her trying to persuade her to come down to FBI HQ to make a statement.

She'd rather stick needles in her eyes.

"You two know each other?" asked Special Agent Dickwad.

Marsh smiled. She looked at his calm features and envied his cool authority. Marshall Hayes drew power around him like Superman wore a cloak. Arrogance and integrity shone from the lean lines of his face—Mr. By-the-Book. But he was more than that. Much more.

He returned her gaze unflinchingly, those intense eyes looking deep inside her soul as if searching for something…

What had the cop asked? Did they *know* each other? Reacting instinctively, knowing she'd shatter if Marsh showed her the slightest kindness, Josie laughed, wincing inwardly at the brittleness of the sound.

"Oh, we know each other, all right." She flashed a suggestive smile, knowing the effect it had on most men. Except Marsh. He was immune to her charms, suspicious of anything except her barbed tongue.

The NY detective grinned, spreading his moustache in a wide arc. Special Agent Dickwad colored up and fed-number-two coughed up his sleeve. Marsh stared at her as if she were a small child whom he was patiently waiting to behave. Anger rose inside her, frustration and fear coalescing into anger. Anger was good. Sure beat the hell out of being scared out of her tiny mind.

"You want the keys to your handcuffs back, Hayes?" Propping one hand suggestively on her hip, she grinned at him, super-confident, super-sexy. The last thing she expected was the savage flash of anger that flared in his eyes. Involuntarily she took a step back, and banged her heel on a riser.

"Cut the bullshit, Josephine. Tell me what happened."

Alarm bells jangled as her survival instincts took over. She shivered. He was more dangerous than most people realized. She'd never forgotten that about him. Had never forgiven him for not falling for her act.

"I don't think Ms. Maxwell knows much, sir," Special Agent Dickwad whispered in an undertone that suggested she was a simpleton. As she'd spent several hours fostering that image, it shouldn't annoy her so damn much.

The fed's manner turned even more obsequious and she rolled her eyes. "The victim—a woman called Angela Morelli—was found dead in the ground floor apartment. We believe Ms. Maxwell disturbed the killer as he was leaving the building. Maybe he figured he'd risk taking a second vic, but one of the neighbors came home and raised the alarm."

She sucked in shallow little breaths to hide her distress, but was dismayed when tears blurred her vision. A woman had died here tonight and this guy spoke like she was just another data point.

She used both hands on the banister for support and closed her eyes. *Is it my fault?* If she hadn't been back late from her appointment would he have left Angela Morelli alone? Except, being an artist, she didn't have a fixed schedule. The bastard had been hiding in the stairwell waiting to ambush her, but he'd already butchered Angela in cold blood.

She wanted to run and hide but everywhere she turned there was someone in her face, pushing at her for answers she refused to give. She sensed Marsh standing close. After all these months she still recognized his scent; his heat. Her mouth went dry and her heartbeat raced. She opened her eyes, nerves exploding, all her panic buttons screaming to get the hell away from him because he was one of the few people with the power to hurt her.

"You fought him off? This experienced serial killer?" Marsh's hazel eyes swept over her with disdain. "With these?" He poked her bicep and she jumped.

Rubbing her arm, she pinched her lips over words too dangerous to say. Anger boiled beneath the surface of her skin, circling like a shark looking for a kill. She was stronger than she looked and the sonofabitch knew it. Never the model of restraint or propriety he was trying to goad her into making another mistake. They had too much shared history for her to con him and she'd treated him too badly for him to swallow a single word she said.

She should never have drugged him all those months ago. She'd planned to kiss him until he passed out and she could escape, but that plan had blown up in her face. They'd had sex, once, blisteringly hot sex. But he hadn't seen her naked, didn't know the secrets carved into her skin. No one knew except the man with the knife.

"Leave me alone."

Detective Cochrane sniggered. The two feds supposedly running the show looked at each other with raised brows and a great big question mark. Marsh went to touch her again, but she flinched and one side of his mouth twitched, telling her how much she'd given away with that one small movement.

Backing up a step, she addressed the second fed, who'd questioned her in the apartment. "I've told you everything I know. I'm done here."

Marsh followed. "Is that right?"

His eyes were so intense they glowed. He grabbed her around the waist and she gasped in shock at the contact. Somehow he turned her around in his arms, slid her effortlessly in front of him like she weighed nothing at all, her feet dangling uselessly over the step.

"Get off me!" She struggled, kicking and hitting, but her fists bounced off him with no real effect. His scent enveloped her, crisp expensive cologne over strong healthy male. The sensation of his hands burning a familiar path over her skin excited and infuriated her all at the same time. But after what she'd been through tonight, the last thing she wanted was some guy manhandling her like a freaking doll.

Through her fury she watched the stunned

expressions of the men below her. Then she realized Marsh was lifting her sweater.

No. No. No. Dammit!

She panicked, grabbed onto his forearms, felt the strength in those muscles. She twisted harder, but his arms were a vise, holding her to him.

Cold air caressed bare skin for the second time that night. His arm shielded her nudity, one hand cupping her breast like it belonged there. His absolute determination burned through her struggles and she went rigid with fury.

So much for honor and integrity.

"Did you mention *these*, Josephine?" Anger brushed the shell of her ear.

She didn't need to look down to see the long silver scars that lined her abdomen in diagonal crosses. Rage heated until it was a white-hot mist as Marsh exposed her biggest secret—her greatest shame—to the whole world. The shocked expressions on the cop and feds' faces should have been comical, but the obvious repugnance and pity she saw there made her stop fighting.

"You have blood on you, miss." Detective Cochrane's eyes were troubled now and Marsh's grip tightened, driving the air from her lungs.

"It's nothing." She hadn't had time to clean up after that sonofabitch had attacked her, but she hadn't told the cops that. She hadn't told them that he'd hurt her or what he'd said. She looked over her shoulder into Marsh's grim, unsmiling face. "Let go of me or I'll rip out your fucking throat."

Fire lit his eyes, but his voice was soft. "You don't scare me, Josephine. At least, not that way."

Marsh lowered her to the stair, held her securely while she regained her balance and jerked her sweater back into place. Fury and pride demanded she hurt the bastard, but when she turned to face him, he showed an impressive display of psychic ability, and took a step away.

Tears swam in her eyes. She bit her lip. How did he know about the scars? Despite his badge, she'd never doubted his almost overbearing sense of honor.

Now she wasn't so sure.

"Let's go." Special Agent Dickwad grabbed her arm like he'd solved the case and hustled her toward the door.

Jerking out of the idiot's painful grip, she glared over her shoulder about to curse Marshall Hayes with every foul word she'd ever learned, but her anger evaporated as quickly as it had come. Something about his haunted expression tore at her. He looked like she felt—as if he'd been in a fight for his life and had barely escaped alive.

***

His toes tingled painfully with cold. Transferring his weight from one foot to the other helped, but if the cops didn't give a statement soon, he was leaving. Job or no freaking job.

A cup of Starbucks helped ward off the chill. He sipped the creamy sweet brew and noted it too was beginning to cool. He was too old for this crap. Twenty years on the job and the crime-beat still sucked.

Nelson Landry glanced around the crowd, noticed small huddled groups whose breath rose as a cloud of steam through the sodium vapor of the streetlights. They reckoned serial killers got off watching the action from the sidelines. He peered closer. Were any of these guys the Blade Hunter? His gaze ran over the figures but no one stood out as a sadistic psycho and he grew bored looking at those young eager faces.

The guy to his right looked respectable enough, but who knew what that overcoat hid or what the guy's fingers were jangling deep in his pockets. Nelson huffed out a laugh at the image he'd conjured. God help him, he'd been doing this way too long.

Cops and feds began pouring out of the building like ants on a mission. Stretching his five-foot-five frame to the limit, Nelson peered past an NBC cameraman's shoulder. Cops were loading up cars and trucks with evidence bags and equipment. The body was long gone.

One of the feds was coming across the street to give a statement. Heaving a sigh of relief, Nelson took the digital recorder out of his pocket, shifted his weight, thankful he'd soon be in the comfort of his own bed. The G-man moved like he had a poker shoved up his ass, almost on tiptoes. Out of the corner of his eye, Nelson spotted a blonde being escorted to a black Lincoln sedan.

Who the hell is that? A real looker. A model or film star he wouldn't wonder.

"Check out the list of residents," he spoke into his voice recorder and raised his Nikon with his other hand, reeling off a few shots of the fed. Then he turned the camera toward the blonde, and centered the shot through the viewfinder. One of the men walking beside the woman made his lips draw back over his teeth.

SAC Marshall Hayes.

The man who'd gotten him busted back down to the crime-beat only a couple of years from retirement, because he'd written an article about a cover up over the death of some curator from the Museum of Modern Art.

Asshole.

The guy worked art fraud, so what the hell was he doing at a murder scene? On autopilot, Nelson thrust his recorder toward the guy giving the official statement and watched the man who'd wrecked his life lean up-close and personal to the blonde before climbing into a Beemer parked further along the street and speeding away.

Marshall Hayes hated the press. Loved making their lives as difficult as possible. The world clicked into place in a serendipitous moment and Nelson grinned. He was about to return the favor.

Chapter Three

Back at the FBI New York field office, Marsh watched the interview through the one-way mirror. Josephine flashed an award-winning smile and sipped delicately from a cup of coffee Special Agent Sam Walker had fetched her—in a china cup, no less.

She had that effect on men.

Long blond hair was tied into a messy knot on top of her head. Her lips were pink and sweetly bowed, her face pretty enough to make you believe any lie you told yourself to justify those unprofessional thoughts about getting her naked.

He hadn't realized exactly how badly he'd missed the irrational, foul-mouthed vixen until he'd seen her again. And it was galling to know that this woman, who loathed him with a passion, was the only one he wanted in his bed.

He rubbed the muscles jammed tight in his neck.

"So why didn't you mention that this man cut you?" Walker asked, placing a hand on her elbow, trying to inspire trust. *Mr. Benevolent.* Playing good cop to Agent Nicholl's scowling bad cop.

Studying her closely, Marsh saw Josephine freeze for that fraction of a second before she laughed self-deprecatingly and forced herself to relax. She put both hands flat on the table in front of her, probably to stop her body language giving her away when she lied her ass off.

If they thought they were going to get anything out of her this way, they were as dumb as she made herself look.

"I didn't even know he'd cut me, until Marsh, Agent Hayes…" Her voice grew husky and she glanced at the mirror, "…flashed you all like that."

Color crept into her cheeks and he frowned. Everything about Josephine's façade was highly polished deceit *except* her embarrassment about those scars. They weren't pretty, but unfortunately, they weren't a turn off either.

His cell phone buzzed against his hipbone.

"Dancer, what have you got for me?" God help him, he still had an art-theft investigation to run.

"Philip and Gloria Faraday are siblings. Born in England," Dancer reeled off. "Parents deceased. No police record, no suspicion of dealing under the table." He gave a big yawn that reminded Marsh it was well after midnight.

The one-way glass was smeared with handprints and the effect was like looking through a soft focus lens. Josephine made a big show of checking her statement. Sentence by sentence as the agents quizzed her. Walker leaned over her like some proprietary wolf and Marsh gritted his teeth.

Dancer carried on. "The lab agreed to send a crime scene tech to us because of the unusual circumstances. Once they're done, Aiden can examine it for authenticity and get the paint analyzed. There aren't any field agents available to help out at the gallery. The SAC said tonight's homicide got priority."

Marsh had no problem with that. Human life was more important than art or money and this case had been cold for years. "Go back to the hotel and get some sleep. I'll meet you at the gallery at nine to interview the Faradays again. See if we can shake something coherent out of Gloria this time."

"Is it true this serial killer attacked Josephine Maxwell?" Dancer asked.

Marsh sighed. They'd worked together for years and Steve Dancer knew him better than anyone. Dancer also knew Marsh and Josephine had shared one night of sex that had led to deep-seated mistrust on both sides.

"Yeah. He killed another woman in her apartment building, and then attacked Josephine in the lobby. Lucky for her they were interrupted and he fled the scene."

Lucky...

Clamping his molars together, Marsh fought the urge to retch. The bastard had actually cut her; he'd had his hands on her flesh and it was a miracle she wasn't dead.

Shit.

There was a long beat of silence on the other end of the line.

"But how did you know? In the bullpen..." Dancer cleared his throat. "I mean the way you ran out of here when you saw those pictures...how did you know?" One of Dancer's greatest strengths was uncovering classified information, but Marsh had never told anyone about Josephine's scars. Tomorrow, he'd be lucky if they weren't national headlines.

So what difference did it make if he told Dancer?

She'd hate him, but then she already hated him.

"This doesn't go anywhere else. Josephine was knifed as a kid. Cut up bad enough that the cops didn't think she'd make it." Marsh closed his eyes against the graphic images still engraved on his memory from the photographs he'd seen. "I had that evidence file copied to me when we were looking for Elizabeth."

He'd also seen Josephine's scars in the flesh when he'd drugged her and injected a tiny transmitter below her shoulder blade. He'd used her to track Elizabeth Ward, her best friend, and his undercover agent who'd gone missing last spring. Josephine didn't know about the transmitter and he'd do his damnedest to make sure she never found out. Their relationship had taken an unexpected turn when she'd used those same tranqs on him, with startling consequences for both of them.

"She has the same pattern of scars the murder victims have."

Dancer was silent, though Marsh heard the other man pulling all the threads together and forming an unbreakable weave. "So you think this is the same guy?"

"Maybe, I don't know. Josephine isn't talking." Switching tracks, Marsh asked, "Have you notified Admiral Chambers we found his painting yet?" Another political string-puller, his father's buddy was going to be delighted they'd finally found that piece. Especially if experts reappraised it as a Vermeer.

"I figured you'd do it." Dancer's tone turned hopeful.

Normally, Marsh would have called the admiral immediately, but Josephine's safety was more important than anything else. Through the window, he watched her smile get more strained. The grip on her pen was so tight the tips of her fingers were bloodless.

His own fingers tightened around the phone because he knew whatever she was writing down wasn't the whole story. Josephine had a problem with telling the truth. Hell, maybe they both did. "You let him know ASAP."

"Yes, sir," Dancer replied smartly. "By the way, I still have that photograph of you in handcuffs..."

Marsh wanted to curse, but other things weighed too heavily on his mind. "Yeah, yeah, just make the damn call."

He hung up and stared through the window. The clench of her jaw and hunch of her shoulders screamed nervous tension, but he doubted she'd break. Not here. Not yet.

What was she hiding? Why the hell was she hiding it?

But the only thing that really mattered was she was back in his life and he had no intention of letting anyone hurt her ever again. A hum ran through his blood, an excitement he hadn't felt in months and he wished to God he didn't feel now. Josephine was in danger—he didn't believe in coincidence. The Blade Hunter was trying to finish a job he'd started twenty years ago, and that *job* was murdering Josephine Maxwell.

***

The urgent need for a shower ate at Josie's nerves. The scent of sweat, blood and fear clung to her, the memory of her attacker's touch eroding her skin, gradually being absorbed into her bones and settling there like a bruise.

She bit the end of the pen. If it wasn't for

Marshall Hayes she'd be in her apartment right now packing.

To go where?

She hadn't figured that out yet. She had options. Connecticut? Montana? Or maybe she should just get on a train with no set destination in mind.

Squinting at the page she'd written, she put down the pen and glanced up at Special Agent Sam Walker, who sat on the table swinging his leg, the gentle motion rocking the surface beneath her forearms.

He and Nicholl were reading the latest report on the murder of Angela Morelli. Discussing it quietly between them. Her stomach clenched.

Despite living in the same building for the last few years, Josie had barely known the woman. And now Angela was dead because of her.

She worried a loose thread on her jacket, snapped it off. The room was dreary and stuffy, nothing but industrial gray and green. Walker's gun sat on his hip, close to her elbow.

Maybe I should become a cop? Too bad she wasn't big on honesty or law enforcement. She wiped her fingers on her jeans and looked at the black holstered weapon again. Guns were something she'd always avoided—only wise guys and cops carried guns where she came from, and she didn't trust either.

Christ, she wanted to get out of here. She scanned what she'd written.

I checked the mail and someone grabbed me from behind.

The sharp blade of the hunting knife flashed before her eyes and Agent Walker's big black gun looked tempting as hell.

Mrs. Lauder from number three opened the front door and screamed. Attacker jumped up and ran away.

There were a few more details she could add, but she hadn't lied.

The door off the street had opened with a rush of wind and Janet Lauder, her downstairs neighbor, had taken one look at the scene, dropped her groceries and run shrieking into the street.

Josie had held up her portfolio as a shield in a last desperate defense.

Mrs. Lauder's screams had gathered support and loud male voices had responded—if they hadn't, Josie wouldn't be sitting here right now. She'd be laid out dead in the morgue. The predator had slid the knife into his pocket and walked toward one of the ground floor apartments. He'd paused long enough to make her a parting promise. "Next time, you're dead."

Asshole.

She signed the statement neatly with her trademark *J Maxwell* signature. Her shoulder itched the way it did sometimes but she didn't try to scratch it. It seemed important not to show any weakness in this bastion of law enforcement.

"Can I go now?" She shifted her feet, preparing to stand. Despite fatigue that dragged at her eyelids, she smiled. It went against her nature, but the *system* had taught her that looking miserable got you nothing but therapy and pep talks from dumpy-looking social workers. She was far too old for that crap.

Nicholl picked up her statement and skimmed through it, frowned at her in that condescending way some men had.

"Madam, I think it is time you started to tell the truth about your association with this murderer and not some half-cocked story about running into the guy in the hallway. Are you his accomplice? Are you helping him?"

Now they're gonna pin this on me? Never trust a frickin' cop. Rolling her eyes, she threw a look at the mirrored window where she knew Marsh was watching.

Time for another inch of honesty. "I don't know what else I can tell you. I got my scars when someone attacked me when I was a kid in Queens. There was a police report." Holding Agent Walker's gaze she let sincerity shine through. "I thought he was going to kill me."

"How old were you?" Walker asked, frowning. He was watching her lips.

She withdrew eye contact. "Nine."

"Where did you grow up?" Walker crinkled his baby-blues, trying to catch her gaze again and charm her. This wasn't going where she wanted it. She'd wanted to deflect them away from herself but had nothing else to give them.

"Brooklyn. I was visiting a friend in Queens." She rested her palms on her thighs. Held them still and then relaxed against the hard back of the chair as she realized she wasn't going anywhere soon.

The room was warm so she slipped out of her jacket and crossed her legs. Both men followed her actions in an automatic male response. She might not be Sharon Stone, but she had moves.

Josephine glanced at the mirrored window and knew Marsh wouldn't be so easily diverted. Heat rose in her cheeks as memories of exactly how she'd distracted him returned in vivid detail. Virgins should not dabble in sexual manipulation unless they were prepared to get more than they bargained for.

"I think I took him by surprise being there, when I was a kid." She frowned. She'd never really figured out why he hadn't killed her. Even in the darkness she'd seen the shocked expression in his eyes. Of course, she shouldn't have been there. Should never have been peeping through that window from the fire escape. So she hadn't made a sound when he'd gathered her up—hadn't wanted her mother or her mother's lover to find out she'd been sitting outside that window watching them.

She pushed down a sob that came out of nowhere.

"How old was he? It was a *he*, right?" Walker persisted.

Walker was a good-looking guy. Shorter than Marsh, solid, square-jawed, there were lines at the corners of his eyes that suggested he smiled a lot. Lucky him. She concentrated on him and not his crane-like partner, nor the darkly intense man who exuded power even from a room away. Hell, distance was no object for Marshall Hayes.

"It was definitely a guy." She conjured up old memories that were always fresh in her mind. "He had blunt fingers, square hands." She looked at her own tapered fingers, swallowed as she recalled the intimate caress of his hand over the knife handle. "I don't know how old he was. Hell, I was nine. Anyone over sixteen was old back then."

"Was he an adult?"

"Physically or legally? I don't know." She ran her fingers through her hair, pulled. The room spun slightly because she was so tired. "Why don't you

45

go get the police report? It's bound to have more details than I can remember."

"We will," Nicholl assured her with a glare.

He was the prick she voted Most Likely to Succeed.

"Why do you even think it's the same guy?" she demanded, picking up the pen and scoring the writing pad with the nib. "It was, what, eighteen, nineteen years ago? I figured he's dead or in prison with all the other psychos."

Maybe her memories had betrayed her...maybe it was a different guy.

Sam Walker opened a file and laid a picture on the table. Angela Morelli's dead eyes stared up at her, her torso patterned with exactly the same marks Josie carried on her flesh.

Bile rose in her throat and she covered her lips with her palm. *Son of a bitch.* Other photos appeared on the table. Body after body of butchered women, blood soaking beneath them in dark pools.

"Josie, I know this is hard, but you're the only lead we have on this guy." *The only one left alive.* Walker's voice was coaxing and gentle, totally at odds with the horror laid out on the table. He squatted beside her, put a hand on her knee and she held very, very still.

She didn't like to be touched. Never had. But she couldn't afford to freak out in Law Enforcement Central. Rubbing her arms, she tried to hide her reaction until he removed his hand.

When he did, she forced herself to try to breathe. To try and remember. It wasn't like she wanted this nutcase on the loose any more than they did.

The bastard had knocked her unconscious and

carried her down some godforsaken alley. "I really don't know how I can help."

As a child she'd lain frozen as that sharp blade had sliced her skin. Not deep, but deliberately searching out raw nerve-endings. *I won't kill you if you don't make a sound.* She frowned, kept her hands on the tabletop in front of her. There'd been *something* about his voice, but it was so long ago...

She'd been too scared to move—just like today. And when he'd flipped her onto her stomach she'd expected him to kill her, but instead he'd scored his blade across her flesh some more, carving a pattern that had defined the rest of her life.

It had stung like a bitch, but she hadn't made a sound. At some point she must have passed out because when she'd woken up, he'd been gone.

That's when she'd staggered to her feet and run for help.

She remembered having her fingerprints taken and desperately trying to wash the greasy blackness from her hands even though the movement had pulled her stitches. "The cops got his prints, I think. Off the knife that pinned me to the ground."

***

Marsh waited in the corridor, checking the latest bureau mandates pinned neatly to the corkboard outside the interview room. The door opened and Josephine walked out, closely followed by Special Agent Walker. She kept her eyes fixed on the floor and would have marched right past him, except he blocked her way.

Cold fluorescent light emphasized the hollows beneath her cheekbones. The blue of her eyes was the only splash of color in this sterile stretch of corridor. Even though he didn't trust her, he was helpless in the face of his fascination for her.

Nicholl hustled out of the interview room checking his wristwatch. Seeing Marsh, he slowed down and shot out a modulated smile.

"Thanks for the lead, sir."

He felt Josephine bristle. Her childhood scars were more than a lead in a case. Shrugging off the thought and knowing he might need Nicholl's help if he wanted an inside track on this investigation, Marsh shook the man's hand. Special Agent Walker stood patiently beside Josephine, resting a proprietary hand on the small of her back.

Marsh stuck out his hand to Walker, just to get him to stop touching her.

"I'll see Ms. Maxwell home." Walker smiled grimly.

Not in this lifetime. "I've got it covered." Marsh released the agent's hand fully expecting Josephine to argue, but her eyes held only fatigue and defeat. "We've got a lot to catch up on."

She flashed a narrowed-eyed scowl at them both. At least she didn't look defeated anymore.

Moving quickly she got into the elevator. He shoved his arm through the gap to prevent it from closing on him and followed her inside. Finally they were alone.

There was an air of fragility about the normally fierce woman as she leaned against the stainless steel walls, her finger pressing the button for the ground floor. It shot a little ache into his chest.

"What now?" she asked quietly.

Her hair was caught inside her battered army jacket. Unable to resist, he slipped his fingers inside her collar and pulled it free, smoothed the silky silver tresses over the worn olive canvas. Her lips parted, nostrils flared.

She felt it too. He could see the echo of uncertainty reflected deep in her eyes, the dance of awareness that ignited between them even though they were both exhausted and wary and burnt from their last encounter. Small white teeth bit pink lips and heat kicked through his groin like a supernova.

Too smart to play with the jaws of a gin-trap, Marsh withdrew his hand. "We go back to your place and I sleep on the couch."

He expected her to argue, but whatever else she might be, Josephine Maxwell was no fool.

The delicate skin beneath her eyes was darkened, but she still managed to look fierce and battle-ready. "Tomorrow I'll clear out of town."

Her MO was to run. He should have known that would be her answer and couldn't explain why it pissed him off so much. "And leave the UNSUB to kill more innocent women? I figured you were braver than that, princess."

It was a low dig and Josephine responded by baring her teeth. Something about her had always reminded him of a wild animal—most dangerous when cornered. "It's your job to catch the bad guys, Superman. Why don't you concentrate on that."

There was nothing defeated about her anymore. This was the grit and balls Josephine he'd gone a few rounds with in the spring. Theoretically they'd come off even, but he wasn't so sure. He'd never recovered, and aside from her encounter with a serial killer, she seemed fine.

It pissed him off.

"He'll come after you."

She narrowed her eyes at him, but not before he'd seen the terror flash in their depths. Why couldn't she drop her guard for once? Why couldn't he? Marsh crowded her against the elevator wall conscious of the security camera that monitored every move. He wanted to kiss her, wanted to keep her wrapped up safe until the danger passed. But Josephine rarely allowed anyone to sense weakness, certainly never accepted compassion or help, especially not from him.

They stared at one another, emotions shimmering in her eyes, his heartbeat thudding angrily in his chest. He bit down on words that wanted to spill out. What were they both so scared of?

The elevator dinged and he stepped away, but not before she swept a scathing look over his frame and tossed her hair over her shoulder with a derisory flick. Like he was nothing. Like he was no one. He almost smiled. One thing was for certain, she knew how to push every one of his buttons. He stuffed his fists into his pockets, waited for her to exit in front of him.

They made their way through security, then to his car, their footsteps echoing across the plaza and ringing off the tall building. The Stars and Stripes snapped in the brisk wind and Marsh welcomed the chill on his skin. A foghorn sounded across the bay, mournful and sad. New York, New York.

Josephine caught her heel and stumbled slightly, but Marsh caught her arm. Some primal triumph pumped through his blood when she didn't shrug away. Pathetic. He was totally pathetic. What he needed to do was use his brain and figure out how to catch this killer.

A thought struck him. "Are you listed in the phone book?"

Frowning, she shook her head. "I can give you my number—"

Marsh already knew her number. He'd chosen not to call it because he was a stubborn ass. "Assuming this is the same guy from your childhood, how did he know where to find you?"

Traffic was light, the air faintly tinged with brine.

A puzzled expression creased her brow. "I'm not listed anywhere. I have a website, but it doesn't give my address."

That's what he'd been afraid of.

"You a registered voter?"

She shook her head and they carried on walking. "Elizabeth is. I don't vote."

Marsh shook his head, pissed. People died for the right to vote and it irritated him when they didn't bother. But it wasn't important right now.

She walked around to the passenger door of his car. "Politicians are all the same anyway."

He ignored that sentiment because she was probably right. "He might have hired a professional to track you down." Marsh wondered if it would give the investigation a lead or waste more time.

It was better than nothing.

A siren whooped, a flash of red light in the distance.

"He could have gotten my name from the newspapers all those years ago. They reported everything in all its glory." Josephine climbed into the car, closed her eyes and rubbed her temples. "Can we stop talking about this now? I have a headache."

51

Looking at her strained profile, he kept silent and started the engine. It responded with a smooth purr and he pulled out onto the almost empty street, heading toward the Village. They didn't speak. Not even when they reached the relative quiet of Grove Street.

Parking the car, he cut the engine, but Josephine didn't stir.

The glow of streetlights swept over her face and gilded her with gold. The gentle rise and fall of her chest told him she was asleep and a kernel of satisfaction moved inside him because he knew damned well she wouldn't have slept if Agent Walker had driven her home. Though what the hell that said about his sex appeal he didn't know.

He wanted to lean over and brush his lips across hers. She wasn't as cold as she wanted the world to believe and some days it broke his heart, how ruthlessly she pushed people away. Since the day he'd first seen her, she'd stirred a ferocity inside him that no one else skimmed, no one else even guessed existed.

A strand of hair fell across her cheek. Gently he brushed it aside, absorbing the soft skin and ignoring the ache in his body. What he felt for her wasn't just physical; that's why it scared him. She opened her eyes slowly and for a moment he thought he saw his conflicted desire reflected in their depths. She jerked at the door handle and got out.

He blew out a breath before following her, stopping to retrieve an overnight bag out of the trunk. It was nearly three a.m. People were still on the street, between clubs or walking home after a night out. Drunken laughter tumbled down the avenue, curiously lighthearted for an evening filled with murder.

"What were you doing in Queens eighteen years ago, Josephine?" It was a question that had nagged him since he'd found out about her childhood attack.

She stopped in the middle of the street, raised her face to the sky. "Can we leave it alone?"

She was hiding something—nothing unusual there. Everyone lied to the authorities; it was a question of figuring out which lies mattered. Something told him this one mattered.

There were no lights on inside her redbrick tenement. Marsh climbed the steps beside her and inhaled the subtle hint of citrus from her hair. Consciously he held his breath as she inserted her key in the lock and pushed the door wide. Tried to hold onto that soft fragrance rather than the faint odor of blood that clung to the ground floor apartment. It wouldn't surprise Marsh if the other residents stayed elsewhere until the stench of violent death faded enough for them to regain the illusion of safety. He'd suggest a hotel but knew she'd never go for it.

Josephine stood stiff and uncertain on the threshold. Her skin looked waxy. Marsh reached forward and flipped the switch and light flooded the hallway, shining off the mosaic tile floor and white walls that were smudged with patches of fingerprint powder.

The door to the lower apartment was taped shut—it could be days before evidence response teams released it.

The hairs on the back of his neck lifted.

"Did the feds clear your apartment before you

left?"

"No." Her eyes blazed at him. "Why would they? He left through the ground floor window." Pointing at the sealed off door, she looked like she wanted to hit him. "Are you actively trying to freak me out or does it come naturally?" She closed the front door behind him.

"A killer comes after you with a knife yet I'm the one scaring you?" Hoisting his bag over his left shoulder, he popped open his holster and took out his SIG-Sauer.

Open-mouthed, Josephine watched him. Shaking her head, she started up the stairs. He let her lead. Let her unlock her door and then touched her arm and motioned her behind him. Despite the way she rolled her eyes he detected a frisson of alarm pass through her, as if she were only now realizing that she could actually still be in danger. The guy could have come back here. He'd know that her guard would be down after being questioned by the cops. He wouldn't expect her to have an escort.

The solid weight of his pistol felt reassuring as Marsh pushed open the door and flipped the light switches. There were no shadows, no monsters ready to jump out from behind the door. Marsh dumped his bag inside and waved her forward, setting the lock behind him. If the UNSUB was here, he wanted to nail the bastard before he hurt Josephine again.

"He's not here," she hissed.

God save him from civilians. "Unless you want to be terminally wrong, why don't you stick close to me while we make sure?"

He held out his hand, watched her reach

uncertainly for his fingers. There was a jolt of awareness between them that widened her eyes on contact. Her skin felt satin smooth. He tugged her behind him, searched closets and each of the rooms, ending in her bedroom.

Releasing her hand, he opened the tall slatted doors and searched the built-in closet, poked his head under the bed and when he was one hundred percent certain that the apartment was clean and secure, he holstered his weapon.

Josephine sank down onto the bed, shrugging out of her jacket. Her head sagged and she looked as strong as a blade of grass. Her forearm got stuck and she jerked uselessly at the heavy sleeve. He went down on his knees, caught her hand which fisted instantly and eased the cuff over her palm, letting the coat slide off her shoulders.

His elbow rested on her knee, heat sparking between them like static. The blue of her eyes was half-hidden by the fall of her hair. Her gaze settled on his lips and then shifted away. "I'm not sleeping with you."

He eased away and raised a sarcastic brow. "What? No condom? Wasn't a problem last time." It was a mean thing to say, but she brought out the worst of him as she purposefully reduced everything that had happened between them to casual sex. There was nothing casual about his relationship with this woman.

She hissed and raised a hand as if to slap him, but he grabbed her wrist. She started to jerk up her knee, but he applied just enough pressure with his elbow to protect himself.

"Kick me in the balls again, princess, and I'll handcuff you to the bed faster than you can say *date rape*," he growled.

"I didn't *rape* you."

"You put Rohypnol in my scotch and said '*Make love to me, Marsh*' and then dragged me off to bed and screwed me senseless. What would you call it?"

"They were *your* drugs and you drugged me first. You kissed *me*." Her mouth thinned. She strained to pull out of his grasp, but he wasn't letting go until he got answers. He knew why she'd done it. She'd been trying to knock him out so she could escape protective custody, but things had gotten out of control. Desire had consumed them both.

He needed to hear the words from her mouth, to know whether or not it meant anything to her.

"I didn't mean to have sex. I never meant to go through with it, dammit." She closed her eyes.

"Then why did you?" His voice cracked. With one act the woman had ruined him for everything except pining after her like a lovesick puppy.

"I—" Her chest heaved. "I must have gotten the dose wrong and then…" She opened her eyes and the stark blueness of them speared him. "I'd never done it before and it felt…good."

Dropping his head, he stared down at the hardwood floor and wondered if she was finally being honest or whether she was so skillful at reading men that she was playing him again. He let her go and she turned away, hiding her face behind a blond veil. The delicate line of her throat rippled as she swallowed.

She rolled over the bed and got out the other side. Her face was white, her eyes flat. "I'm sorry. You're right. I drugged you and forced you. It *was* rape. You should have me arrested."

He sat down on the bed and rubbed his eyes. *Damn*. He'd wanted to know if it affected her the way it affected him. He hadn't meant to attack her with false accusations because they both knew he'd wanted her from the moment they'd met.

Standing slowly, he dug his fingers into his hair, knowing he had to be honest, knowing he had to try and regain some of the integrity and honor that he strived to live by. He walked over to her, put his hands on her shoulders. Stiff as a Barbie doll she stared into his eyes, pride and shame battling in the tilt of her jaw, clearly expecting a sharp jab to finish the job.

"It was the best sex I ever had," he told her grimly.

Her eyes flashed with surprise as she processed his words. "Are you crazy?" The walls went back up. "Or just trying to get in my pants again?"

Marsh shook his head and walked over to the door. "You're a piece of work, you know that?" He wanted to tell her he never wanted to get inside her pants again, but he wouldn't let any more lies stand between them. Sweeping his gaze over her body he had one last question about that evening six months ago. "You didn't get pregnant?"

Putting a pale, long-fingered hand over her stomach, she shook her head.

"That's good." Marsh held onto the doorknob and said thickly, "Get some sleep." Closing the door behind him, he leaned his forehead against the cool wood and wanted to bang his head. *Good*? So much for no more lies.

Chapter Four

There was a stillness in the air, an expectancy that excited him. A gentle mist of rain sprayed his face and cooled his feverish skin. This wasn't his neighborhood, this wasn't his town, but it was his hunting ground.

He blinked twice, winced at the soreness of his left eye. He'd covered the scratches with makeup, but that bitch was going to pay. The bite on his wrist smarted, but he'd covered it with antibiotic cream and bandaged it carefully. His knife nestled reassuringly in his pocket. Solid. Real. Safe. Sharp. Vengeful. Memories crowded in, stirred his blood and made the breath catch in his lungs.

The bloodlust wouldn't let go. It was getting harder and harder to think about anything except killing, and that worried him. The woman in the downstairs apartment had been too old to truly satisfy him. But who could resist the symmetry of getting to Josephine Maxwell through another blond-haired bitch?

Not that she'd been a real blonde.

Trees rustled as a cold blast of air raced up the street from the Hudson bringing with it the stench of rotten seaweed exposed by the receding tide. A couple strolled along the sidewalk, arm in arm, tensing slightly as they neared him.

Invincible, the Blade Hunter smiled, nodded his head and said, "Evening." His fingers tightened around the handle of the knife until his knuckles ached.

The woman smiled back with the slack focus of one who'd had too much to drink. She was a blonde and he would love to teach her a few lessons about letting her guard down, but he didn't linger. The boyfriend had jarhead written all over his Cro-Magnon face.

Something slithered around his legs.

"Ow!" He let go of the knife in his pocket and went down hard on the sidewalk, breaking his fall with his forearms, skinning his palms.

Meow.

A cat sat on the sidewalk looking at him, flicking its tail.

"You okay, bud?" The jarhead turned back toward him, leaving his girlfriend wobbling uncertainly in high heeled inebriation. If he had her to himself he'd slide his knife expertly across her skin...

He shook himself. Clambered to his knees. "Yes. Thank you." The guy picked him up, almost lifting him clean off the floor by his collar.

"You need help getting home?" The guy's voice was gruff, fierce and unexpectedly considerate.

'*I will deal with them according to their conduct, and by their own standards I will judge them...*'

"I'm good, thanks." He smiled. Brushed off his pants, no damage done.

The guy lowered his brows and muttered, "Get off the streets, man—there's a freaking lunatic slicing and dicing people like you for breakfast."

Meow.

The dark haired stranger shot his boot in the direction of the cat, sending it fleeing between parked cars into the gutter.

He watched, fascinated, as the Good Samaritan strutted back to his girlfriend. *New York City.* The city that never sleeps. A siren blared far off in the distance. A blast of hip-hop music poured out of a passing car. He grinned. He *loved* this city. Maybe he'd stay awhile.

Chapter Five

Dancer thrust a copy of *The NY News* so close to his nose Marsh could smell the newsprint. He grabbed it out of Dancer's hands, straightened up from the desk where he was overseeing Philip Faraday as the man accessed the galleries' private inventory records.

Front page and center was a picture of him and Josephine taken at last night's murder scene, and alongside that, was a picture of him here with Lynn Richards.

For fuck's sake. He groaned. Hadn't figured anyone would care enough to focus a lens on him. Then he read the byline—Nelson Landry. The little shit.

Rubbing the bridge of his nose, he squeezed his eyes shut at the big, bold headline.

SUPERCOP ON THE JOB.

He was going to catch hell from his boss. The chances of this not getting to the director's ears were less than zero. Good thing that financially he didn't *need* to work.

Philip Faraday craned his neck to see. "Looks like you had a busy night, Agent Hayes." Turning back to the computer monitor, the man's fingers tapped rapidly over the keyboard, calling up data. "That the woman you brought to the opening last night?" Faraday nodded to the newspaper.

Marsh shot the guy a tight smile. If he could find out who sold the stolen art to the Faradays, he still had a slim chance of chasing down a lead, making an arrest and getting the hell back to Josephine before she figured out a way to leave town. "Do you have that information for me yet?"

Wearing a burgundy shirt with gold cufflinks, designer sunglasses and black slacks, the art dealer looked sharp. And he was a damn sight easier to deal with than his flaky sister, Gloria, who teared up whenever Marsh asked her a simple question. He'd sicced Aiden and Dancer on her, which seemed to be working because she'd stopped crying, except when she looked at him.

"I'm going as fast as I can." Philip stopped typing and scowled up at him, the light glinting off his thick glasses. "Maybe I should get my lawyer in here."

There'd been a time when people had thought him charming. BJ. *Before Josephine.*

"If you want a lawyer, feel free. But selling stolen property in this country will get you jail time. So why don't you work a little bit harder on getting me that name and I'll work hard at remembering you cooperated?"

Philip averted his gaze and began printing out documents.

Marsh's cell phone rang. He pulled it from his suit pocket, moved toward the floor-to-ceiling glass frontage that faced West Broadway.

"Hayes," he answered.

"I'm being followed." Josephine's voice sounded clipped and breathless.

"What the hell do you mean you're *being followed?* You were supposed to go into protective custody with Walker and Nicholl."

"Yeah," she said, "about that..."

Sweat broke out along his brow. He could hear her footsteps echoing off the sidewalk, her breath raspy.

"I changed my mind," she said, like that was a sane option with a serial killer on her tail. *Shit*, she'd done the same thing with the mob after her so he should have been prepared.

"Lied your ass off more like." Deliberately Marsh bumped his forehead on the enormous windowpane and absorbed the reverberation through his brain. "Where are you now?" *Don't let it be somewhere deserted and quiet. I don't want to listen while some bastard cuts you up—*

"The middle of Washington Square."

Okay. "See any cops around?" He waved at Dancer, tried to get his attention, but the agent was handing Gloria coffee and patting her shoulder.

"No," Josephine laughed, "for once, no cops." Beneath the laugh there was a whisper of fear that dug into his sternum.

"Go sit on a bench near the fountain, and stay on the line. I'm on my way." He held his hand over the phone, shouted to his coworker. "Dancer, Josephine's slipped her FBI leash and now she thinks she's being followed."

Dancer shook his head as he came toward him. "That woman has a death wish."

Marsh closed his eyes.

"Sorry, boss, probably *not* what you wanted to hear." Dancer tugged his ear.

She was in a crowded area. He doubted a predator as savvy as the Blade Hunter would risk such a high profile murder location. Not when the thrill was in inflicting pain.

The Total Mastery Gallery was situated between

Prince and Houston St., SoHo. Only a few blocks from Washington Square.

Marsh looked over at Philip Faraday, who'd swiveled to face them, shamelessly eavesdropping on their conversation.

Turning his back, Marsh lowered his voice for Dancer alone. "Arrange warrants for the bank and phone records and find out where the hell the Faradays got that painting. If they don't give us a name by noon, take them downtown and charge them both with possession of stolen property. That'll do for starters."

With his cell to his ear, he strode out through the huge glass doors and onto the street. "Keep talking to me, Josephine."

"What do you want me to say?" Josephine's voice was calmer now. "You were right, I was wrong?"

Taking one look at the bumper to bumper traffic, he jogged north on foot, dodging pedestrians. "Sounds like a good place to start."

She laughed, just enough to take the edge off his skyrocketing nerves. Then he cursed his colleagues at BAU. *What the hell were Walker and Nicholl thinking?*

"How did you know about the scars?" she asked suddenly.

Now there was a question he'd been waiting for and didn't want to answer.

"You checked me out that night you drugged me in Boston, didn't you?" Her voice sounded distant as if she'd disconnected from him. That night he'd saved her from a mob hit and then drugged her so he could implant the transmitter and set up his plans without having to watch her every single moment.

But if Josephine thought seeing her skin was an invasion of privacy he was pretty sure she'd flip if she knew about the microchip.

"I put you to bed, remember? I started to undress you, but then I saw the scars..." Damn. At least that lie was better than admitting the truth, even though he sounded like a pervert. "After I saw them I figured you'd rather I left your clothes on." This wasn't a conversation to have over the phone.

The silence drew out. He didn't like the sensation of her pulling away.

Dead leaves gathered in gutters, black and soaked from last night's rain. The sky was overcast and heavy moisture damp in the air. A siren screamed going fast in the opposite direction. It was only eleven a.m., but Marsh hoped the park was packed full of people enjoying an early lunch.

"Josephine? You there?" Fear soared at the silence and his heart punched against his ribs. "Josephine!"

It took him less than two minutes flat out running. His leg muscles burned, hot air fired his lungs, but he was right there, heading for the centre of Washington Square, frantically searching the area for the blonde termagant who'd taken over his life.

And there she was.

Relief surged through him like a hot wave as he spotted her dressed in the same olive-drab jacket from yesterday. She was sitting hunched over on a bench, phone to her ear, one arm folded over her chest, legs tightly crossed, glaring at some guy who wore a banner proclaiming, 'Are *You* Going to Heaven? *Take a test.*'

She was safe. Pissed as usual, but safe. And not

going to Heaven if he could help it—not today anyway.

The trees were almost bare, a few orange sycamore leaves clinging tenaciously to survival. It was more than a little ironic they were standing on an old burial ground. He took a moment to regain his breath. Searched the area for possible threats, all the time keeping Josephine in his peripheral vision.

There was one guy, sitting on a nearby concrete bench, *The NY News* spread over his knees as he munched on a sandwich. Mid fifties, jeans, thick rust-colored sweater, balding head with a compensatory beard. He looked like a university professor.

Marsh watched him glance and squint over at Josephine. Then the guy turned the page of the newspaper, fighting with a brisk breeze that whistled through the streets, flattened the page against his knee. He glanced up again. Then Marsh realized the guy was looking at the photograph of him and Josephine in the newspaper.

People didn't forget a face like that.

Marsh dismissed him. On the far side of the park, behind the Arch, Marsh spotted Walker and Nicholl in a Lincoln town car parked along The Row. Narrowing his eyes, he shook his head, placing his hands on his hips. They were staking her out to see if she led them anywhere. She was a freaking suspect. Or bait...

Suddenly she was beside him, holding out a can of cola. Accepting the drink, he pulled the tab and swallowed deeply, letting the sweet lick of sugar calm his blood.

Handing back the can, he slanted her a look that dared her to share. Josephine didn't like to share anything. She was more closed off than Fort Knox. But she took a sip anyway, which gave him a juvenile thrill. He'd once again regressed to high school.

Avoiding his gaze, she reclaimed her spot on the bench. The pallor of her skin reminded him she hadn't had much sleep last night and this was her second time going head-to-head with the killer. She wasn't a rookie. The first time had scarred her for life—literally and figuratively. Who knew what yesterday's encounter had done.

Taking out his wallet, he hunted for Agent Walker's card and dialed his number.

"Walker." The man answered on the first ring.

"This your idea of protective custody?" His voice was cold and clipped.

"Ms. Maxwell wouldn't accept protective custody, *sir*." Walker's tone made Marsh stare hard at the Lincoln.

"So what are you going to do? Wait until he cuts her up before you nail him?"

"I don't need you to tell me how to do my job." Walker's voice rose and Marsh heard Nicholl in the background telling his partner to back off.

But maybe the guy was right. Josephine wasn't exactly known for her cooperation. Marsh rubbed his forehead. Walker was a good agent with several commendations in his file and Marsh was screwing with the investigation because he was personally involved and because he could.

Shit. He'd always detested people who abused power and yet look how tempting it was. He took a deep breath. Then another. The one thing Marsh believed in was the law. He needed to let the bureau do their job, while he protected Josephine.

67

"You're right," and though it cost him, "I'm sorry."

The tension eased a little on the end of the line.

"Did you get the evidence from the old case?" he asked. "Because I can go over to Queens right now and pick it up—"

"No, sir, that won't be necessary..."

"You got it?" Marsh heard evasion in his voice. The guy wasn't telling him everything.

"No, sir." Walker paused as if debating what to tell him. "The evidence disappeared. About a month ago a beat cop was murdered, his uniform stolen and someone used it to sign out the evidence on Ms. Maxwell's old case. It was never returned."

"What?" Marsh fisted his hand in his short hair, pulling at his scalp. This UNSUB was bold and not missing a trick. "Did you get anything from the station cameras or the log?"

Walker hesitated again, and Marsh was starting to get seriously pissed.

"The only thing we got was your name, sir."

What the...? "I told you I examined the files six months ago," Marsh frowned. *Had he told them?*

"Yes, sir, but the UNSUB signed your name when he took the file."

Why the hell would he do that? Marsh gritted his teeth on a curse. "Maybe he checked the log to see who else checked out the evidence..."

"Maybe." But Walker replied too quickly.

"Do I need an alibi for last night, Special Agent Walker? Because I'm pretty sure I can provide one." Marsh didn't have time for this shit. Turning his back on the black Lincoln, he sat on the bench next to Josephine, aware of her scent, her interested blue eyes.

"I have over two hundred people, plus my partner, plus a date, who can place me at the Total Mastery NY Gallery on West Broadway for most of last evening."

Josephine raised a single eyebrow, but he didn't know if it was the fact he was supplying an alibi or the fact he'd had a date that surprised her.

"Why'd you sign out the evidence six months ago?" Walker redirected his questions.

No way was Marsh exposing Elizabeth Ward, his former agent and Josephine's best friend, to this investigation. Not when Elizabeth had sacrificed everything and finally got her life back.

"Josephine's father was worried about her." Marsh felt her stiffen beside him, but refused to look in her direction.

"Walter Maxwell?" Walker probed.

Marsh let his head drop back, his neck stretching as he gazed up at the thin veil of gray sky through half-naked branches. "That's right," Marsh replied, hearing the unspoken question, *Walter Maxwell who turned up dead twenty-four hours later?*

"I think we need to get a statement from you, sir."

He was a ballsy bastard, Marsh gave him that.

"You clear it with Director Lovine and I'll be happy to tell you everything I know." Like *hell*.

Marsh usually resented the power and influence that came with his family name and fortune, but right now it saved him from dealing with a ton of bullshit that would not help solve this case. Director Brett Lovine and he had grown up together in the best schools. Though he rarely used his personal connections for his own benefit he wasn't going to get embroiled in some screwed-up conspiracy theory while the real killer murdered more women.

Josephine tapped her fingers against a wooden slat of the bench, scraping at the flaky paint. There were no rings on her fingers; her nails were scrubbed clean and short. Wanting to calm her agitation, he placed his hand over hers and was shocked by the coldness of her flesh.

"Maybe in the meantime you could actually start looking for the UNSUB?" Marsh cut the connection and reached over to take Josephine's other hand from where it clasped the strap of her bag. Electricity bounced crazily in his stomach from the contact. She resisted for a moment, but then she seemed to give up. She sagged against his shoulder as he rubbed her fingers between his palms until they started to warm.

Her skin was smooth as silk and despite the drugs she'd spiked him with that night six months ago, he remembered other parts were even softer. Desire shot through him. An answering awareness lit her eyes, but there were tears there too. Her eyes shone with a cauldron of emotions. Physical awareness, yes, but sadness and grief also. Elizabeth Ward's disappearance had led to both her father and Marion Harper, the woman who'd raised her, being murdered by mobsters trying to track them down. He squeezed her fingers. No wonder she was messed up.

"My, my, what do we have here?" A deep Southern drawl rasped off Pru Duvall's lips.

Marsh grimaced and looked up at the wannabe First Lady. What was she doing on this side of Manhattan? As far as he knew, the Duvalls had an apartment in the exclusive echelons of Gramercy

Park.

"You are a fast worker, Special Agent *in Charge*, Marshall Hayes." Pru raked her eyes up and down Josephine's figure. "I see you like them young, skinny and blonde."

Josephine's muscles vibrated like a strung bow. He let go of her hands, which fisted into bony knots, and placed his palm on her knee.

"Mrs. Duvall, what a pleasure." Marsh didn't bother to stand. "Let me introduce a very good friend of mine, Miss Josephine Maxwell."

Pru Duvall smiled tightly at Josephine, who stared mutinously back at the older woman.

"Ahh, now I recognize you, my dear. You're the victim of that awful person who's running around Manhattan with a knife."

Flicking her blonde hair over one shoulder, Josephine pushed his hand from her knee and stood, hoisting her bag over her shoulder. "I'm nobody's victim."

Turning her back on Pru—*bad move*—she stared down at him, the light in her eyes forged from hellfire. "Coming?"

The alarm and frustration of the last twelve hours were wiped out by admiration for her indomitable spirit. Without a word to Pru, he stood and followed Josephine down the path out of the park, knowing that if she truly wanted him to, he'd follow her anywhere.

***

"Where are we going?" Marsh's gruff question irritated the hell out of her. She didn't know what to do with the feelings he evoked by racing to her rescue and then holding her hand while sitting on a park bench in Washington Square.

The terror that had gripped her after she'd left the apartment had knocked her off balance. And she wasn't happy about the fact that when she'd panicked she'd phoned Marsh, rather than dialing 911.

She looked over her shoulder, waited for him to catch up. Pru Duvall watched them with a catty expression on her face—she'd looked at Josie like she was something nasty scraped off the sole of a shoe.

"She's got the hots for you." Josie glanced up into hazel eyes that sparked with amber and jade like fall leaves scattered about the city.

He shook his head, "She's a power-monger. She wants me on my knees groveling."

"She wants you on your knees all right, but I don't think groveling is what she has in mind."

He grinned and she looked away.

He disturbed her. Made her thoughts scatter. Made her think about sex.

Everything about him appealed to her senses, from the way his suit molded those wide shoulders, the strong length of his legs, and that perfect face with the lean cheekbones and full bottom lip. He even smelled great, clean and fresh like the ocean.

She wanted him.

Her mouth went dry. She was stunned to think this way. The whole time she'd been growing up "sex" had been a dirty word. Her father's favorite nickname for her had been *whore* and that was on a good day. All these years later, her father's vicious words still hurt. She made a fist, clenching her fingers so tight her knuckles pulled at her skin.

She'd done everything to prove him wrong, to prove she wasn't a whore and that she wasn't going to get dragged into the gutter like her mother or the whisky-soaked alcoholic who'd spawned her. That's why she hadn't touched a guy until she'd seduced Marsh last year. That had been a disaster, but at the time it had felt amazing.

Somehow this ultraconservative government agent had flipped a button inside her that made her want to get naked and busy, and it scared the hell out of her. But not as much as the man with the big knife did.

She shivered.

He put his arm around her shoulders, startling her, and guided her around a group of college students all wearing shorts despite the cold weather. Some of the guys were checking her out. She knew she should be flattered by the stares and murmurs, but the scars that branded her flesh reminded her how superficial beauty was.

So maybe it wasn't the desire to prove her father wrong that kept her from indulging in physical relationships. Maybe it was nothing more than simple vanity. Touching Marsh like this, pressed so close against him, made her heart speed up and excitement flutter along her veins. She'd always pushed heterosexual males away because she was afraid to let anyone see her scars. But right now she had a heterosexual male by her side who'd seen all her many flaws. It didn't seem to be such a problem anymore.

But if scars had been her only issue she'd have just turned out the lights.

She was screwed up and the bottom line was she didn't want to let anyone close. Relying on anyone but herself was dangerous. She pushed away from Marsh. He only looked surprised it had taken so long.

"What happens next?"

"I'll set up protective custody," his voice went deeper, seductive and compelling, "get you into a safe house—"

"I'm not going to a safe house." He drew in a breath as if to argue, and for the first time in her life she felt compelled to explain. "Look. Social Services made it their mission to take me away from the one person in the world I trusted." A piece of lint clung to his lapel; she concentrated on brushing it off rather than the emotions that went hand-in-hand with thinking about Marion. Her gaze settled on the strong column of his throat, above his starched white collar. "There's no way I can stand to be locked up again."

"You'd rather be dead?"

"*I* wanted to leave, remember? To disappear? You're the one who wants me to stay and, yes, frankly I'd rather be dead than locked up in some 'safe house' waiting for someone to kill me." A lump swelled in her throat. "But I'd rather not be either."

The wind blew her hair in a wild flurry around her face. "I thought you wanted to catch this guy?"

"I want to nail him." His fingers squeezed her shoulders and her gaze rose to meet his. "But not if it means you getting hurt." His fingers were warm through her jacket, the pressure increasing, as if compelling her to trust him.

Slowly, he leaned forward and touched his forehead and nose to hers, hot flesh against cold. This was the most intimate gesture she'd shared with anyone, this one-on-one stare with a G-man she'd spent months hating, months fantasizing about. Flecks of gold glinted in his hazel eyes, and the banked heat of desire glowed deep and hot.

"I'll hire private protection—"

"I can pay for my own damned protection." She was unhappy at being vulnerable to a killer and inexplicably disappointed Marsh wouldn't be the one watching her. *Watching* her. *Right.* She drew back.

"There's no way I can protect you 24/7. I'll stay with you at night, but I have a job to do. And I'm hiring the bodyguard, so get over it."

Frustrated, she blew out a breath and remembered what Elizabeth had told her about Marsh's core sense of honor and justice. Poor deluded bastard.

"Where are you going right now?" He looked along the street as if suddenly noticing the throngs of tourists and shoppers.

"There's an art gallery on Mercer that sold two of my paintings last week, I was going to talk to the owner about what they might want to replace them with."

He glanced at his fancy wristwatch, as if mentally tallying up the minutes he needed to spend in her company. Sliding her teeth against one another she narrowed her gaze at the cracks in the sidewalk. Why was she so angry at him for doing his job? Why was she so angry, period?

"I'll walk you there. Dancer can swap with me later if I can't get hold of a friend of mine who lives in the city. You remember Steve Dancer, right?"

She nodded. Hard to forget Marsh's sidekick with his techno-gadgets. Steve Dancer had been nice to her even when everybody in the world, including Marsh, had hated her guts. Not even Nat Sullivan, Elizabeth's new husband, had wanted her around after she'd inadvertently brought Andrew DeLattio to his remote ranch. She could hardly blame him. Elizabeth had almost died and it had been her stupid fault.

Her shoulders sagged as Marsh herded her toward her appointment, already on the phone to a bodyguard whose number he knew by heart. She wanted her life back. Her nice, safe, insular little life that now seemed as cold and desolate as a wasteland.

There was a hot dog vendor on the corner of West Broadway, the aroma invading every particle of air she breathed, reminding her she'd only had one measly piece of toast since lunchtime yesterday.

"You want a hotdog?" she asked Marsh, groping for change in her purse.

The sun flared between clouds and light flowed over his dark hair, catching a hint of silver she hadn't noticed before.

"You're going to eat on the move?" Disapproval in every word.

"Yep." She wished she didn't find him quite so attractive, wished she'd never discovered what she'd been missing as a twenty-seven year old virgin. Life had been fine before that.

"Let's go somewhere decent—"

"This is decent." She shook her head, blew the hair out of her eyes. He was such a snob.

One hand on her elbow he pointed to the flies hovering on the ketchup dispenser. "This is a health hazard," he said.

Seriously… She rolled her eyes at him.

The sun broke fully through dissolute clouds, glinting warmly off his tanned skin. He tugged her away from the succulent aroma and reluctantly she fell into step beside him.

"Well, it better be quick—"

"Why, Josephine?" He stopped and looked down at her, a hard light in his eyes. "I thought artists were Bohemian, free spirits? Why are you always in so much of a damn rush that you don't look after yourself?"

"I'm hungry, you idiot." Angry at being so unfairly judged lit a fuse within her. "And I know how to look after myself." She planted her finger on his chest. "I've had plenty of practice looking after myself and aside from this stupid freaking serial killer on my tail, I do a pretty good job of it."

People streamed around them in the street. Marsh swept a pitying glance over her frame, from her Doc Marten boots to her favorite army jacket. She glared back, wanting to cross her arms over her chest, but knowing that would put her on the defensive rather than the attack.

"You're too damn thin. I could push you over with one finger." He copied her move and stuck his index finger in her sternum, between her breasts.

The world stopped. Time hovered. The people rushing past them ceasing to exist. There was nothing but the heat in his eyes and the energy that sizzled and circled between the points of contact of each finger on each chest, round and round, firing sparks through her heart and breasts, making her breath squeeze tight into a tiny ball.

Suddenly it was the flat of her hand against his white cotton shirt as if holding him off—but she wasn't and he knew it. He dropped his hand slowly away from her.

Speechless for once in her life, she finally let her hand drop away.

"Come on, woman." He took her elbow gently and steered her down the sidewalk. "Let's get some food."

***

They settled on a small Irish pub. Marsh ordered a steak sandwich. Josephine ordered beef pie, French fries and orange juice.

Marsh sipped water as they sat in silence. That pulse of desire that had rushed them on the street rattled him. Six months ago, he'd let her get way too close and he wasn't sure he'd ever get over it. Lust for her had clouded his judgment, affected his thinking and made him break the law. Not to mention nearly gotten his agent killed. Right now, he couldn't afford distraction, because this time it would be Josephine who wound up dead.

A huge mountain of food arrived in front of them and they both dug in. No way was she going to be able to eat all that. First she smothered the fries in vinegar, then ketchup, and she started eating like she was ravenous. One French fry after another disappeared between those delicate lips. She licked salt off with a darting pink tongue.

She looked up. "What?"

Marsh shook his head and stared at the rapidly disappearing food. "I hope you're not doing that to impress me."

"I'm starving." Wiping a napkin over her mouth, she paused. "And you know I rarely do anything to impress anyone."

"Except Marion?" He watched her reaction.

The fork paused in midair, and she went completely still. "I'd have done anything for Marion" she admitted.

"What happened to your real mother, Josephine?"

Pain was buried beneath the angry look she threw him and he immediately regretted pushing her when she put down the fork and stopped eating. The woman needed building up. She was thinner than she had been in the spring. Couldn't afford to drop another pound.

He didn't understand why she attracted him so much. She was too skinny and had issues the size of the Empire State Building. The pulse above her collarbone fluttered delicately as she shrugged and he wanted to kiss her there.

"She took off." Her eyes flicked right, which would have been great except Marsh knew she was left-handed and the physical clues for lying usually got twisted around.

So why lie?

"How old were you when she left?" He watched her lips pucker as she thought about his question.

"Nine."

Same age as when she'd been knifed.

"So what? Your mother abandoned you just after some psycho attacked you?" *What kind of woman did that?*

Silver blonde hair fell around her face as she shook her head. She picked up the fork again and stabbed a piece of beef out of the rich fragrant gravy.

"She left before that." She put the meat in her mouth and chewed. "Ran off with some guy from

79

our church."

"Did you say *church*?" Marsh raised a shocked brow.

Josephine gave him a bad-ass grin. "Yeah. I was a devout little Catholic girl right up until the day I found out it was all bullshit."

"And you never heard from your mother again?" He persisted, unsure why, except for the desire to find out what made her tick. The blank expression on her face made him wish he could read minds.

"Never saw her again." She smiled without humor. "Not that I blame her for getting out." The blue of her eyes deepened. "Well, you met my daddy, right?"

He nodded. He had indeed met her father, a scumbag who'd been willing to sell his daughter's life for the price of a bottle of whisky. But what sort of mother abandoned her child into the care of such a man?

Josephine polished off the last of her fries and downed her juice while he toyed with his food. Walter Maxwell's tiny apartment had been cockroach ridden and filthy. His stomach rebelled at the memory and he pushed away his sandwich. Josephine had gone through hell as a kid. She didn't deserve to die at the hands of a psychopath. Then again, who did?

His phone rang. It was Dancer. "Do you mind if I take this call?" he asked.

She shook her head.

"I got a name for the source of the painting, but you're not going to like it," Dancer said.

What else is new? "Go on."

A giant walked through the entranceway of the

restaurant and searched the room until he spotted Marsh. Marsh waved him over.

"The company that sold the allegedly-stolen possible Vermeer is one Blue Steel Trading Corporation. Owned by the wife of Senator Brook Duvall. Prudence."

"You have got to be kidding me. Hold on a minute." Marsh put his hand over the mouthpiece and stood. Looking up at the ebony-skinned colossus who'd once served under him in the Navy, he grinned as he shook Vince's hand, grateful they were friends and not enemies. "Good to see you, Vince. Vincent Brandt, meet Josephine Maxwell. Josephine, meet Vince."

They eyed each other like a snake and a meerkat.

"I've got to go. Don't let her out of your sight until I get back tonight, Vince." Marsh looked down at the angelic countenance of the Blade Hunter's first victim. "And don't trust a word she says. She's a liar, and she's damn good at it."

Chapter Six

Marsh leaned over the table where the accounting records were laid out. He was back at Federal Plaza and beginning to wonder if he'd ever see his Boston office or home again, although New York City was getting more attractive by the minute.

Dancer peered out the window twenty-three flights down, where traffic resembled matchbox cars and people were two-legged ants scurrying from point A to B. A sparrow hopped onto the sill and Dancer tapped the glass and the bird flew away. Marsh ignored him, knowing the guy was frustrated with the turn of events in the investigation. They were about to wallow in a political quagmire and couldn't afford to screw up.

"Blue Steel Trading Corp sold the painting for $100,000, six months ago?" he asked.

"Yes. Which doesn't jive with the assumed value of the painting either." Aiden Fitzgerald, a renowned art expert who was also an undercover FBI agent, stared at a photograph of the painting blown up on a massive scale. "Even with the *De Hooch* signature, it's worth half a million, easy."

"Maybe the seller needed fast cash?"

"Or they knew it was stolen and wanted to get rid of it," Dancer added.

"At least someone went to the trouble of having it professionally cleaned." Aiden leaned back in his chair—model perfect, impeccably dressed. He steepled his fingers together, put the manicured tips to his lips. The New York art scene was his patch and he wore it well. "The De Hooch signature looks like it has been there for years. Assuming there is a Vermeer signature buried there—a big assumption at this point—why did they cover it up?"

"Maybe because a Vermeer suddenly coming to light would cause an international stir? Maybe they didn't want that sort of media spotlight."

Aiden's eyes cut to Marsh. Both World Wars had been a time of great disruption when many valuables had changed hands for many reasons. People had hidden their wealth and their spoils in a variety of disguises.

"The last Vermeer find, which is still doubted by many, sold for thirty-million in two thousand and four." Aiden placed his hands on the crisp white copy of the bill of sale. "Johannes Vermeer is only known to have created three-dozen paintings in his life. Most are in Museums, one, as you know, is listed stolen from the Gardner Museum." He blew out a big breath, tugged his lips as he examined the photograph one more time—the painting itself was still being processed for evidence in a nearby lab with more security than POTUS. "I still think, assuming it isn't a damn good forgery, this could be the real deal. The use of light..." His voice dropped away in admiration. He looked up. "It could go for as much as fifty million at auction today."

"So what the hell is it doing at a small gallery opening in New York City?" Marsh asked, rubbing his eyes. The Faradays had to have known it was more valuable than what they'd paid...but that was the point of being a dealer, right? To make a buck. "What was the price tag on it at the gallery last night?" Marsh asked.

Dancer pushed away from the window and crossed over to the desk. Pointed out a figure on a separate list. "Eight hundred grand." He whistled and flashed his boyish grin. "I'll take two."

Marsh drummed his fingers on the desk.

Pru Duvall had stood next to him, directly in front of that painting and hadn't even glanced at it, hadn't shown the slightest interest in anything except his date. It was possible she didn't have anything to do with the day-to-day running of Blue Steel Trading Corp and had never seen the painting before. But if she wasn't interested in art, what the hell was she doing at a NYC show? He didn't trust Pru Duvall and her husband was an asshole. But he was a well-connected asshole.

The Duvalls were staking out their political patch and the art scene in NYC was brimming with affluent, influential people—who else could afford to spend eight-hundred grand on a painting?

"Set up an interview with the Duvalls, Dancer, but keep it very low-key, very non-threatening. In their home if possible." Marsh checked his wristwatch, wondering how Josephine and Vincent were getting along. He pulled out his phone and dialed Vince's number. "What did the admiral say when you told him we'd found the painting?"

A flush of color made Dancer's freckles disappear and he had the grace to look ashamed. "I, ah, didn't reach him." He shuffled his legs as he leaned on the table. "The housekeeper said he was on a fishing trip to Alaska."

"Pretty sure they have phones in Alaska, Steve." Marsh ground his teeth at the sound of the dial tone. Dancer was the best electronics experts he'd ever known, but the man didn't deal well with power brokers. He could charm women with nothing more than a dimpled smile, but got tongue-tied with the brass. "Call the FBI office in Anchorage, have them track him down."

It was four o'clock in the afternoon. Marsh rubbed his temple and wondered what Vince and Josephine were up to. *And why weren't they answering the telephone?*

***

"It's too big."

"You're holding it wrong."

"How the hell do you walk around with this thing?" Josie strained her neck to peer up at Vince. His laugh started somewhere in his stomach and worked its way out of his lips—she felt the vibration move up her back as he stood behind her. With one enormous hand he took the gun out of her two-handed grip, replaced the magazine and slid it effortlessly back into his shoulder holster.

The cannon looked tiny in his hands.

"It's a Desert Eagle pistol, ma'am," Vince's eyes were darker than chocolate, with a hard polish of military. "Weighs more than four-pounds with the magazine loaded."

She shook her hands and rubbed her aching wrists. "Well damn. That won't work."

He frowned down at her, a diamond stud winking in one ear. "You looking for a self-defense weapon?"

"No, I'm thinking of invading Washington." She planted a hand on her hip and glared back at him. "Of course I'm looking for a 'self-defense weapon'."

God, even the thought made her cringe. She'd felt nothing but desperation when she'd looked through the sights on that monster pistol. And desperation meant fear.

She hated fear. Hated guns. She caught her bottom lip with her teeth. *Life sucked.* Get over it.

Elizabeth was on a delayed honeymoon in the middle of the Outback or she'd have phoned her for advice. She wasn't due back till next week and Josie doubted Nat would appreciate her interrupting their time together.

Her fingers ached from being so tightly clenched, so she relaxed her hands. Wished she could concentrate enough to do some painting, but even that was beyond her right now.

A flash of white teeth caught her by surprise. Vince smiled.

"We can arrange that."

"You'll help me get a gun?" Grinning from the relief of actually doing something proactive as opposed to sitting on her ass waiting for this killer to turn up, she grabbed her bag and raced up the steps to the door. "Where do we go? Do I need cash? How much?"

Vince stared at her narrowing his eyes, assessing. "Well, we'll need two recent photos—head and shoulder shots." He walked over to the big windows at the front of her apartment, examined the blinds and then closed them. Shutting out the sunlight. "And you'll need some ID. Birth certificate, probably, and money orders for the fingerprint and application fee—"

"Application?" Standing by her front door, her shoulders sagged as her mood plummeted. She reached for the doorknob.

"For a Special Carry License. Don't touch that door until I say so, young lady."

Rolling her eyes, she asked, "And how long will it take to get a Special Carry License?"

"Long enough to teach you how to use a handgun." Vince gave her one of those *God Almighty* stares that Marsh had down pat. They must teach them at Navy boot camp.

Irritated beyond politeness, she put an index finger to her lips and cocked her hip. "Hmmm, I wonder if that murdering bastard remembered to pick up his *concealed-knife* carrying permit before he started butchering women? I guess we should put out a news alert, huh?"

"You think this is funny?" Vince's intensity made her uneasy and uneasy pissed her off.

She grabbed the doorknob.

"Don't you—" Vince didn't yell, but his voice was like a sonic boom penetrating the brick and despite his bulk he lunged toward her quick as a crocodile. But she was faster.

She yanked the door wide open then fell back in shock when she realized a man stood there. Her heart scrambled into her throat. Vince drew his weapon and leapt toward her.

"Get back!" He pushed her against the wall as Special Agent Sam Walker drew a deadly looking pistol and pointed it at Vince's massive chest.

"No, no, no! FBI!" Josie struggled to move, tried to put herself in front of Vince, but his hand was like a metal brace across her chest. "He's FBI! FBI!" she gasped. Josie watched their expressions alter from warlike to wary.

"ID." Vince's voice brooked no opposition.

Thankfully, Sam Walker didn't argue. He

flipped his jacket to reveal that gold badge with the eagle on top and Vince lowered his gun, but didn't release her. In fact, the pressure of his palm on her sternum increased and Josie found it difficult to suck in a breath. Funny how there were no sexual fireworks, unlike when Marsh touched her.

Funny as a heart attack.

Slowly, with infinite care, Vince put his gun away, pulled his wallet out of his pocket and dug out some ID. "I'm this *lady's* bodyguard. I apologize for pulling a gun on you, sir."

Walker had the gall to look amused as he returned the ID and Vince continued to pin her to the wall. Her cheeks felt hot, and her lungs struggled to function with that much weight working against them.

"I only opened the door," Josie panted.

"You disobeyed a direct order, missy."

"I'm not in the..." Her vision started to gray. She wasn't about to apologize. She hadn't asked for this guy's help. "I'm not... in... the freaking Army..."

"Navy." Vince turned his head to trap her gaze. "If you want to get people like me and Special Agent Walker killed, you just carry on acting like a spoiled brat."

Josie ground her teeth, unable to squeeze the words out of her burning lungs. She was the target and yet she was the only one without a weapon. How the hell was that fair?

I didn't ask for your help...

Dark eyes pinned her as the world started to spin on the inside, but there was no way she was apologizing for opening her own front door, dammit.

***

The door to Josephine's apartment stood wide open. Marsh looked up the stairwell and started running, flicking the snap on his holster and putting his hand on the SIG's grip. He already had a round in the chamber.

Someone shouted out as he got to the top of the staircase.

"Don't get excited, Hayes." Special Agent Sam Walker came out the front door, fatigue digging trenches at the sides of his eyes.

Marsh put his back weapon and redid the snap. "Where's Josephine?" Shouldering his way past the other fed, he stopped abruptly as he caught sight of Vince leaning over a prostrate form.

"What the hell happened?"

Vince straightened and shook his head. "My fault. I underestimated the amount of pure stubborn pigheadedness running through her veins. She passed out rather than admit she might actually be in the wrong."

There was a snort from the couch. She fought to sit up, but Vince placed his palm on her head. "Lie down for another minute. Okay?"

To his surprise Josephine nodded and lay down. The blinds were drawn, probably against snipers, though Marsh doubted the Blade Hunter would get to her that way—not personal enough. Something moved at the edge of his vision. Sam Walker strode past him and down the steps into the sitting area.

"Can I have a drink of water, please?" Josephine's voice was sweet and seductive. Marsh felt a shot of heat. The last time he'd heard that tone was when she'd asked him to make love to her.

Would she use that tack on anyone? Sam Walker went into the kitchen and Marsh watched him go, anger burning beneath the surface of his skin. *Shit.* He shook his head, jealous as hell.

"Your bodyguard nearly killed me." She looked pathetic and frail lying there on the big scarlet couch, the giant looming over her. The same woman who'd once nailed him in the balls so hard he'd almost passed out.

"Yeah, I figured Vince was the type to knock a woman around. That's why I hired him." He exchanged a knowing look with the former SEAL. "Somehow I doubt this is Vince's fault."

Sam Walker came back into the room carrying a glass of water.

"Special Agent Walker saw it—didn't you, Sam?" Josephine sent the sonofabitch a tremulous smile and he nodded, a return smile on his face.

Dark emotions twisted through Marsh's gut. *Great.* Once again she'd reduced him to emotion rather than logic.

He sighed, sank down on the couch beside her. She curled up her legs to accommodate him. A pair of scruffy boots lay an inch from his suit pants. He picked one up, undid the laces and slipped the boot from her foot, dropped it onto the floor before laying her foot gently back on the couch. Repeating the action with the other foot, he saw Agent Walker watching him, a speculative gleam in his fatigue-rimmed eyes. Marsh dropped her other foot, which bounced on the cushion, didn't even have the energy to smile when she curled her feet beneath her pert bottom as she sat upright.

Enormous canvases covered the wall behind

Walker's head, distracting Marsh's gaze. The colors were white flames with the occasional intense splash of color that writhed and twisted as if trying to escape. He remembered the first time he'd seen them. Stunning, evocative—like the woman who'd painted them.

"Want to tell me what happened? Or shall we move on?" Marsh asked. Tension joined forces with a headache that beat the crap out of his skull.

Beetling his brows, Vince said, "I don't know if I can protect her if she refuses to cooperate with basic instructions." His eyes were on Marsh, intelligent, loyal and playing Josephine like a pro. Except she'd never played well with others.

"I don't need you anyway. I'll disappear. I know how—"

"Yeah, that worked out *so* well last time." Marsh was careful with words in front of Sam Walker, but her flinch of pain told him he'd struck home. The Mafia had tracked her down after torturing and murdering her father and the woman who'd raised her. If Marsh hadn't found her first, she'd have been dead. Their gazes locked, the blue of her eyes so vivid they looked like they'd been daubed on a fresh canvas.

Sam Walker took a seat next to Vince on the opposite couch, looking short by comparison.

"I don't think it's a good idea to take off." Walker's tone was subdued.

Josephine's hands gripped each other like tangle weed.

"Why? What do you have on this guy?" asked Marsh.

Walker pulled a folder out of his case. The sober quality of the man's stare made Marsh pay attention.

"Detective Cochrane pulled up a list of possible victims linked to this killer as far back as the mid-nineties, two cases from New Mexico and two from D.C. I've been going back through the records trying to link more possible victims—"

"What are you using to assess linkage?"

Sam shot a look around the room. "Whatever I say is classified. If any of this information is leaked I'll get you all charged with obstruction." He rested his elbows on his knees, a pen held loosely between his fingers. "Even you, sir." He nodded at Marsh.

Marsh figured he must have checked his alibi for the murders and he was off the hook. *About time.* "Then why are you telling us?"

"Because I know you have the clout to get the information anyway and I like the illusion of control." Walker didn't look impressed with Marsh's status and Marsh respected him more because of it. But he'd do whatever it took to keep Josephine safe from a killer. Walker stared hard at Josephine. "And because I think you're the first victim."

"I'm *not* a vic—"

"Are you sure?" Marsh cut across the denial that was an integral part of Josephine's existence.

Walker nodded and reached for a picture from the top of the pile. "I was initially concentrating on this woman in New Mexico because I thought she was the first victim. Her name is Donna Viera, murdered in the early nineties."

The photograph slid across the surface of the coffee table with a whisper of sound that stirred the hairs on Marsh's nape. Blonde. Skinny. Her body covered with a series of crisscross patterns that had bled profusely, streaking her skin.

"Cause of death?" Marsh asked.

Josephine averted her eyes and sipped water. Vince hunched over the table, staring at the photos of ritualized slaughter.

"She bled to death." Walker pulled out another photo and placed it beside that of Donna Viera. *Angela Morelli.* The woman from downstairs. *Two decades apart and the sonofabitch was still killing.* Marsh tried to control the fury that surged through him.

"These victims are almost definitely the work of the same person. Both vics are blonde, Caucasian women, late twenties to early thirties—attractive women."

Josephine put her water down abruptly, spilling it. "I'll get a cloth." She was halfway to her feet, but Marsh planted a hand on her thigh and held her in place. Vince got up to search for a towel. Marsh knew she wanted to avoid this, but it was important that she understood exactly what she was dealing with.

"Angela Morelli was a dyed blonde." Walker pointed to the woman's pubic region. "He skinned her genitals, probably as punishment."

A wave of revulsion rose in his throat, but Marsh shoved it down. Josephine had her hand over her mouth as Vince handed her the cloth. It dangled uselessly from her fingers so Marsh took it from her and wiped up the water she'd spilt.

"What about his MO?" Marsh asked.

Walker glanced across at Vince. "I know you're a decorated soldier and a war hero and all, but if this gets out…"

"I had top security clearance as of three months

ago and you think I've forgotten the rules already?" Vince's amused expression didn't fool Marsh. The slur on his character insulted the ex-SEAL.

"Vince is *the* most discreet person you'll ever meet," Marsh stated.

"And the most law abiding." Josephine shot Vince a glare, but he returned it with a quiet smile and a wink.

"I figure you need to know what the danger is." Walker pulled out two more photos. Two more women brutalized.

"These women were attacked in their own homes. They're single and were alone during the time of the attack. He spends considerable time with the victims. Several hours according to the evidence."

Josephine opened her mouth to speak, but closed it again, no words escaping.

Walker carried on. "Evidence suggests he gags them, ties them to their beds and then he cuts them. Repeatedly."

"Any DNA or trace evidence?" Marsh asked, hoping against hope.

Walker shook his head. "Nothing yielded a viable biological sample until the blood we found on the floor downstairs when you bit him. Analysis isn't back yet but they have a rush on it. Let's hope he's in the system." Looking at Josephine, he said quietly, "From what you've told us we figure he wears some kind of hat or mask, at least until he has the victim secured."

Josephine shuddered and turned away. Her skin was so pale the blue of her veins was visible beneath the surface on the backs of her hands.

"Why does he cut them?" Josephine's voice was

high pitched.

Walker shrugged. "Piquerism? Some people get sexual gratification from the act of cutting or stabbing. Or get off on the victim's pain."

"Sexual assault?" Marsh asked.

Walker shook his head.

"He didn't rape me." Josephine's tone held relief. Marsh reached out and took her hand, rubbing her cold fingers with his. She turned to face him, eyes stark with confusion. "Why not?"

"Maybe he's impotent." Marsh shrugged. He really didn't know what drove a man to kill for fun. The fact the victims hadn't been sexually assaulted was a plus, but he still made them suffer.

Walker fingered another file. Marsh recognized it and gritted his teeth. His secretary Dora had sent a copy of the report on Josephine's attack from his office in Boston to the NYPD and FBI at his insistence. Walker took out another photograph, this one a thin hollow-eyed child who lay sleeping in a hospital bed.

Every muscle in Josephine's frame tensed to stone. Then she started to shake. Slowly she extended a hand and stroked the edge of the photocopy like it was alive and the child might wake if she disturbed her.

The form in the picture was flat-chested, narrow hipped. Androgynous. Sexless.

"I think you were lucky on several counts." Josephine flinched but Walker continued. "His behavior hadn't escalated to murder yet, or you didn't fit his victim profile."

"You don't think he chose her specifically? You think she was an accident? Or an opportunistic attack?"

Walker shrugged. "It's a theory."

Vince stared hard at the table, mouth turned down, eyes focused on the images. "Is that you?" He nodded to the picture.

Picking it up, she nodded, her eyes wide with shock.

His deep baritone stirred the air. "So how many women do you think this animal has killed?"

Sam Walker looked grim, rubbed his hands over his face.

"Well, after interviewing Ms. Maxwell, I decided to run the information through ViCAP again, only this time I omitted the MO and just used the knife wound information."

They locked eyes and Marsh held his breath, dread settling into his marrow. "How many?" he asked.

"I've found ten that fit with what we already had—all blondes, with their skin sliced rather than stabbed, some found in remote locations, others pulled out of rivers, some even burned."

"He's destroying evidence."

Walker nodded at Marsh's grim statement. "And now Interpol is involved..." The silence stretched on and on until Marsh wanted to grab the man by his jacket lapel and shake the information out of him.

"How many?"

"We're setting up a timeline of disappearances going back as far as nineteen ninety-three when Josie was attacked—"

"How many?" Marsh repeated harshly.

"Maybe fifteen since ninety-three," said Walker. "Sometimes it's impossible to tell if decomp is too advanced."

Vince swore and turned away.

Fear and unease radiated from Josephine's taut frame like a violin string being plucked. Walker stared at her, but Marsh didn't know what the man expected her to do. *Feel guilty? For what?* He doubted she knew her attacker, though she wasn't telling them everything.

Marsh hated seeing her scared. It tied a knot in his gut and scrambled his brains when he needed them most. He stared at the hardwood floor, knowing this situation was going to get worse before it got better—unless they got very, very lucky.

"Why does he cut them?" Marsh repeated Josephine's question.

Vince frowned, hunched forward, his hands clasped together.

"Scarification is big on the S & M scene. Lust murderers are often involved in sadism." Walker shrugged. "We don't know, we're guessing at this point."

"So have you guys worked up a profile?"

"The guys at the BAU are working on it now we have more information—unfortunately there are more murderers than FBI resources." Walker frowned down at the coffee table, ran his hands along the hard edge. "We know we're looking at a geographically transient, organized offender."

"The hardest type to catch." It wasn't news to any of them that they were dealing with a smart bastard, but even smart bastards made mistakes.

Walker flipped some pages in his notebook.

"Age," he pressed his lips together. "This new information revises our age estimate. Assuming he was between eighteen and twenty-five when he first attacked Ms Maxwell, that puts him around thirty-eight years to forty-five years of age."

Which gave him a lot of good killing years left…

"Caucasian?" Vince queried.

Walker looked at Josephine who nodded in confirmation. "Yes, average height, white male with gray eyes is about our only solid point of reference right now."

"What do you want from me?" A single silvery tear tracked down her cheek. She didn't wipe it away, perhaps thinking they wouldn't notice it if she didn't draw attention to it.

Marsh answered for Walker. "In serial murder cases, the first and last victims are the most revealing about the UNSUB."

He moved the photograph of Angela Morelli next to the picture of Josephine as a child, mentally recoiling from both. She was the key.

Her gaze was transfixed on the gruesome photographs.

"What were you doing in Queens that day, Josephine?" Marsh asked.

Pain filtered through the deep blue eyes, followed by denial. She shook her head and then opened her mouth to speak. Shut it again. Frowning, she picked up a shot of Donna Viera.

"Oh, god." Shock made her sit up straighter, balancing on the edge of the cushion.

"What?" Walker pushed. "What is it?"

"My mom. This woman looks like my mom." Josephine covered her mouth. "Maybe he was stalking her, the night he found me."

"I thought you said your mother disappeared before you were attacked?" said Marsh.

She went silent and Marsh wondered if she'd finish telling her story or clam up the way she usually did.

Mouth half obscured by hair and fingers she said, "I followed her that night. That's why I went to Queens." She squeezed her eyes closed, clearly torn with indecision, a pink flush rising up her cheeks and neck.

"Why did you follow your mom, Josephine?"

"It was so long ago." She slouched back against the couch, staring at the high ceiling.

"*Try* to remember." Sam Walker barely contained his frustration. Marsh knew exactly how he felt.

She gave a bitter laugh. "That's the trouble. I remember every detail."

The slight tilt of Walker's lips gave away his skepticism. Eyewitnesses were notoriously unreliable. And after all this time…

"I was worried she was going to leave me again. She'd left for a few weeks when I was younger and…" Her laugh was bitter. "Well, I was right wasn't I? I never saw her again."

Her eyes glazed over as she looked into the past. "I was on my way home from school when she got on a bus I was riding, but she didn't see me because I was sitting toward the back."

Marsh had to strain to hear her voice as it grew softer.

"She'd been acting strangely, dressing nicer, wearing make-up, smiling." Josephine caught her lip with strong white teeth. Continued to stare at the high vaulted ceiling. "So I followed her. She got off in Queens, went into this big red-brick building with a fire-escape that snaked up the outside.

"I climbed onto a Dumpster and managed to catch the lower bar of the fire escape and hauled myself up. I was a gymnast back then so it was easy." A slight frown touched her brow.

Exchanging a look with Walker, Marsh wondered if this was the break they needed.

"I peeped in different windows searching for her and finally, I found her." Disgust dripped off her words. "Being fucked against the wall by a guy from St. Mary's Church." Slowly, carefully, she picked up her glass of water and drained it. "Nice, huh? Brought a whole new meaning to *Come all ye faithful.*"

"You remember the guy's name?"

She shook her head.

"So what happened next?" Walker prompted, stone-faced.

Josephine glared at him, rubbed her hands over her knees in an unsettling repetitive gesture. "It got dark, but I hadn't realized. I just sat on the fire-escape, watching, waiting for Mom to go home."

Marsh's chest tightened as he fought for breath. Imagining the child on the fire escape.

"Then all of a sudden this guy wearing a mask was beside me." She looked up, eyes stark in her pale face, "He clamped his hand tight over my mouth and dragged me to that alley." She shrugged. "Everything else is in the police report."

Special Agent Walker tapped a pen against a notepad that had appeared in his hand. "Could your attacker have been the same man who was in the room with your mother?"

Her hair fell out of its knot. She shook it out in an untidy halo. "I don't think so. They'd gone into the bedroom or bathroom, out of sight. I was watching the front door, and I never saw him leave."

"But is it possible?" Walker pushed.

Josephine shrugged, looking confused, "I suppose, but why'd my mom let him hurt me? Oh…" Her mouth opened and closed. Ashen-faced, she caught up with where Agent Walker had been trying to take her. Marsh wanted to cradle her in his arms and soothe her rigid muscles. He didn't dare touch her.

"You think my mother's dead?" Her voice rose and she lurched to her feet. "How could she be dead? There was no report of a murder."

"Maybe we never found the body," Walker suggested gently.

"Why leave me alive?" She paced toward the covered windows, her black pants clinging to slender hips, her droopy sweater hanging loosely across her shoulders.

"Maybe he couldn't bring himself to kill a kid?" Marsh suggested. "When you passed out he took the opportunity to get rid of the body before you woke up?"

Josephine stopped pacing, her hands coming up to cover her face, sobs wracking her shoulders.

"Dammit." Kicking himself for forgetting the *body* might be Josephine's mother, Marsh moved to where she stood and wrapped his arms around her, forced her head to rest on his chest as her body shook.

"The interview is over." Marsh stared at Agent Walker whose mouth tightened with annoyance. "Read the police reports, check the tenant records of the buildings Josephine was found near and see if any Jane Does matching, damn, what's your mother's name, Josephine?"

"Margo, Margo Maxwell. Margo Thomas before she got married." The words were mumbled into his shirt, tears wet against the thin fabric, making it stick to his skin.

"See if any Jane Does matching the profile turned up in the six months after Josephine's attack, or if Margo Maxwell surfaced alive elsewhere— check her Social Security number and driver's license—that should tell you whether or not she's dead."

Josephine's sobs grew louder. *Christ*, he was as sensitive as a neutron bomb. He held her tightly, trying to offer comfort, but the muscles in her back were cast-iron beneath his fingers.

"Will we see you tomorrow, Vince?" He stared at the big man. There was something unsettled about Vince that suggested he didn't want this job. Who could blame him?

Ebony eyes looked up, the diamond stud glinting briefly in his ear. "Oh-seven-hundred, sir." Gathering his huge frame, Vince stood. "She gonna be all right?" He nodded uncertainly toward Josephine's worsening cries.

"Yes." Marsh inclined his head to Agent Walker who'd retrieved his files and stood, hesitating as if he was reluctant to leave.

"I'll need to interview her again tomorrow." Tiredness etched his features like decomposition degraded a corpse.

Marsh knew the guy was a good cop but right now Josephine was his priority. "She'll be ready." Ready to help nail the bastard who attacked her so many years ago and who might also have killed her mother.

Chapter Seven

There was pain in her chest. It expanded and grew. Crippled. Ripped. All these years, she'd tried not to hate her mother for abandoning her, for leaving her behind with an abusive father. But maybe, rather than leaving, her mother had been murdered and dumped, and no one had cared enough to look.

She couldn't bear it.

Warm safe arms engulfed her. Heat and strength cradled her in a protective cocoon as tears dripped down her face and off her chin. *Why hadn't someone asked questions?*

Her father had drunk himself into oblivion and blamed her. And Josie had stupidly believed him. She'd seen her mother with another man and had decided with childish certainty it was her fault. She'd driven her mother away because she'd never been good enough.

It was classic. Classic and stupid and self defeating. Nine years old. *Nine years old* and responsible for everything that happened in the world—a belief confirmed when she'd been punished by the man with the big knife.

I won't kill you if you don't make a sound... She hadn't made a sound. The bastard had murdered her mother and she'd never made a sound.

She stuffed her fist over her mouth, still trying to quiet the sobs that wouldn't stop. She didn't break down, she didn't break. Ever. But right now there was nothing she could do but weep for her mother and the little girl she'd been. Warm hands rubbed her back. Strong arms held her upright. Finally the tears slowed and she remembered exactly who the arms belonged to.

She gripped the soft cotton of Marsh's shirt. Her throat felt raw. "If he killed her...I need to know. I need to get this bastard."

His eyes glittered as he ran his hands down her arms, supporting her at the elbows. "We'll get him." His voice was firm, the undertone urging her to believe in him—in the system. But would he do whatever it took? Or would he play it by the rules like Vincent?

"I need a gun."

"I hired you one. His name is Vincent Brandt."

By the book.

Counting on Marsh and Vince felt like juggling hand grenades—not good for her mental health, but she wasn't dumb enough to take on this predator without all the help she could get. She just wished she could defend herself. She moved away from him. The sun had set and the apartment was clothed in deep shadows that reminded her too much of that long ago night. She turned on a lamp. There was an unsettled feeling in the pit of her stomach; more than grief, more than fear, more than hatred. She was a loner. She didn't work well with others. It wasn't what she was used to.

"What if he kills you and Vince?" Unexpected pain sliced into her at the thought. The words revealed too much weakness so she gave them a twist. "And I'm left with him and he has all the weapons? I'll have nothing to defend myself with."

"If he's shooting at me or Vince, or any other law enforcement personnel for that matter, you run like hell, scream like crazy and get yourself to a safe place."

Marsh drew a handkerchief from his pocket and handed it to her.

"You must be the only guy left in the world who carries handkerchiefs." She sniffed, knowing she'd never win this argument. No way would Marsh trust her with a gun. Frankly she didn't blame him. She wiped her face, blew her nose and then pocketed the white linen in her pants. "I like that about you."

"Well, at least that's something." His smile crinkled the corners of his eyes but it didn't hide the sadness. Or the regret.

They hadn't done well together because she didn't know how to act like a normal person. She'd never been normal. She was damaged and insecure. Had grown up trying to survive. Something in his gaze made her wish things were different, that she was different. She held her breath, but he looked away as if suddenly uncomfortable. A thought struck her and she looked down, concentrating on her hands. Marsh was dating someone. She'd forgotten.

"You should go. I'll be okay tonight. I'll lock myself in and promise not to open the door for anyone. Go back to your girlfriend. I'm sure she's missing you."

"What are you talking about?" Marsh's brows pinched as his frown deepened. Then his expression cleared and humor lit his eyes, making them gleam wickedly. "Ah, my date from last night?"

Was it only last night since her safe narrow little world had shattered? It felt like a million years ago. Jealousy stirred low in her breast, unfamiliar and ugly. "Did you have the *best-sex-ever* with her too?"

Whoa, where the hell had that come from? And why did she feel so angry with a man who was doing so much to help her? She was an idiot.

"Lynn's eighteen and hot as hell." Marsh moved toward her in a way that made her jealousy morph into unease. There was grace in his movements, banked heat in his gaze.

"And I thought you were too old for me." She eyed him apprehensively, but forced herself to remain still. On many levels he made her feel safe—all except one. Her awareness of him as a man scared the crap out of her. He stepped closer. Suddenly she was brought up short by the wooden mantel against her shoulders and the realization she'd been backing away.

"I am too old for you." The wicked gleam turned molten as he glanced down at her lips. He lowered his head, slowly. She watched, fascinated, powerless to move because she wanted him to kiss her. And for all her faults she'd never been a hypocrite, so she rose onto tiptoes and braced her hands on his wide shoulders. Surprise radiated through suddenly taut muscles. Her soft, hesitant lips met a warm, hard mouth. She closed her eyes and let herself kiss him. Savored the careful exploration, the sweet hesitancy. It was so unexpectedly gentle, so foreign and so heady.

He placed his hands on the small of her back, brought her flush against him, every point of contact cycloning excitement through her body like an electric shock. Her breasts tingled, nipples grew aching and tight. She ran her hands through his hair, wondering why every sensation was heightened just because *he* touched her.

His lips released hers, cruised her neck, her ear. Shivers danced along her skin, heat thrumming along her veins like liquid craving. He lifted her off the ground and she wrapped her legs around his hips, his erection rubbing against her center, feeling so amazing she wanted even closer. He braced her against the wall. The unrelenting hardness at her back felt good against her spine. Solid and reliable while the rest of her world crashed around her. He stroked her and sensations exploded between her legs, making her muscles clench and her breath gasp.

"I want you. I always want you even though you drive me crazy." His breath blistered her ear, his hand rough on her breast, playing with her nipples, making her damp. Making her tremble with desire. He ground against her and she wished he was inside her, filling her as she cascaded over that inexplicable edge, lights flashing, sirens blazing, crying out with astonishment.

It was as spectacular as she remembered. She closed her eyes to absorb the pleasure, but the image of her mother being fucked against a wall drove all the passion from her mind and she shoved away from him.

"Oh, god." Nausea whirled through her. *Whore. Slut.* She stumbled toward the bedroom.

Marsh grabbed her arm and swung her round. "What's wrong? Are you okay?"

"I'm like her." She wiped her hand over her mouth, trying to rub away the memory. "Just like my mother."

"You're normal." Frustration roughened his voice. "Sex is normal."

But she wasn't. She pulled away and he released

her, anger glowing in the depths of his eyes.

"You have a girlfriend," she whispered.

"No, and the fact I let you think I do shows how low I've sunk. I don't usually play games, Josephine. I'm not that kind of guy." He dragged his hands through his hair and took a deep breath. "My mother is trying to set me up and marry me off to any woman who'll have me. I do *not* have a girlfriend. The whole time we were out I felt like her goddamned father." He looked so pissed her heart clenched. The thought of him getting married—being permanently unavailable gutted her. And she didn't want anything to do with him—*remember*?

"I haven't been with anyone since you...since *we*...had sex. You've ruined me for anyone else." There was a raw honesty in his tone that froze her to the spot.

"That was six months ago."

His smile was pained. "I know. I can't get you out of my head."

She stared at him. She couldn't get him out of her head either. It wasn't only sex although that was confusing enough. She wasn't some shy miss, but this was unfamiliar territory. Complete with forbidden fruit. Bottom line was she was clueless about sex. Sure, she'd seen it in movies and during biology class and god help her, she'd drugged Marsh and seduced him, never thinking she'd *enjoy* what they did. But it seemed so long ago, the pleasure he'd stirred inside her moments ago was so fresh, so...incredible. She wanted it again—to repeat it and try to learn how to be a *normal* woman. But one way or another, sex had been her mother's downfall and it had cost Josie her childhood. And sex was all there could ever be between a girl like her and the ultra-conservative federal agent.

If sex was dangerous, relationships were warzones.

Marsh turned and walked up to the front door. For one awful moment she thought he was leaving, but he flicked the locks and the deadbolt. Relief surged through her and it wasn't all to do with evading a serial killer. She watched him stroll down the stairs, graceful as a tiger, charming as the devil, wishing like hell she was good and mad, and could deal with him. Instead his eyes were on her body with *that* look again and she reacted with a sharp inhalation.

They needed a distraction.

"Food." She dove for the kitchen.

"This isn't finished, Josephine." His voice was soft and warm, sending tingles running down her spine.

It was definitely finished.

His laughter chased her and she foolishly thought it *was* over until he followed her into the kitchen, where she was digging into the bottom of a cupboard, searching for a sieve. She glanced over her shoulder. Marsh loosened the knot of his tie and shrugged out of his suit jacket, slinging it over his arm.

Sinful. Gorgeous. Suave and strong. The words didn't begin to describe how the look of him affected her. And when he wasn't being an arrogant bastard she actually *liked* SAC Marshall Hayes. And that scared her more than the idea of them screwing like rabbits.

"What are you doing?" He arched a single dark

109

brow, his eyes roving her ass like he couldn't help himself.

Ignoring an answering pull, she dragged her hair back from her eyes, spotted the white handle of the sieve and grabbed it, straightened up.

"Baking a cake." She glared when his mouth dropped open in surprise. "What?"

"I didn't think you even knew how to boil an egg."

Opening a drawer to find measuring cups, she paused for a moment and took a breath, rather than just reacting. Time to confront this thing. "That's because we don't know each other very well, do we?"

"We know each other better than you want to admit."

Turning to face him, she was rocked by the full force of his gaze.

"I know you've got a bitch of a temper, which hides a whole arsenal of insecurity." His voice was soft and made her shiver. "I know you fight dirty especially when frightened." He took a step closer and she wanted to bolt. "I know you make a funny little sound in your throat when you come."

Blushing furiously, she looked away. He was the only person on the planet who knew that about her.

"I know you were a brave little kid who overcame a hell of a childhood to go on to become a successful artist." He paused and she looked up, unable not to. "And I know you're true and loyal to those you love."

His image of her rocked her. She was bitchy, and abrasive, and had spent most of her life running away from her reality. She didn't know how he saw any good beneath the surface she showed the world.

He took another step bringing him within arm's length, trailed his index finger gently down her forehead, sweeping her nose and coming to rest on her lower lip, which trembled.

"I know I want you."

Rattled beneath his perceptive gaze, she fought the pathetic sensation that invaded her limbs. She couldn't afford to let this man in. She'd never survive losing him too. "Even if I don't want you for anything but protection from a madman?" She narrowed her eyes against the intensity of his gaze.

"What if I said I don't want you for anything but sex?" he countered, then tipped her chin up. "But then I'd be lying and I promised I'd stop doing that when it came to you."

The thump of her heart against her ribs was so violent, she was sure he could hear it. Shoving past him, she crashed out of the kitchen and into her bedroom, slamming the door behind her. So much for not running away, so much for facing her fears. There was no laughter, no joy. Only bleak knowledge that Marshall Hayes was more dangerous to her soul than any knife wielding maniac.

***

He looked at the dead girl on the bed. Wrists and ankles bound. Blonde hair splayed across the dark sheets, almost gold in this light. Blue eyes, fading from bright and terrified to opaque and lifeless. Decomposing before his eyes. *For they have sown the wind, and they shall reap the whirlwind.*

111

It was her own fault.

"I won't kill you if you don't make a sound..."
Only the child had remained silent. But she wasn't a child any longer. A shiver ran through his flesh as he remembered the scars. Perfect silver marks against pale white skin.

His.

The same way this pathetic creature was his.

Blood soaked the mattress. It spattered him too. He stepped out of his coveralls and stuffed them in a black garbage bag that he'd incinerate. The knife handle was solid in his hand. Weighty. Familiar. Latex gloves made his palms sweat. A necessary evil. Duct tape quieted her screams. Another concession to the neighbors.

Killing in the city was more difficult than killing in the great outdoors, but even though he missed the thrill of the noise they made when he cut them, he had no intention of getting caught. Once he'd finished what he'd started all those years ago, once he'd completed the circle, he'd move on. He'd change his identity and stop for a while. Experiment with other ways to calm the bloodlust.

The scars on his chest itched. He couldn't stop forever. God knew he'd tried.

Memories of violence ricocheted inside his head like a hammer smashing a steel drum. The tightness in his chest made breathing difficult. *Only boys and women scream. It's time to be a man.* He opened his eyes wide so he could see his power, not remember his weakness. He was a man now, not a child. It was his turn to dominate and control.

He started to shake. It was too soon to have done this again, but the rush was too hot, too intense to fight for long. The drums grew louder. He craved the domination, despised the weakness.

He looked down at the girl's bloody perfection and breathed deep, trying to calm the fierce contractions of his heart. *He* was the last thing she'd seen on this earth and the knowledge filled him with power that no one could ever take away. He eyed the area of flesh he'd skinned. She'd had a tattoo marring her body. She was his canvas. His work, and she'd been tainted by graffiti. Not a masterpiece, not even close. But she'd served her purpose and now it was time to get out. He picked up the garbage and stroked her face one last time. Maybe once he killed the child he could move on from the past. He'd destroy it all if he had to.

***

A Queen Anne desk and matching chair were positioned before the window overlooking Gramercy Park. Light streamed through the sheer drapes, casting a soft almost spiritual glow over the room. Marsh squinted against the brightness. Josephine wasn't talking to him. He forced himself to relax his jaw, hoping to alleviate the headache that drilled his temples. It had been a long night on a hard couch, staring up at a dull ceiling while trying not to think about the woman in the next room.

Fresh peonies and gardenia sat in a fat crystal globe adding an overpowering scent to the picture-perfect room. A *Degas* sketch hung over the Adam's fireplace. Elegant. Expensive. The décor reminded him of a thousand other sitting rooms of a thousand other society matrons whom he'd visited over the years, including his own mother's.

Leaning against a damask-covered settee he tried to picture Pru Duvall in this setting and failed. Somehow the image didn't jive. Despite her Southern hauteur and classy pedigree, the hard edge of her personality made her more suited for chrome, marble and splintered glass.

With his expensive suit and highly polished Italian shoes, god help him, he fit right in. Adjusting the strap on his holster allowed him at least the illusion he was something more than society dead weight. The memory of a sulking Josephine sipping coffee and staring silently out of her loft window flashed through his mind. They came from totally different worlds but he didn't care. He'd almost lost her a few days ago. Tragedy had brought them together but this time he was determined to work things out. Somehow.

So how the hell did I manage to screw up last night so badly?

Pru strode in, followed by the aide he'd seen at the opening. Marsh stood as Dancer straightened from where he'd been examining a *Meissen* snake-handle-vase.

Marsh flicked an uneasy gaze at his agent. *Please, don't bug a US Senator and his wife.*

"Marshall Hayes." The crackle in Pru's voice was husky. "You turn up in the most unexpected places. If I didn't know better I'd think you'd taken a fancy to me."

Inside Marsh recoiled, but quashed it. Maybe Josephine was right, maybe Pru was looking for a little extracurricular bedroom action and though he'd rather suck battery acid, he sent her a smooth smile. "A woman as lovely as you must have many admirers."

Tilting her head courteously, she seemed to accept his compliment at face value, or accept the society dance the way they'd both been raised. Her baby-pink sweater was cashmere, her A-line skirt mauve-colored tweed. Everything screamed conservatism, except for the scalpel-edged glint in her eyes.

Turning her head, she faced Dancer with another predatory smile. "And who are you?"

With his floppy red hair and freckles, Steve Dancer looked more like a Catholic schoolboy than an FBI Special Agent. Something that usually worked to his advantage. Right now Pru Duvall looked like she dined on Catholic schoolboys for breakfast.

He walked over and shook her hand. "Special Agent Dancer. Pleasure to meet you, Mrs. Duvall." Marsh had a sudden vision of Huckleberry Finn being made into a fashion accessory by Cruella De Vil.

"And this is Geoffrey Parker, Brook's PA." She wiggled her fingertips in the aide's direction and he nodded briefly, clearly uncomfortable with the situation. "I've stolen him for the morning."

The perfect society hostess, Pru rang for coffee and made herself comfortable on the loveseat opposite. Never mind they were here to interview her for something as tawdry as art fraud and theft.

Marsh waited for the coffee to arrive before he got down to business. He set down his dainty porcelain cup on its dinky saucer and felt like a bumbling giant. Dancer looked as uncomfortable with his, holding it protectively like a quarterback shielded a ball.

"Mrs. Duvall, Pru. I need to ask you about a

painting you sold to Total Mastery Galleries last spring—it was on show at the same gallery opening you attended the other evening."

She waved her hand in a way that suggested talking trade was crude. "I have a business manager who handles all that. Geoffrey can give you his card."

"Your business manager will need to answer some pretty serious questions, Pru. Possibly criminal." Marsh watched her pupils dilate.

"Why?" Geoffrey ventured, trying to diffuse a potentially volatile situation.

Marsh drew out a photograph of the painting from his jacket pocket. Slipped it onto the table. "Do you recognize it?"

She shook her head.

Despite his many years being a lawman he couldn't read her. "Blue Steel Trading Corporation sold the picture for a fraction its actual worth, about six months ago." He didn't mention that the painting was a suspected Vermeer and worth much more. *De Hooch* was valuable enough. And regardless, it was stolen.

Pru picked up her own coffee and sipped delicately. "What does my having an incompetent business manager have to do with the FBI?"

"The painting was actually stolen in February nineteen-ninety from Admiral Chambers." Marsh watched for a reaction.

"That old coot?" The light in her eyes was cold, but she laughed. "He probably lost it in a poker game after drinking too much and forgot about it the next day."

Marsh had figured Brook and Pru Duvall might know the admiral, though laughter wasn't the reaction he'd expected.

"Be that as it may, he reported it stolen and your company sold it to Total Mastery Galleries this year. We need to know where it's been the last decade and, more importantly, where you obtained the painting."

The lines around Pru's eyes creased infinitesimally. More power to plastic surgery. "Like I said, Marshall." Her fingers gripped her cup lightly, tendons straining beneath her pale skin. "My business manager handles all that."

Geoffrey cleared his throat, but Marsh ignored him.

"Are you telling me you have no knowledge of this painting?" He tapped his fingers on the photo she hadn't even glanced at.

Pru picked it up and made a big show of focusing, as if she needed glasses. Marsh bet his badge her sight was 20:20, laser-quality.

"I don't pay much attention to art." She raised a brow and looked straight at him as if daring him to disagree.

"Can you tell me why you were at the gallery opening on Friday night then?" Picking up his ridiculous cup of coffee, he finished it in one gulp.

"We received an invitation. We went."

"So you don't actually know the Faradays?"

Something altered in the light of her eyes. Leaning forward she held his gaze. "Have I done something illegal, *Special Agent in Charge* Hayes? Because if you are hinting at indiscretion on my part I'll call my lawyer."

Marsh had wondered when the big guns would be drawn. Seemed they'd reached Pru Duvall's very low tolerance for the US justice system. And she hadn't answered the question. Although given her impatient nature maybe that wasn't such a surprise.

Geoffrey moved toward Pru. "I'll get you the contact information you need, Agent Hayes."

Interview over.

Marsh tilted his head. His smile was sweet as honey. "I'm sure your business manager can clear up any misunderstanding." He stood. "I certainly don't want to cause trouble for Brook so close to the race for nomination." His smile was flat.

Dancer hid a guffaw behind a cough and drew Pru's attention. She stared at him the way a cat scoped out a mouse.

"That's a bad cough you've got there, Agent Dancer," she purred. "I hope it doesn't turn into something nasty."

Dancer sobered quickly. "I'm always extra careful with my health, Mrs. Duvall."

"Good." The reply was accompanied by another icy smile. Prudence Duvall was hiding something and he was going to find out exactly what it was. As they left he eyed the *Meissen* vase. Marsh hoped Dancer had bugged the witch.

Chapter Eight

Josie combined work with a pilgrimage. The Statue of Liberty loomed overhead, three hundred and five feet, two-hundred and twenty-five tons of American pride. Designed by the French. Celebrating independence from the British.

And didn't that say it all.

Oil pastels made her hands greasy. Her sketchbook rested against a mini-easel Elizabeth had bought her a couple of Christmases ago, expensive as hell, and not something Josie would ever have indulged in.

Her mood plunged. The scent of brine was thick in the air, but when she closed her eyes for a split second she was back in Montana and Andrew DeLattio had her crowded into the back of his van, his hand up her shirt as he taunted Elizabeth on her cell phone. She missed her best friend. Thanked god Andrew DeLattio had gotten his head blown off before he could hurt her again.

A shudder of revulsion snaked down her spine. He was dead, dammit, and the Blade Hunter was going to join him in hell.

A gull screamed overhead and broke her reverie.

Vince lay twenty feet away stretched out on the grass. He looked asleep, but she figured ex-Navy SEAL war heroes could look asleep without actually being asleep. Took years of training, but no one ever said being a SEAL was easy.

The sun felt hot on her cheek. She picked up a

pale blue pastel, squinted at it then switched it for a darker shade instead. The sky was a brilliant ultramarine. Pristine and perfect and peaceful.

A deception as every New Yorker knew.

Her mouth turned down at terrible memories that had changed her and her city forever.

They said that what didn't kill you made you stronger but if that were true she wouldn't be such a coward about everything that really mattered.

Concentrating on the only thing she knew how to do well, she started shading in some of the background, having blocked out the statue and pedestal with broad strokes. There was something vibrant about the way the green of the statue shimmered against that bright blue sky and she wanted to capture it. Photographs helped, but she knew from experience they wouldn't reproduce the colors exactly. Nor would pastel but she had her paints too. Using combinations of all three media she hoped to do the lady justice.

As a native, she'd been commissioned by the Tourist Board to do a series of NYC paintings. It was good reliable work in a career that rarely had good reliable work.

The first two paintings had been of the Chrysler Building and the Empire State. One, a close up of the art deco detailing; the other a monument to a more ascetic architectural period. Rubbing the bridge of her nose she sighed. It was hard to draw skyscrapers in this city—too much associated pain. She looked over her right shoulder at the place where so many people had perished and her throat closed.

Bracing her shoulders, she raised her chin. She wouldn't be a coward because one man wanted to hurt her. People from this city were stronger than that. They weren't easily cowed, especially when they had a hulking bodyguard at their beck and call.

Sleek gulls buzzed overhead. Determinedly she rubbed the pastel over the paper, getting on with her life. They'd catch this bastard and Marshall Hayes would get the hell back to Boston.

The oil pastel snapped beneath her finger. "Dammit."

Concentrating on the statue, she picked up the pale green and a dark leaf-green that was almost black for deeper shadows, holding both in the same hand as she sketched in details. Grabbed cadmium-yellow and white, and with a couple of strokes gave Liberty her fire.

To get the sharp edge she needed for the spikes of the diadem, she pulled out her little penknife and sharpened the edge of an iced green.

"You have a permit for that?"

She jumped a half-inch off her seat. Marsh squeezed a hand on her shoulder and blasted a hole through her determination to keep things between them strictly professional.

Lines cut deeply around his mouth, sunlight molding his stubborn jaw. She rolled her shoulder away from his touch, didn't like the fact she was so happy to see him. "You gonna arrest me if I don't?"

"I do still have those handcuffs."

Heat flooded her cheeks as unbidden memories rose. A whiplash of heat coiled low in her body, a touch-light to passion. The brightness of his gaze made her blink, his eyes more green today than brown—clear, complex, changeable. She knew he wanted to protect her, but those deep hazel eyes also promised something else. Soul scorching sex.

What single unattached woman in her right mind wouldn't want to have sex with a rich handsome federal agent who'd promised to protect them from a monster? It didn't make her a slut. It finally made her ordinary.

Taking off his charcoal-colored jacket he slumped on the bench beside her, his knees brushing hers. He stared at the sketch with a thoughtful expression, but said nothing, his frown intensifying with his silence. It took every ounce of control not to ask him what he thought. But her work had always been her own, not influenced by the opinions of others or the contrary moods of the market.

A bit like her.

The rumble in her stomach told her it was lunchtime. Unable to work with him watching, she packed away her pastels and placed the sketch in her portfolio. She looked around for Vince, but he'd taken off.

"You on duty?" she asked with a sinking heart. *Why else would he be here?*

"He went for a walk." The lines beside his eyes deepened as he squinted up at the statue. "I came to let you know I probably won't be at your apartment tonight."

Her fingers curled. *Dammit,* she wasn't completely helpless. "I can go stay with Pete for the night—you remember Pete? My ex-roomie?"

A red line burned across Marsh's cheeks. "There are some people you never forget—Pete and his lover definitely fall into that category." He closed his eyes and a shudder rippled across his shoulders.

Neither he nor Pete would say what had passed

between them. "You don't like gay people?"

Marsh threw his head back and laughed deep and loud. His throat was pale bronze against the pure blue sky, his Adam's apple clearly defined. Josie grinned. She didn't remember the last time she'd heard him let loose with a laugh and despite trying to hold onto her irritation, she liked it.

"Gay doesn't bother me one bit." Then he shifted to face her, his thigh brushing hers as she held his gaze. "In fact, finding out your roomie was gay and not your live-in lover made my freaking day."

She swallowed. "Oh."

His smile told her he'd revealed more than he wanted to and changed the subject. "Vince said he'd stay over at your apartment, until I got back," Marsh told her, "which could even be late tonight but will probably be tomorrow."

"Okay." There was a serial killer who had a blade with her name on it and, despite appearances, she wasn't stupid. In truth she was unbearably beholden to them both and one day soon she needed to be brave enough to tell them that.

Bending down she finished packing her stuff into her knapsack. She had enough detail and color information to carry on the work at home. And she couldn't concentrate with Marsh so close. That bothered her because normally nothing distracted her.

Spotting the urn at the bottom of her bag she paused. She'd planned to scatter Marion's ashes to the four winds today. But she couldn't do it. As much as she tried, as much as she'd promised herself, she still couldn't let go of the past.

Pain welled up, but she didn't want Marsh to

sense anything was wrong. The fact that Marion was dead had a lot to do with him and she hadn't even begun to deal with her feelings over that yet.

Maybe that was the reason she'd run so hard from him? Punished them both for being alive when Marion was so horribly dead? Or maybe it was just good old-fashioned terror of getting involved and getting your heart tenderized with a meat mallet.

"Where are you off to?" she asked.

"Savannah."

"Oh." *What the hell was in Savannah?* She refused to ask, knowing how seriously he took his job. Craning her neck she stared up at the image of freedom and independence, ignored the gnawing under her heart at her lack of those qualities in her life. A pigeon landed on the ground in front of her, a puddle of feathers strutting and pecking for scraps of food.

"You ever been up to the top?" She indicated the malachite green Greek monolith with a tilt of her chin, surprised when he shook his head.

"No, but I know the arm has been closed to visitors since 1916 when German collaborators set off dynamite on the New Jersey shore." His eyes held a wealth of sadness. "Terrorism is nothing new. You?" It was a lazy question, them sitting in the sunshine chatting, but this statue meant so much more to her than that.

"I used to come here every year with Marion. The weekend *after* Independence Day." Marion hated crowds, yearned to travel to her grandfather's homeland across the ocean to Ireland. She'd never got her wish. The tightness in Josie's throat burned. "I... I didn't come this year."

Marion's death had been too fresh—the guilt

almost suffocating and she didn't think it would ever go away. She glanced at her knapsack. Today was the first time she'd had the nerve to return and that was only because she'd had to, putting Lady Liberty and the memories off as long as she possibly could.

Now visions of all those childhood visits welled up inside and even six months on, the pain of losing the woman who'd taken the reins of Josie's life when she'd had no one else was overwhelming. She knew deep down that it wasn't Marsh's fault Marion had been killed. It was hers. A sob rose up and she cupped her hand over her mouth so it didn't escape.

She could feel Marsh's gaze, feel the weight of understanding in those hazel depths. But he didn't move to touch her. Didn't try to help. This wasn't something he could solve or fix. She had to get past it herself. The silent empathy in his eyes suggested he understood her pain, her need for penance and her inability to get past the guilt.

He pressed his lips together and shoved his hands in his pockets. Leaned forward and the pigeon flew away. After a couple of minutes silence, he asked, "Did Special Agent Walker get in touch this morning?"

"No." She reached up to shake her hair out of the elastic band she'd tied it back with. The sea breeze immediately grabbed it and played.

"Maybe he hasn't found anything yet." Marsh's jaw flexed.

Found anything... Like an old blonde corpse matching my mother's description. Mingled grief and guilt formed a kaleidoscope of torment that knotted her stomach. Knowing she was about to

125

lose it, she grabbed her belongings and strode away, aware of one very solid body scrambling after her.

Marsh snagged her arm and spun her round to face him, "I don't have time to chase you around. This isn't a game!"

Trying to destroy the evidence of her tears, she blinked rapidly. But he must have spotted the wetness on her cheeks because suddenly every inch of her body was pressed to his, her face against the cool fabric of his shirt, inhaling the male scent of his cologne and the slight musk of sweat. She couldn't breathe or see, but she craved comfort so badly it didn't seem to matter.

"Jesus. I'm sorry. I keep forgetting this is your mother we're talking about."

Strong hands roamed her back, soothing and therapeutic. It felt good to lean on him. So damn good. And far too dangerous. Being alone was what she did. How she survived. The pain of being hurt and abandoned had cut deeper than any knife and she wasn't sure how to deal with things any other way. She pushed back and sniffed inelegantly. She wiped her eyes and blew her nose.

"Wanna climb her?" she asked. She knew she'd surprised him. She'd surprised herself except she wanted to go up, to scatter Marion's ashes on the wind, but this was one thing she couldn't do alone.

He took her hand and squeezed. "I can't. I have a flight to catch shortly. Anyway it's closed today. Vince will stay with you tonight—"

"Okay. Great." She slipped out of his grasp. "We'll hang out. Catch a movie." She kicked a stone, bit the inside of her cheek to stop herself saying anything more junior-high. All ten-foot-six, ex-Navy SEAL walked up behind him.

Marsh's cell phone rang and she used the opportunity to head toward the ferry terminal. His hand snaked out and grabbed her before she'd gone two paces.

"Hayes," he answered the phone. "When?" He paused for a second and Josie knew something bad had happened from the way his eyes sliced to her. "Yeah, she's here. I'll bring her right over."

She felt the blood drain from her face. "Did they find my mother?"

Their eyes locked, his febrile bright. "No. There's been another murder."

***

Marsh negotiated traffic toward Federal Plaza, one hand gripping the wheel tight as he blasted the horn at a cabby trying to cut him off.

Josephine sat beside him, pale, tense, withdrawn.

"They have any leads?" Vince asked from the backseat.

"They wouldn't tell me anything on the phone." Tension rose within him triggering an ache in his jaw and a fear that ran all the way to his fingertips. And he had to go to freaking Savannah.

He glanced at Josephine's stark profile.

"Come with me." The suggestion was out of his mouth before he could stop it, but now he thought about it, it was a damn good idea.

She shook her head, blonde hair brushing her slender shoulders. Too slender to carry the weight of this monster.

"Your flight is in less than an hour." Her voice was subdued. Sad. "If we're ever going to stop this

127

man I need to go through everything I can possibly think of with Agent Walker."

Marsh bit down on what he was going to say. She could do all that tomorrow after she'd spent the night with him in Savannah—and that had nothing to do with sex and everything to do with keeping her alive.

But what if this bastard killed another woman in the meantime?

Marsh filled his lungs with a deep breath and tried to relax. He caught Vince's dark stare in the mirror, read the unspoken pledge in his eyes. He nodded.

Working his shoulders to loosen the stiff muscles, he checked the time and knew he had to pull out all the stops if he was going to get to the airport on time. "Promise me one thing," he spoke to Josephine.

The fragile look disappeared. Instead, suspicious eyes turned on him, reminding him she didn't normally do promises.

"What?"

"After you're done with Walker, go home with Vince and don't leave his side for anything. And I mean *anything*."

"Anything?" Josephine smirked with her trademark pissy attitude that Marsh finally figured out was a front to cover fear. "Showering will be fun, but I'm game if you are, big boy."

He met Vince's eyes in the mirror and recognized the determined glint in his wide smile.

"Sure thang, Missy, you think you can handle me, that is." Vince put on a Southern twang that made Josephine scowl and then laugh.

She did have a sense of humor. She just tried to

bury it.

Then they were there, Vince getting out and opening Josephine's door, scanning the area even though Special Agent Sam Walker stood there glowering through the windshield. Marsh grabbed Josephine's hand before she got out.

"Be careful." He wanted to say something else, something meaningful but he didn't know what. Instead he stared dumbly into wary blue eyes. "Please?"

She nodded, got out and slammed the door behind her. Marsh winced, grateful for solid German engineering.

Sam Walker stuck his head through the open window. "I need you inside too."

Judging from the guy's appearance, he'd had another rough night. Marsh glanced at the clock on the dash. "I can't." BAU saw more burnout than all the other fields, but if anybody could help catch this killer, it was those guys. "I have a job to do in Savannah. I'll be back late tonight or tomorrow morning. You can schedule an appointment then."

Ignoring Walker's glare and shout, Marsh rolled up the window. *Jesus. What was wrong with the guy?* Was he back to being a suspect? Walker stepped back, turned to Josephine and smiled briefly at something she said.

Marsh pulled out and maneuvered the car through heavy traffic. Gritting his teeth, he ignored the anger, the ache and the desperation that crawled along every nerve fiber. He had a job to do. Vincent was more than capable of keeping her safe. The trouble was—he finally admitted to himself—he didn't want anybody else getting too close to her and that bugged the hell out of him too.

His cell phone rang, a welcome distraction. Turning on the hands-free, he wove in and out of lanes, heading for the Manhattan Bridge. Did a full body cringe when a female voice announced the director was on the line.

Shit.

"Marsh, what the hell are you doing?"

"Brett, good to hear from you—"

"This isn't a social call." Brett Lovine sounded harassed and pissed. Not a good combination for an FBI Director, though probably not an uncommon one.

"Then what can I do for you, *sir*?" The names they'd called each other as kids echoed through that short title. Enough to have Brett blowing deeply into the receiver.

"I am just off the phone after talking to Montgomery Able. You know him?"

"Ahhh—"

"Senator Brook Duvall's lawyer, *Special Agent in Charge* Hayes." Brett's tone edged toward a sarcastic snarl.

Ahhh. "Director, I have solid evidence connecting Pru Duvall to a stolen painting. I have to investigate the lead." Checking his mirror, he changed lanes, roared onto the expressway and put his foot down. "Just because Brook is odds on favorite to win the party's nomination is not a reason to back away from this. In fact, I'm doing him a favor by investigating the matter thoroughly."

Brett snorted, but Marsh plowed on. "We have reason to believe Admiral Chambers' stolen painting is actually a missing Vermeer that could be worth as much as fifty million dollars at auction and will cause an explosion in the art world when it's revealed. Any hint of impropriety will sink Duvall like a stone."

The line went quiet.

Brett was obviously weighing the good publicity the FBI might garner if they recovered that painting, versus the bad karma associated with pissing off a potential future president.

"We both know Chambers is such a crazy old goat he might have given the thing away and changed his mind the next day," Bret said slowly.

Marsh acknowledged the truth of that statement. "But he has photographic evidence the painting was in his collection and he reported it stolen to the FBI."

His boss seemed to be listening. "I don't want a word of this leaked to the media. Not one word. Understood?"

"Yes, sir." Marsh smiled. *Nothing like getting your own way with one of the most powerful people in the western world.*

"And what the hell are you doing involved in this serial killer fiasco in New York City?"

"The case involves a close personal friend of mine—"

"Yeah, I saw the photos." Back to being his friend, Brett scoffed. "Just your type. Do us both a favor, screw her and get the hell out of that sit—"

"Or what? You'll fire me?" Fury forged his tone.

"Maybe I will."

"Do it." Marsh cut the connection.

Heat poured from his body as a wave of adrenaline fed the rage that simmered like lava inside his brain. Suddenly his wool jacket was suffocating. He lowered the window and let the cold breeze whip around the interior of the car and flay his senses.

Brett had never questioned his professionalism before. He counted to ten as he contemplated turning the car around and heading back to Manhattan.

Controlling a coarse exhalation he took his foot off the accelerator and considered what had gone down. The all familiar stench of politics and power, poking meddling fingers into law and order, stirred up the murky water. It stank.

But Brett hadn't fired him.

Yet.

Until he did, Marsh was going to track down the thief of Admiral Chambers' painting and hope like hell the evidence was compelling enough to stand up in a court of law—no matter who'd stolen the damn thing. And Josephine?

Brett's words had struck a raw nerve. Picturing her clear defiant gaze made him pause at his over-the-top reaction to the Director of the FBI. Her distaste for authority was rubbing off. She'd had a bad effect on him from the moment he'd first met her—spitting nails at everything he represented. But he wasn't quitting on her. Ever. He just didn't quite know how to get her to trust him.

He pressed his foot to the metal and sped toward duty and the job.

Josephine was safe.

That was all that really mattered.

***

Nelson bent over the photographs on his desk. It had taken fifty bucks and some genius detective work to discover the ID of the latest chick to get sliced and diced by the Blade Hunter. Lynn Richards—the woman he'd snapped two nights ago attending an art gallery opening with SAC Marshall Hayes. Nelson couldn't believe his luck.

The babble in the office was cacophonous. The atmosphere in the city starting to buzz with fear and paranoia and all of a sudden Nelson's mundane dealings with death, drugs and despair were getting the sort of attention normally reserved for movie stars and pop icons.

"Landry!" His pre-menstrual bitch of an editor stood at the door to her office and yelled across the floor.

He looked up uneasily, unable to measure her mood by anything except the glint in her eye. "Yes, boss?"

"Got anything new on the latest Blade Hunter vic?"

"Yup. Everything from her parents being at a VIP dinner at the time of the murder, to her dating a fed." He waved Saturday's *NY News* at her and pointed out Lynn Richards' picture. Sweat dripped down the side of his face because this story could put him back in the game.

"That's the vic? You're sure?" Stalking over to his desk she examined him with a distrustful expression. Her natural look.

"Yup."

There was a pause that spread across the whole office, everyone holding their breath.

"Get me copy in fifteen minutes and I'll hold the front page."

He grinned. "No problem, boss." Excitement hummed through him even as he started typing his piece.

"What about the other girl?" She pinned the other woman on the front of *The NY News* with a crimson nail.

Nelson shrugged. He hadn't got anywhere with that yet. "I don't know who she is. I'm working on it."

"The fed?"

Gonna wish he'd never fucked with this particular reporter. "Not available for comment."

Her finely plucked brows arched. "I have my own sources. I'll see what I can find out."

Chapter Nine

"**D**o you ever sleep, Agent Walker?" Josephine eyed the deep lines gridlocking the fed's face.

Sam Walker stretched his mouth grimly, shook his head, blue eyes lacking any real spark. "Not anymore." He called Nicholl to say they were on their way back inside.

Vince hovered as her shadow and suddenly she was grateful. They started walking toward the concrete-and-glass building, flags snapping behind them with sharp cracks in the brisk wind. Walker touched her elbow with his hand and all Josie could really think about was the big gap at her side where Marsh should be.

And that freaked her out.

"There was another murder?" Vince's deep voice rumbled like a bulldozer.

Walker glanced over his shoulder at the ex-SEAL. Nodded, but didn't give any details. Cold stole over her flesh. Maybe if she'd remembered sooner, or admitted following her mother all those years ago, none of these women would be dead.

They passed through security, where Vince surrendered his weapon, before entering the building's atrium. The doors of an elevator opened and a group of people poured out. One woman sobbed openly, her pale blonde hair raining down in an untidy mess. Josie sidled away, unable to bear witness to such raw hurt.

The woman saw her and stood rooted to the

135

spot, oblivious to the people crowding behind her. "You." Her face froze in a grimace of anguish that morphed into rage. "You know who did this. You know who killed my baby!" She launched herself, and for all her street-smarts, Josie stood there, immobilized by the hatred in the older woman's eyes.

Bracing herself for the rake of nails down her face, she was stunned to be pulled backwards and placed firmly behind Vince's broad back, unable to see a thing.

Bodyguard.

She'd forgotten about him.

The weakness in her knees surprised her. She leaned back against the wall as the poor woman was hustled away, the ensuing silence loud and echoing as people stood and stared.

Vince herded her into the elevator. Agent Walker got in beside them, rubbing his forehead. Maybe it *was* her fault. The killer's malignant spirit was an essential part of the flames that had forged her.

"Sorry about that." Walker sounded pissed.

She opened her mouth, but nothing came out.

Getting off the elevator, Walker said, "Wait here for a moment." Then he left them hovering in the corridor like unwanted guests at a party.

She and Vince watched him approach Special Agent Nicholl at the coffee maker, then pull him by a narrow lapel through an open doorway and out of sight.

"Looks like trouble." Vince bobbed his eyebrows toward the doorway.

"What d'you mean?" Josie frowned at him—not getting it. Until suddenly the fog cleared. Nicholl had orchestrated that little scene downstairs.

But why?

To knock her off balance? That seemed the most likely reason, but why? What the hell could she tell them that she wasn't already moving heaven and earth to remember?

Walker came back into the corridor with the look of a man who'd planted a punch on someone who deserved it.

"He really thinks I have something to do with this, doesn't he? That I'm conspiring in some way?" Josie said. It was amazing that Nicholl could have such a low opinion of her.

Sam Walker said nothing as he led them to an interview room much like she'd been in before. He held the door for Josie, but put his hand in front of Vince to stop him entering.

"I'll have to ask you to stay outside."

Vince gave him a *no way* stare.

"If we'd done this at my apartment, Vince would have been there." Josie pointed out. "Unless you want to take a break, Vince? Meet me back here later?"

"I told Marshall Hayes I wouldn't let you out of my sight, ma'am." Vince stated in a monotone. "Bathroom breaks excluded, provided I clear the room first."

She crossed her arms and gave him a look. "Seriously?"

He cocked a brow. "Seriously."

"That's what I was afraid of," Walker muttered under his breath. "Hayes leaves you a bodyguard but can't be bothered to answer some basic questions—"

"What do you have against him?" She was

baffled. The two feds were so alike—both dedicated, tenacious and so law-abiding they made her sick. She'd have thought they'd have been law-enforcement buddies.

"Nothing," Walker answered quickly, then nodded Vince into the room. "Don't interfere, okay?"

Vince settled his weight on one of the orange plastic chairs that had been born in the seventies. It creaked ominously, but Vince ignored it, braced his feet and crossed his thick arms.

Putting her knapsack—complete with Marion's ashes—carefully on the floor beside the chair, Josie sat, realizing from the way Agent Walker refused to hold her gaze that something terrible had happened.

"Mind if I record this?" Walker asked.

Josie didn't give a rat's ass.

He flicked a switch and began by reciting the time, date and their names for the record.

"Where were you last night, Josephine?" Walker looked down at the table in front of him, staring at the files as if they were the most interesting things he'd ever set eyes on.

"What?" She squinted at him. *Hadn't he been there at her apartment until Marsh had kicked him and Vince out?* She didn't even know what time it had been, she'd been too wrapped up in memories. "You know where I was." Her fingers gripped the corner of the table, her nails scratching at the thin veneer.

"Can you say it for the tape, please?" Walker looked innocent enough. Tired and weary. Maybe this was routine.

"I was in my apartment."

"Did you leave your apartment at anytime last

evening or before seven a.m. this morning?"

She straightened her back, the edges of her vertebrae cutting into the unforgiving plastic. "No."

"Were you alone in the apartment?"

"No." She frowned, her fingers tapping a rapid tattoo on the table and wondered what that said in the police handbook on body language.

Walker looked up, and she felt the temperature drop forty degrees. "Who was with you?"

She stopped tapping. "*Special Agent in Charge* Marshall Hayes was there with me. You know all this."

"Marshall Hayes was in your apartment *all* last night? You're certain?"

Damn, what the hell was going on?

"Absolutely," she said loudly for the benefit of the tape.

"You're positive Marshall Hayes never left your sight?" Walker's eyes bored into hers. After her and Marsh's heated exchange last night, she'd locked the door and never come out. Marsh had knocked on the door at eleven and told her he was sleeping on the couch. She hadn't seen him 'til dawn. She stared straight at Sam Walker's tired eyes and lied. "Marsh spent the whole night right next to me."

Walker's lips pinched together. Vince shifted, clearly ill at ease.

Playing the slut suited her better than playing the victim and she'd found over the years, people would rather believe the worst anyway. "Why?" Josephine asked.

Sighing deeply, Sam Walker pulled out a headshot of a young woman. The eyes were dull. Mouth flaccid. She'd been young once. And beautiful. "Do you know her?"

Josephine picked up the photograph of the woman. Tears blurred her eyes. The bastard had done it again. Her finger hovered over the girl's face. They could have been sisters. The woman in the lobby could have been her own mother...

"I've never seen her before." She bit her lip. "Who is she?"

Agent Walker slid the cover of the yesterday's *NY News* in front of her nose.

A glossy photo of her and Marsh leaving for this building two nights ago was emblazoned front and center.

"I was on the cover of the *NY News*? I still don't get—" But then her eyes slid to the picture beside it, and she picked up the photograph of the dead woman and placed it next to the picture of Marsh attending a gallery opening earlier that same evening.

"Oh, no." Her eyes swung from Walker to Vince. "Does he know?"

Vince lumbered to his feet. Leaning heavily on the table, he stared down at the picture. "I doubt it—he wouldn't have gone off like that if he did."

They both turned their gazes on Walker, but Josie got the question in first. "You really think he's capable of this?" Marsh was the most decent human being she'd ever met. He was so decent it was nauseating. "Marsh would never do this to anyone." He was going to be devastated—blame himself for putting the girl in a killer's bull's eye. "And why would *I* be within a thousand yards of him if he were the guy who attacked me—"

"You said you didn't see his face."

Walker's reply was stony—like she'd blown his most viable suspect. Well, the FBI must be grasping at straws to want to nail one of their best.

"You don't need to see someone's face to recognize them—it's in the voice, the shape and breadth of someone's shoulders." She opened her palms wide. "It's in the feel of someone's hands, the scent of their skin." Holding Agent Walker's gaze, she willed him to believe her. "The guy who attacked me wasn't Marshall Hayes."

Vince straightened and moved back to his orange seat. "You know she's right, Walker. You just don't wanna let go of your nice juicy bone."

Walker pulled his lips up in a bitter smile and shrugged as if conceding the point.

"Fine," he shuffled the papers, "I ran your mother's Social Security and driver's license numbers through the system—neither has been used since she disappeared the night of your attack."

The breath whooshed out of her body like she'd been slammed against a wall. "So she's dead." She stared down at the table, noticed graffiti marked the well-worn surface.

"Not necessarily…"

Josie jerked up her head. "What do you mean?"

"She could have moved abroad. Or be living under an assumed identity."

Josie frowned. "The guy she was with was a missionary from Africa—"

"Africa?" Vince straightened up, suddenly attentive.

"Didn't I say so yesterday?" Josie frowned.

Walker shot Vince a glare that told him to be quiet, then bent to check his notes. "You just said some guy from St. Mary's Church."

"He'd only been in the country a couple of weeks."

"Where in Africa?" Vince demanded.

Walker glared at him again and looked like he was about to curse, but he glanced at the tape as if remembering it was on.

"I don't know." Josie shook her head, thoughts moving so fast they were spinning. Vince stood, all six-foot-seven of uncompromising muscle and stalked over to the recorder and turned it off.

"What are you doing?" Walker spluttered and then stopped as Vince shrugged out of his jacket and started unbuttoning his shirt, the holster where his Desert Eagle pistol usually sat empty, dangling beneath his left arm.

"Putting a different perspective on things." Vince spread his shirt wide open, revealing a magnificent ebony chest and marks that made Josie's heart knock against her ribs.

Six long deep scars ran over each side of his torso emphasizing his ribs. A tiny row of dots punctuated the top of each scar.

"A few years ago, I traced my family history back to a small village in Mozambique." Satisfied he'd made his point, Vince pulled his shirt front back together and started redoing the buttons. "I went to visit and they tried to pressure me into a scarification ceremony—told me I wouldn't be a *real* man unless my body matured in the way of my ancestors.

"I told them there was no way I was letting them near me with their old rusty knives." He laughed, a boom of sound and shrugged his massive shoulders. "But I got sterile instruments from a nearby clinic and let them cut me—not because I wasn't already a real man, you understand, but because I thought it looked cool." He cocked a brow and tucked his shirt into his pants. "Lucky for me, I was already circumcised."

"I'll take your word for it." Josie tried to wipe the shock off her face, but failed. "So *that*," she placed her hand on her ribcage, beneath her breast, "is common in Africa?"

"Not as much as it used to be, but yeah." He nodded his head. "Tattoos don't work well on black skin."

"Did it hurt?" Walker couldn't hide his distaste and she caught the look on his face. His eyes dropped to her chest. An involuntary male response? Or was he thinking about her scars? She looked away.

"Like crazy, but women love it." He winked and his diamond stud flashed.

Josie snorted, "Probably says more about the women you date than your sex appeal."

"My point is…" Vince suddenly turned serious, "the cutting could be a link to Africa. I didn't mention it before because I didn't want anyone jumping on the race bandwagon. But even if this dude is white, he could have a connection to Africa," Vince concluded.

Walker pulled on his lip with his thumb and forefinger. "If I recall some of my basic anthropology courses, scarification is also big in other indigenous populations in Australia and South America."

All the moisture in her mouth dried up. "He uses those women like they're a canvas to work on." She shuddered.

Walker turned the tape back on. "Josephine. Let's go over everything you remember about the man you believed ran off with your mother."

***

The headache raging in Marsh's skull had nothing to do with the naphthalene that radiated from Pru Duvall's business manager's office and everything to do with the staggering humidity of a brewing storm. Although, come to think of it, his head hadn't stopped hurting since he'd found out Josephine was the target of a serial killer.

Despite being early October, the temperature was in the high nineties and the humidex was off the charts. Moisture clung to his upper lip and rolled a pathway down his body.

His hand tailored wool suit might be perfect for the insidious cold of the eastern seaboard, but was like wearing a wet blanket in Savannah, Georgia. He took off his jacket, waited for Thomas Brown to finish pouring a glass of iced tea. The cool liquid condensed on the outside, pooling on the dark wood for a moment before Brown handed it over.

"Thank you." He took the glass from the neat little man and swallowed half of it in one gulp. His body temperature dropped a fraction of a degree.

"You're welcome." Brown smiled back. "More?"

Marsh accepted gratefully.

Brown was nothing like the hotshot Marsh had expected. The guy had the look of indentured manservant about him. Meek, mild, nothing like Pru Duvall.

"Is it always this hot in the fall?" Slowing down, he sipped politely. The cool brew slid down his throat with icy welcome.

A ceiling fan whirred softly overhead, sending

waves of hot air back to the ground and providing all the relief of a hairdryer. A curtain twitched in the light breeze. The sound of children's laughter rode the sultry atmosphere with featherlike snatches of delight. Marsh was impatient for answers, but experience told him a little small talk and courtesy would get him further, faster, than barking demands. Especially in the south.

The room was stuffed full of period clothing and antiques. Enough to start a store. Mothballs, musty and pungent, were scattered around the place like little white marbles. Marsh surreptitiously dug one out from beneath his thigh, dropped it to the floor, wiping oily hands onto his pant leg.

"Keeps the cats off the chairs and moths out of the clothes." Thomas nodded toward the railing full of old dresses that looked like they came from the film set of *Gone With The Wind*.

"Excuse me?"

"The mothballs." Brown's eyes crinkled softly in amusement. "Keeps the cats from damaging the fabric." On cue a fluffy Persian stalked out from behind the desk, tail straight up in the air as it sashayed past Marsh.

"Are you some kind of collector?"

"No, sir." Thomas smiled. "The opposite in fact. This all belonged to Miss Pru's parents and grandparents. She asked me to get rid of the lot." He took a seat behind the small desk that was cluttered with papers and files, a big hulking computer monitor and an old ring dial telephone.

"Does this house belong to Mrs. Duvall too?"

The house was a moderately-sized Regency, painted a ghostly pale-blue. Shutters and intricate iron balconies added to its visual appeal and it faced onto a square with a stone fountain at its center and giant oaks providing shade and shelter from the relentless heat.

Thomas nodded. "Yes, sir. Was her grandmother's house originally, but Miss Pru had all her things moved here when her mother, Miss Virginia, died. She grew up in one of the big mansions on Abercorn Street, but she sold it. It's a hotel now."

Marsh nodded. He could see Pru growing up in decadent style and splendor, much like himself. But what he didn't see was Pru selling up and moving to this house, which though beautiful and historic, wasn't magnificent or grand like her childhood home must have been. Mansions were good for entertaining political cronies.

"Any idea why she sold up?" Marsh queried.

The whites of Thomas' eyes were tinged with yellow. "I don't rightly know, sir. Miss Pru doesn't confide in me, just pays me to look after her property down here for which I'm very grateful."

Thomas Brown was at least fifteen years older than Pru—Marsh wondered what family skeletons he knew about. *Had they been lovers?*

"How often does Miss Pru come down here, Thomas?" Marsh asked.

The other man looked down at his brown leather shoes that stuck out the side of the desk. They were well worn, but not shabby, a bit like the man himself.

"Not often." Thomas glanced over, squinting his eyes as if considering. "Maybe twice in the last three years...well, she's been living in Australia on and off for the last little while."

The lovers angle seemed a bit of a stretch.

Marsh pulled out a photograph of Admiral Chambers' painting. "You sold this painting to a company called Total Mastery NY about six months ago. Do you remember it?"

Thomas sent Marsh a look that suggested he was an imbecile.

"Of course, I remember." Thomas folded his hands across the front of his belted pants. "I was mighty pleased to get such a good price."

Marsh didn't tell the man that it was worth many times what he'd received for it—or nothing at all if it was stolen.

"Where did you get the painting, Thomas?"

"From the mansion." Swollen knuckled fingers rubbed slowly through close-cropped black hair. "Miss Pru told me to sell anything that wasn't needed to furnish this house. She'd already taken any pictures she wanted to keep." The man nodded toward the clothes and porcelain that cluttered every space. "It's taken me five years, but that's all that's left of it now."

This wasn't helping. "Do you remember when that particular painting first arrived at the mansion or how it got there?"

Chocolate eyes gleamed. "I don't even recall exactly where I found it," he said, frowning. "But I figured when I did find it, it might be valuable because it looked so old. I sent it off to a local firm to get it cleaned." He shrugged, bony shoulders stretching the thin cotton. "When it came back it was almost unrecognizable. All that black dirt gone." Those wide lips smiled. "The only thing I cared about was getting the money back for the restoration and making a tidy profit. What's all this about, Agent Hayes?"

The painting had been cleaned *since* it was stolen from the admiral. "Do you know if Mrs. Duvall saw the painting after it was cleaned, but before it was sold?" Marsh scrubbed his hand over his face, recognizing a looming political nightmare. Establishing provenance was going to be much trickier than he'd anticipated. Could there be two identical paintings in circulation?

"I don't rightly know, sir." The gentle eyes held a hint of pity. "But I don't think so."

"Do you have any proof of provenance?" Marsh asked. This was rapidly turning into a waste of time.

Thomas smiled, cheeks balling into tight brown apples. "All the important papers were lost in a fire after the War Between States." Thunder rolled in the distance and white light flickered around the room. He pushed back his chair and peered out the window as the clip-clop of horses' hooves passed by. "Ironic to be spared by Sherman only to be brought low by a scullery maid, don't you think?

"Here comes that storm," Thomas commented.

Marsh nodded. His whole life felt like a storm right now and here he was sitting in Savannah learning absolutely nothing. His phone vibrated in his pants pocket.

He checked the number—*shit*.

He returned the unanswered phone to his pocket. He had one more question. "How do you sell the items, Thomas? At an auction house?"

"Miss Pru sent a shipment of finer antiques and such to a fancy auction house, left me to deal with the rest." Thomas nodded toward the computer. "I put them on the web."

Surprised, Marsh's eyebrows stretched high. "You sold that painting online?" Holy crap.

"Yessir." Thomas slowly nodded his head up and down. "The beauty of the Internet."

Folding his jacket over his arms, Marsh thanked the man and said goodbye. There were no answers to be found in Savannah. Only another layer of old wealth and a mystery that was screaming at him through the distance of time and space. The journey here was nothing but a waste of time. Marsh's cell rang again and this time he had to answer it.

He stood on the front steps overlooking a moss-draped Savannah square. "Hayes here."

"Marsh..."

It was Josephine, and his heart was kicked into high gear by a bolus of adrenaline and then jolted by a crack of thunder overhead.

"Are you all right?" He told himself not to panic. Vincent wasn't some chump.

"I'm fine. Vince is right here beside me." She lowered her voice, the words becoming muffled as if she'd put her hands over her mouth. "Did the FBI talk to you about the latest murder yet?"

"We can't talk about this over the phone." They were on an unsecure channel. He didn't intend to give anything away to some bastard listening in.

Josephine's swallow was audible—more of a gulp. "It was your date. The girl you took to the art gallery opening. He killed Lynn Richards."

Chapter Ten

Darkness filled the unlit stairwell. A thin strip of light shone beneath one doorway, but the others were black and empty. Propping a hand against the doorjamb, Marsh concentrated on breathing. In and out. Deep calming breaths that slowed the blood in his veins to a stultified roar.

The murder of Lynn Richard had shifted something fundamental within him, like the slow grinding of a tectonic plate at a geological precipice.

He'd caught the last connecting flight back from Atlanta. And though it was nearly midnight, he'd gone straight to the Richards' home to express his condolences. It hadn't gone well. Their daughter was dead—because of him. Marsh balled his fists with rage. Targeting Josephine was bad enough, and Angela Morelli, and all the other women the bastard had brutalized. But he'd planned the sadistic murder of that young woman based purely on nothing more than her photograph on the front page of a newspaper...

She was so young.

Christ. In the Navy he'd lost men under his command and regrets over their loss sat like shrapnel in his chest. But *this*? He rubbed his eyes, wanted to rage, but instead pushed himself upright and slipped the key in the door. It swung open, Vince's Desert Eagle pointed directly at his heart.

"Good thing I called first, huh?" Marsh

recognized the empathy in the other man's gaze. Vince had done god-knows-what, in more war zones than they had states and he understood loss. They stared at each other for a silent moment before Marsh looked away.

"Pays to be extra vigilant in the kill zone, Marshall. And now is the time to remember that." Vince holstered his weapon, picked up his overnight bag and slung it over his shoulder. "See you in the morning."

"Watch your back, Vince."

The other man nodded sharply. Walked away, his rapid footsteps echoing off the walls with clipped efficiency. Marsh closed the door behind him and locked up. Rested his head against the cool wood as emotion washed through him.

"It wasn't your fault," Josephine said out of the darkness.

He spun at her voice. Watched her shadow hover uncertainly beside her bedroom door.

"Yeah." His voice was gritty. "It was." He rubbed his throat, hoping to rid himself of the knot that threatened to choke him.

Josephine crossed over to the windows and looked out into the dark street beyond. Footsteps echoed faintly along the street, probably Vince hurrying back to his other life. "You can't control everything."

"I never even wanted to go out with her." The memory of how he'd treated her, because she wasn't Josephine, because his mother had set them up, ate at him. He'd been a spineless prick and now she was dead.

His eyes followed her movements hungrily in the dark. The moon caught the edge of her nightshirt, rimming her profile in silver. The outline of her body was visible through the backlit fabric, her shape filling him with an aching need. Bitterness ripped through him; self-loathing crawling through his body. Even Lynn's death couldn't turn off his desire for her; if anything it made it worse. These hours might be all they shared. She might never be his and although he'd die to protect her, there were no certainties in life. The only certainty was death.

"I didn't want to go on a date with her because she wasn't *you*." The words spilled out when he'd thought they'd stay silent inside his head. *Shit*.

Her hands gripped the material at her breast. "I—"

"Don't say it." He dragged his hands through his hair and moved woodenly down the stairs. "I don't want your fucking pity."

She came toward him, stopped a few away. "I've never pitied you, Marsh. I've hated you and the things you make me feel, but I have never pitied you. This wasn't your fault—"

"It was my fault," Marsh said quietly. "If *I* hadn't taken her to the gallery opening she wouldn't be dead."

Her shoulders tensed and her chin lifted. "If your mother hadn't set you up on a date, if the photographer hadn't taken your picture, if the newspaper hadn't put us on the front page together." She advanced until there was nothing between them but polarized molecules of electricity. "If I hadn't survived."

Pain tore his chest wide open. *Jesus*. It *was* his fault. He dropped down to the couch, hands over his face, the smell of naphthalene still embedded in his skin despite endless hand washing. Repugnant. Stomach clenching. Disgusting.

He took a deep, shuddering breath, felt Josephine's arms slide around him, lightly, uncertainly, as if she had no clue how to comfort someone. "That bastard killed her like she was worthless. Slaughtered her because he wanted to give the FBI the finger. She was eighteen."

"I want to help. Please tell me what I can do to help."

Handcuffs would be good. Tie him up and fuck his brains out. That'd work. *Shit.* He wanted to sink into her flesh. Bury every desperate thought in soft folds wrapped around him so tight, no guilt could steal inside his head. Then he could pretend evil didn't run rampant and unchecked through their world. He could pretend the law would prevail and they'd nail this sick bastard and she'd be safe. But it might never happen. They might never catch him.

Josephine cradled his head to her breast and rocked him.

She was rocking *him.*

He raised his head so their eyes were level, the usual vivid blue of hers just another shade of gray in the moonlight. The skin around her mouth was tight, her lips compressed, as if she held emotion forcibly inside, unable to release it, unwilling to express it. He cupped her cheek, rubbed his thumb across the hard line of her lips and felt them relax a fraction as she released a breath. She smelled of grapefruit as if she'd recently showered, skin still slightly damp.

She never railed against fate or the terrible things that had happened to her. No matter what this killer threw at her, she didn't give an inch and

Marsh didn't think it was because she didn't feel the fear, but because she'd barricaded herself behind so many emotional defenses she was almost impenetrable.

Almost.

"I think you're a better man than most." Her hand caught his, pressing it into her cheek.

That's what he wanted—to be better than most—to be good enough to fill the void left by an older brother whom he'd loved. Good enough to catch the bad guys.

His fingers slipped around her cheek, brushed her ear and delved deep into the silken tresses of her hair. He drew her closer to him. Felt the resistance in every muscle, every vertebrae, in every staggered breath she drew.

"I want you."

"I can't—" She pulled back slightly.

"You did last time," he said. The drumbeat of his heart snarled through his ears, scorched blood streaming through his veins making him want to dive in and devour her. But no violation was allowed. No coercion. No drugs. No guilt. Nothing but honest desire.

Lightly stroking the delicate skin of her wrists, he leaned back so his shoulders rested against the couch.

Released her.

She wasn't a coward. She'd put herself firmly in the bulls-eye of the mob last spring helping Elizabeth and hadn't flinched, but when it came to the passion that burned between them, this crazy crackle of heat, she always ran.

"Go to bed," he told her. Baring his teeth in a humorless grin, frustrated and pissed, needing something from this woman that she didn't want or need from him. He closed his eyes so she couldn't see his weakness.

Silence rang loudly. The only noise was her breath, a light indecisive sound.

He didn't want indecisive. "Go to bed, Josephine."

Cool fingers touched him through the soft wool of his pants and he jolted violently, the caress turning a silky ache into volcanic heat that forced a noise from between his gritted teeth that sounded like he was dying.

She hesitated as if unsure.

"Don't stop." *Mr. Cool.* Lightly he moved her slender fingers over flesh that begged for her attention—he didn't want anyone else and he was probably going to freak her out, scare her away, but he needed her to touch him. He needed her to want to touch him.

With one hand she pushed him back against the couch. Moonlight washed in and out of the high windows, leaving her as insubstantial as shadow, as powerful as a prophesy. He let her pin him, knowing he was doomed, knowing she could rule him with nothing more than the pressure of those slender hands or a soft word.

Her hair shone, drifting down to cover her expression when he damn well wanted to see her face. Then she touched him again—an exploration that made him jump and bump his elbow on the wooden arm of the couch. He gritted his teeth, sweat beading along his brow, every pleasure neuron in his body latching onto her touch like iron filings to a magnet. She withdrew her hand and for a second he thought he might howl, but then she tugged on his belt, damn near cut off his blood supply before she undid the buckle and slid the leather free.

Soft fingers brushed his stomach as she undid the button, drew the zipper down with a rasp that sounded hotter than his most erotic fantasy.

"I've never done this before." Her mouth was close to his as she whispered in his ear, sliding her hand along the swelling heat of him.

He couldn't breathe let alone talk.

Her hands moved silkily over his flesh, a hiss of steam rising in their wake. "Tell me if I do something you don't like." Insane laughter rang inside his head. Not possible.

Kneeling beside him on the couch, her knees dug warmly into his thigh and she ran her fingers higher, over the tight drum of his stomach and undid a button of his shirt.

Unable to stop himself, he pulled her across his lap, sensations of light flashing behind his eyes as she straddled him, adjusting their intimate fit in a way that made his brain meltdown—especially when he realized she wasn't wearing any underwear.

His hands gripped the firm flesh of her thighs, fusing her to him, refusing to let her move even though he could feel her desire to do just that in the quivering of her muscles.

"Josephine." His voice was rough.

Opening her eyes, she looked as if she'd come out of a trance. Not what he wanted, but he wasn't playing games tonight and he wasn't having any misunderstandings getting between them.

"I don't want to fool around like a teenager. I want to take you to bed and—"

"Fuck my brains out."

"There's more to it than that." The vehemence in his voice shook them both.

"I don't want there to be more to it than that." She reached up and rested a hand on his shoulder. "Can we just do this? Have sex. Like normal adults? Or are we gonna screw this whole thing up again?"

He grabbed the edge of her t-shirt, too quickly for her to protest and jerked it over her head.

"Normal well-adjusted adults get naked when they have sex," he told her. Neither of them was normal or well-adjusted but he didn't care.

"Normal people don't look like this." Her hands came up to cover her torso.

"Don't," he said, "Please don't. Your scars don't bother me." He palmed a small perfect breast and she rocked toward him. Her head fell forward, hair trailing in a long swathe over her shoulders.

Reminding him she was naked and he was pretty much fully clothed.

A fantasy come true. If he got any hotter he was going to ignite. He ran his hands over her back, skimming the area where he'd implanted the transmitter all those months ago, unwilling to draw attention to the spot but curious. The skin felt satin smooth, no hint of the microchip hidden beneath the supple flesh. Shuddering, he moved on to cradle the soft swell of her breasts with her own palm, letting her feel the beauty and sensuality of her own body. A soft moan escaped slightly parted lips.

Tracing a silver scar, he rubbed lightly the spot where it ended, right on the point of her hipbone.

"You're beautiful," he said.

"No, I'm not." Her head came up, fire flashing in her eyes in the moonlight. "You don't have to flatter me. You *are* getting lucky tonight."

"Exactly." Dealing with this woman was always a challenge and when no blood circulated his brain it was downright impossible. "So why don't you believe me when I tell you, you're the most beautiful woman I've ever seen?"

He held her gaze; saw distrust warring with insecurity.

"I'm going to have you anyway." He trailed his hand lower, slowly trailing his finger down her body and then between her legs. He dipped one finger inside hot flesh. "Why would I lie?"

"Oh god," she whispered as her hands braced against his chest. "I don't know."

She was slick and wet and the desire to dive inside nearly overcame him, but he wanted to give her everything, make her view sex as a thing of wonder, not a pit of depravity.

He held her in place with one hand low on her back, bringing her closer. Gently, he took a puckered nipple into his mouth, and suckled her gently, rasping his tongue across the knotted areole. A breathy moan resonated through the room, bouncing off the high ceilings. Tight panting breaths echoed the rhythm of his fingers. She dug her fingers into his shoulders, nails biting deep as he pressed his palm against her clitoris and found the spot that made her writhe in his arms. She exploded against him, lips parted, eyes closed as she shuddered and trembled naked in his arms. She slowly quieted and rested her forehead on his shoulder. The feel of her breath against his neck had satisfaction ripping through him. A vital piece of his life shifted back into place.

Desire still pulsed through him, but it was

tempered by patience. He wouldn't rush her. Wouldn't rush them. Maybe she wasn't ready for more—

An openmouthed bite to his neck punctured his thoughts. She reared back, a beautiful angel, gloriously naked in his lap. "You're way too controlled here."

"Making up for last time." His voice was gritty, hoarse. He took a strand of silken hair and teased it across the top of her breast.

"You said last time was the best sex you've ever had," she reminded him.

Lightly, he ran a fingertip over the sensitive skin at the junction of her thigh, watched her shiver. "Do you doubt me?"

The sound that came from her lips was a high-pitched intake of breath. "No, but my experience is limited."

Marsh slid them both onto the floor.

"What are you doing?" she asked. There was enough curiosity in her voice that he didn't stop.

"Giving you a crash course of the highlights." He slid down her body to taste her, the scent of woman exploding into every space inside his mind. Thought fled, lust detonated through his veins and tripped a fuse inside his head.

"Oh, god." She arched up as his tongue slipped through her folds. "I can't believe how good that feels. I don't think I can take it."

"Do you want me to stop?" His words were muffled and grim.

"Not yet." And she laughed. Thank God. It was such an unusual sound he almost did stop. Cupping her backside, he teased and stroked, nuzzled and nipped, wanting to be inside her, but also wanting to make it last forever. To make it good for her. As long as he didn't have to think about anything else he was happy watching her control snap and fray. She stiffened, mouth opening in a silent scream, body bowed like some primal vision of femininity.

Beautiful. Sex wasn't tawdry or dirty. It was beautiful. She was beautiful.

He raised his head. She lay panting on the floor. The dim light revealing pale skin and slender frame. Slender, but not weak.

The sight of her lying there naked drove him crazy, but he was also aware of a change in the atmosphere as she started to think again. Warning bells rang, but he was also curious. Tight, throbbing, insane, wound up like a clockwork missile, curious. The thin scars crisscrossing her body were picked out in shadow. Suddenly visions of Lynn Richards haunted his mind. He rubbed his hands over his face, sat up as reality crashed over him.

She tapped her head, voice low in the darkness. "Doesn't matter how far away I go, he's always right here when I return."

He wanted to tell her they'd catch this bastard before he killed again, but he wasn't so sure anymore. "I can help you forget for one night." He held out his hand. "Come on. Let's go to bed."

***

"What did you tell him?" His voice was raspy. The light seeped from the surrounding neighborhood through the uncovered loft windows. His skin tingled, his prick throbbed with anticipation so primal it might burst through his flesh and consume the night. The crop cracked down hard on her bare ass.

"Ow!" A thin dark line bisected her pale white skin. Color leeched in the shadows. "Nothing. Please, please! I didn't tell him anything!" Pru Duvall sobbed against the pillow where he'd shoved her face the moment she'd walked into the room. He'd pushed her tweed skirt up and rammed himself into her until she'd begged.

Then he'd stopped.

A siren echoed around the high loft space. Agitated noise, wailing and screeching. Desperate little people doing desperate little deeds.

There was power *here*. It strummed through the night like the wings of a bat, silent, invisible, as tangible as the crop he flexed between his fingers.

Whack.

"Jesus." Pru sobbed. "I can't take any more."

He touched her skin, absorbed a flinch with his fingertip. Pru Duvall might be a future First Lady of the United States of America, but in her heart, in her soul she was darkness and dirt.

"Please..." Her voice cracked.

He'd thought about killing her, but a little voice deep inside said killing Pru Duvall would be like taking his own life—and he wasn't ready to do it yet.

The worked leather at the base of the crop felt soft and frayed against the sensitive tips of his fingers.

Drums beat in the darkness, but not killing drums, just excitement and pleasure—if only that could be enough for his all needs. He'd cuffed her hands behind her back. Not the velvet-lined cuffs others used, but steel bands he'd stolen from a cop when he first moved to the city. Dead cop now.

"I'm going to destroy him." He ran a gentle finger along the abused line of skin. *Power*. Lowered his lips to blow gently against the skin and kiss the pain better. *Control*.

Pru shivered, the whites of her eyes shining.

"Good," she hissed.

He scraped his teeth over her perfect skin. Bit gently at the base of her spine and rubbed between her legs with the length of the riding crop.

"Please?" Her little girl's voice fractured as she sank back on her haunches.

Whack.

"Damn you—"

He whipped her harder, breaking the skin.

Thwhack.

"I'm sorry, I'm sorry. Please, please, don't kill me. I can help you. I'll do anything you want." She always did. It's what made them so compatible.

Chapter Eleven

A slash of light cut across the ceiling as a car moved slowly along the street. Josephine lay curled against him like a cat, her head nestled beneath his shoulder and he didn't know what he was going to do about her. Some primitive yearning had driven him to make love to her as often as possible during the night like some wild bull staking his biological claim.

And if he were honest, the thought of Josephine pregnant with his child sent a feeling of contentment deep into his marrow. Which was *insane*.

From an early age he'd had plenty of girlfriends. Being rich didn't usually hinder his chances, but it did this time. This time having money worked against him. Having money would make Josephine, who snored gently against his chest, bolt like a rabbit for a safe place.

And he didn't want her to bolt. They'd made love for hours and even now the scent of her skin, her hair, her essence, stirred desire in him. He didn't want to lose her but he didn't know how to keep her. She was too unsure, too defensive, too feral.

There was a clank in the street, metal on concrete, like a can rolling along the sidewalk. Gently, Marsh eased away from her warmth and moved to the window. Looked out into the street.

Dawn hovered out of reach. A man hunched against the chill of the wind, walking a Dalmatian whose tail lashed back and forth like a whip. Leaves skittered in his wake as the dog marked his scent on the metal scrollwork that lined the base of every tree.

Marsh felt eyes on him.

Who else was out there in the night? *Was the Blade Hunter watching right now?*

Why had the sonofabitch made this personal?

Covers rustled in the bed.

"What are you looking at?" Josephine asked. Fear threaded her voice, made his nerves tighten at the insidious threat.

"Some guy walking his dog." He looked back at her.

Groaning, she fell back against the covers. "I *hate* this."

He moved away from the window and sat on the bed. The mattress dipped under his weight. "I hate it too."

Words didn't help. Promising to catch the bastard didn't help. The only thing that might help was locking this animal behind bars. Marsh moved around the bed and picked up his pants—rifled through his pockets for his cell phone.

Checking the screen, he saw he'd missed several calls, but not the ones he'd been expecting.

"I don't understand why Agent Walker hasn't brought me in for questioning."

"Ugh."

"What do you mean *ugh*?" Alerted by her tone he glanced up. Moving back to the side of the bed he dropped his cell next to his weapon.

"I hmm..." Josephine's voice was muffled by the sheet.

"Did Walker tell you something?"

Josephine sat up in bed, gathered the sheet across her breasts and looked sexier than ever with her mussed hair and lush lower lip.

"More like I told him something." She pressed her lips together and met his gaze. The moon had set, but there was enough ambient light to make out the way her eyes skittered away from his.

"What exactly did you tell him?" he asked.

Raising her chin, she swept her hair out of her eyes with an impatient gesture. Marsh recognized the pugnacious tilt of her jaw.

"He was going to pin it on you."

Her words stirred his suspicion. "He wouldn't be doing his job if he didn't consider me a suspect." And that fact pissed him off. All the years of service to his country counted for nothing. And that's exactly how it should be, he reminded himself.

"Well I know you didn't do it." She glared at him like he was a moron.

Uh oh. "What did you tell him?"

"I told him you were here with me." Defiance and certainty radiated from her.

"But for all you or Agent Walker know, I could have crept out of here in the middle of the night and murdered Lynn." He nodded his head toward the locked door that had separated them last night.

She shook her head. "I *know* you aren't that monster."

Did Walker feel the same way? He doubted it.

Again he was getting *the look* like he was too stupid to live.

"I told Walker you were *with* me, all night long," she said.

Shit. A rapier of anger speared through him. Sharp. Deadly. He looked away, suddenly afraid of his feelings. "You lied to an FBI agent during a critical investigation?"

"Yep." She tossed out the word the same way she tossed her hair.

"That doesn't bother you?" His jaw clenched so tightly he could barely speak.

"It isn't exactly the first time." Raised brows challenged him.

Christ—he knew that, but this was a serial killer investigation. A short breath escaped his nostrils in a burst of frustration. He was trapped. If he confessed the truth he branded Josephine with the label "liar" that might put into question every testimony she ever gave. But if he didn't tell Walker the truth, he demeaned himself and his ethics. He'd compromised himself once before and damned if Josephine hadn't been involved that time too.

"What exactly is the problem, Marsh?" She got out of bed, naked and distracting as hell, which knowing Josephine was her intention. "Because I thought the whole point was to catch the bad guy? Getting caught in his tricks won't do that." She crossed her arms over her breasts. His eyes lingered involuntarily. This woman was his Achilles' heel and he resented his weakness.

She hesitated, worried her bottom lip. "What would I do if you were arrested for a murder I know you didn't commit? The real killer is trying to get me alone and unprotected, you know that." A tremor ran through her frame, cold or fear he didn't know. He moved closer, put his hands on her shoulders, the slender bones unyielding beneath the surface of her skin.

This serial killer *was* playing games with the cops. "Vince will be here for as long as it takes. We can hire additional security if we need to—I told you this already."

"I don't want 'additional security' I want you." She raised herself on tiptoes, wrapped her arms around his neck and kissed him. He was so surprised by that unsolicited act of affection he stood there stupidly, only one part of his body reacting. When she released him his brain was blank from lack of blood.

"The Blade Hunter is trying to get you caught up in this investigation, to confuse the police and divert attention away from himself and leave me exposed." She nipped his bottom lip hard enough to make him blink. Ouch. "That means he's watching me—watching *us* and I'm not going to let him manipulate everything the way he wants to."

He knew she was right and he knew she was also very wrong. But with one hand stroking his erection, the other curled around his neck, Josephine dragged him down to the bed and God help him, he didn't exactly put up much of a struggle.

***

Marsh poured coffee from the state-of-the-art coffeemaker in Josephine's kitchen.

"Want one?" He spoke over his shoulder to Vince who'd walked in.

Vince nodded and took the second chair in the galley-size kitchen.

Pouring four cups of the thick brew, Marsh left one on the counter for Josephine who was tucked safely in the shower. Steve Dancer slouched in another chair, his shirt wrinkled, his socks mismatched.

Marsh had been raised in an atmosphere that demanded physical perfection; home, school, the Navy and finally the Bureau, but Dancer had managed to slip through the cracks and under the wire. It should have appalled Marsh's senses that Dancer wore brown shoes with black pants and a navy sports coat, but he didn't give a shit. Steve Dancer was one of the brightest people he'd ever met. The only child of a single mother, Dancer had put himself through MIT by working three jobs. Men underestimated the guy because of his freckles and unkempt appearance. Women wanted to mother him. Marsh didn't know why the guy had signed up for the FBI, but he was smart enough to be grateful he'd been able to wrangle him onto his team.

"Why did you let her lie to Walker, Vince?" Marsh was still pissed he'd been caught in a web of deceit. He didn't like being manipulated by anyone.

"She didn't exactly lie." Vince's white teeth gleamed against burgundy lips. "She implied." He shrugged one massive shoulder. "Walker bought it, but man, he was pissed."

"All he has to do is go back and check the dates of the other murders, which I thought he'd done." Marsh drew in a tight, breath, released it through his nose. "Why would he think I was involved?"

Vince rubbed hands the size of dinner plates over his close-cropped hair, ear stud blinking. He gave him a dry look. "You know why."

Josephine.

Jealousy was a bitch. But having a relationship with Josephine shouldn't interfere with catching the killer. No matter who she was, what she looked like or what she said.

"Did the killer strike again? Anybody hear anything?" Marsh asked, stirring his coffee. Dancer and Vince shook their heads.

"Maybe he took the night off." Dancer sipped his coffee and winced. Not a morning person.

Or maybe they just hadn't found the body yet.

"Where are we at with the De Hooch/Vermeer investigation?" asked Marsh.

Dancer blew the top of his coffee. "I took a look at the internet records. Sale looks legit."

"With or without a warrant?" Vince's eyes sharpened with interest.

Dancer's freckles danced on his cheeks. "No comment."

Vince grunted and went back to his coffee. Picked up a muffin from a box in the middle of the table that Dancer had brought from a bakery around the corner.

"According to Thomas Brown the picture was in the family mansion for years. But according to Admiral Chambers it was stolen from him in nineteen-ninety."

Marsh looked up at the ceiling. Given the prominence of both families he was facing at a royal screw up.

"We need to talk to Chambers again. Verify his account of the theft."

"He's back," Dancer ran his hand through his hair, which flopped awkwardly back in his eyes. "Got a flight out of Anchorage last night."

Anxiety bit along the edge of Marsh's nerves. He had a job to do and a position to uphold. Neither melded with protecting Josephine from a killer 24/7.

"I guess we're going to Boston." He grimaced.

"What about…" Vince glanced over his

169

shoulder and jerked his chin toward the open door.

Marsh rested the base of his spine against the kitchen counter. Leaving Josephine in NYC meant leaving her vulnerable. Vince could protect her, but Marsh needed to *know* she was safe.

"She's coming too."

"She won't like it," Vince stated with a shake of his head.

There was a creak of a hinge and the soft tread of bare feet across floorboards. Josephine padded to the doorway, looked at the three men in her kitchen and silently held her hand out for coffee. He picked up the mug and handed it across, their fingers brushing and the spark of contact making her blush. Dancer caught Marsh's eye. Raised a knowing brow.

Ignoring the other agent, Marsh stared into Josephine's eyes. "You need to come to Boston with us."

A soft breath escaped her lips, "Has he killed again?"

He cleared his throat. *It was a sensible plan.* Josephine would buy it. "No, this isn't to do with the Blade Hunter case. I have to go to Boston as part of the investigation I'm leading." He stared into cobalt eyes that were slowly freezing over. "This way we can keep an eye on you rather than leaving you exposed and threatened in NYC." He tried to hold her gaze, but it was like she was disappearing before his eyes.

"I won't run away from this asshole. Not this time—"

"It isn't running away, it's being smart." Marsh plowed right on over her concerns. "Bring everything you need to paint and we'll set you up somewhere—"

"My canvas is twenty-foot high." Remoteness echoed through her voice like she'd turned herself off.

"Work on something else for a few days." His voice got louder, unconsciously trying to penetrate the armor she was building around herself.

Her eyes turned to his, empty—none of the passion, none of her usual spirit.

"I have a commission to finish." She bit her lip. "It might not be important or worthy—but it's mine and I'm not giving it up for that sonofabitch." She was looking right through him, but not seeing him. She was seeing that knife-wielding bastard. "Vince can look after me." Backing out of the room she smiled vaguely at them all, her pale skin turning even whiter in the morning sun.

"Josephine." Panic crept in to his tone. She said she wasn't running away but she was lying. He'd expected fireworks, but he had expected to get his way. This distance was beyond him and he'd never seen her retreat into herself before. "Pack your stuff because we're leaving at noon."

There was no reply, just the click of the lock on the bedroom door and the expectant weight of silence.

"Well, that went well." Dancer slugged down the last of his coffee, licked frosted sugar off his fingers. "Want me to get the tranquilizers or can you manage?"

***

The light was perfect. If she could concentrate on color, on how to make the folds of the Statue of

Liberty's toga look both fluid and solid at the same time, everything would be fine. Squeezing out permanent green, some phthalo green and a blob of cobalt green deep acrylic, she stared stupidly at her palette. Her hands shook as feeling slowly crept back into her senses.

This was never going to work. Being with Marsh was never going to work.

He couldn't protect her forever and she didn't want him around purely out of obligation. Neither did she want to put him in danger or have to worry about him. She closed her eyes and swayed. She was an idiot.

She should have run that first day but she'd hesitated and that had been her first mistake.

Liberty's upraised arm mocked her. This painting was supposed to represent the indomitable spirit of New York City. It was supposed to represent the phoenix rising from the ashes of grief and the courage of the people of this great city. But how could she hope to do it justice when she couldn't even walk the streets without a bodyguard? She despised what her life had become. She wasn't some weak little drip who hung on a man's word and expected him to take care of her. Neither did she want to be the dumbfuck blonde in a horror flick who got caught by a monster with a big sharp knife.

Marshall Hayes got under her skin in a way no man ever had before. She wanted to believe in him, wanted to lean on him, and knew she couldn't risk it.

Sunlight filtered in through the tall glass windows and worked tiny beads of sweat on her temple. At age nine she'd learned the key to survival was keeping quiet. Keep your head down, don't get involved. Don't expose your emotions. Run, hide, watch, survive, strike out when necessary, and keep your goddamned mouth shut. Her father's image rose up in her mind, calling her names because she'd had the audacity to resemble her mother. What would Walter Maxwell have done different if he'd known his wife had been murdered rather than left him? Josephine frowned for a moment. It would have been another excuse to drink himself to death. No wonder her mother had gone off with another man. Marion had saved her, taken her in, and in the end Josie had repaid that debt with painful death.

Painful death had a habit of following her around and she couldn't stand the idea it might be Marsh this time as a result of some vain effort to save her. But she was not letting a man—not even a good man like Marsh, and definitely not an evil bastard like the Blade Hunter—control her life.

Her fingers closed around the handle of the paintbrush and she dipped it in the thick cobalt green. Stepped across to the stepladder and put her foot on the first rung.

"Are you going to listen to reason?" Marsh's voice came quietly from the doorway and her blood revved.

All last night they'd clung to one another. But he made her feel exposed and she couldn't afford that vulnerability. Shaking her head, she daubed on the first light coating of paint across the right hand side of the statue. She couldn't bring herself to face him.

"Are you going to tell me why not or just ignore me again?" The Boston accent was even flatter than usual and cold enough to make her shiver. In the cottage in Vermont she'd refused to talk to him for thirty-six hours straight. Then she'd seduced him. She didn't know how many mistakes one person could make in a lifetime but it looked like she was trying to find out.

"I can't run away when he's out hunting other women." She lifted her chin, ignored the fine tremor that ran through her when she turned to look at him standing there in a dark navy suit and scarlet striped tie. So beautiful and powerful; her throat hurt looking at him. "I'm staying. You go."

"Didn't last night mean anything to you?" His voice held an edge that started to piss her off.

Wobbling slightly on the ladder she said, "Last night was good, Marsh, but I'm not gonna play in your bed until they catch this guy. I have work to do."

"You think I want you in Boston so I can fuck you?"

She climbed off the ladder and met him head on. Heat and anger burned off him like jet fuel. This wasn't going the way she'd planned.

"You think I can't last a few nights without sex when I've been celibate for months?" Amber battled with jade as his pupils flared.

"I don't know! I don't know about any of this." Her voice rose. "None of it makes sense."

With sharp jerks he took the brush and palette from her rigid fingers and placed them on the table. "One thing makes sense."

Josephine inhaled a jagged breath as he grabbed the material of her shirt in a fist and pulled her flush against his body. His lips crushed hers, fury and frustration ripe in the pressure and clash of his teeth.

His other hand pressed against the small of her back, bringing them in intimate contact and sending blasts of desire pulsing from her breasts to the apex of her thighs.

His lips turned gentle, belying his anger, his teeth nipped at her mouth until she responded and her hands crept up around his shoulders. She closed her eyes against the weakness that assaulted her, gripped him hard as dark emotions rose up. His kiss slowed and she tasted gentleness, opened her eyes and caught a brief glimpse of pain before he drew away.

"This isn't about sex, Josephine. You know whatever is happening between us is much more than just sex and I don't like it any more than you do." His words were weary and tore at her resolve. "But you coming with me to Boston is about stopping that bastard slicing you open with a sharp blade and finishing what he started all those years ago."

Nausea curled through her, as she knew it was meant to. He was trying to scare her. As if she needed any reminders. But she didn't intend to get caught by this psychopath.

She pulled away. "Vince is here."

He paused and looked over his shoulder on his way to the door. "But *I* wanted to do it... *I* wanted to be the one who kept you safe."

175

Chapter Twelve

Paint speckled toes peeped out of turquoise sequined flip-flops. The ragged hem of her jeans tickled the sensitive bridge of her foot. But neither sight nor sensation eased the tension in her jaw or set of her shoulders. Fury burned a thin line of rage through her bones. She seized onto it in a desperate attempt to help herself focus.

Josie grabbed a new size-twenty brush and an industrial-sized tube of China White and threw it in her basket. New sponges, Conté crayons, and a sharp triangular palette knife followed.

Shoving past Vince, she flung him a glare.

Men.

With a smack, she dumped the basket at the checkout, stared stonily at the gum-chewing clerk who slowly registered her presence and began scanning her purchases. So what if she was acting irrationally? None of this was her fault. This bastard was ruining her life and Marsh was trying to control it. She wanted her independence back. She needed the space to think.

"He wants to keep you safe." Vince's low voice murmured in her ear, but rather than easing her mind, he fired the fury higher.

"I thought that's what you were for." She flung him a dismissive up-and-down scowl.

The store clerk stopped chewing and glanced nervously at Vince who blocked out most of the light. Vince's gaze flickered to the clerk and he cocked a questioning eyebrow back at her.

Her hissy fit was attracting the wrong kind of attention. "Don't worry about him, he's my bodyguard and a decorated war hero," she reassured the clerk.

"Anyone ever told you you're about as subtle as a chainsaw?" Vince murmured directly into her ear.

Gathering her supplies, she marched out of the shop and onto the street, fought the wind as it whipped her thin black sweater against her skin. It felt colder than it should have. A frigid wind cutting down from the Maritimes with the sharpness of bear claws. She shivered. Painting and anger had been the only things she could think about since she'd argued with Marsh that morning. Good job she'd been dressed before she'd run out of paint else she'd probably be standing here naked.

Unable to concentrate on her commission, she'd put Liberty to one side and blasted pure emotion onto a fresh canvas. The result looked like road-kill and it turned her stomach when she'd recognized the inspiration for the image.

Skillfully avoiding tourists and New Yorkers alike she strode along the sidewalk. She should contact Agent Walker to see if there was any news. Marsh wasn't running this show; he was just trying to protect her.

The aroma of pizza competed with gas fumes as she stood on the curb, checked for traffic and jaywalked across to Bleecker, not caring if Vince followed or not. Turning onto Grove Street she looked over her shoulder and found Vince in her shadow. Silent, scary, alert.

And it pissed her off.

The Blade Hunter was pulling her strings,

making her dance to his tune, giving her a new life with new rules and she didn't like it. She'd spent her childhood being controlled by others.

The faces of mutilated women flashed vividly through her mind, her mother's face…a girlhood memory distorted by time and gruesome crime scene pictures. Cupping her hand over her mouth, she came to a standstill in the street.

"You okay?" Vince asked from behind her.

"No, but I'll live." *Hopefully.* Then she spotted Marsh standing across the road outside her apartment building looking upwards at the windows. She thought he'd already left for Boston, but he looked like he'd been standing there for hours.

Vince put a hand on her shoulder. "Be smart."

"Why? You need a vacation, sweet-thing?" She squinted up at the big man.

White teeth flashed like headlights on high beam. He gave her shoulder a squeeze. "This *is* a vacation, cupcake." He gave her a gentle push.

Great. She was a wimp surrounded by superheroes with big frickin' guns.

Marsh turned toward her as she stumbled forward. "You come to your senses yet?" His words grabbed her temper by the scruff of the neck and gave it a good shake.

"I'm staying."

Disappointment flickered in the hazel of his eyes and it hurt. *Dammit,* this was why she didn't get involved. Being alone was a damn sight easier than trying to live up to someone else's expectations. And knowing she'd miss the SOB when he left sat about as well as waiting for a serial killer to strike. But maybe it was better this way.

Hoisting her bag of supplies under one arm she unlocked the front door. Marsh stepped up behind her and she glanced sideways, watched Vince raise a hand in farewell.

"He's grabbing enough food and gear to last the next forty-eight hours." His voice was neutral and gave nothing away. It didn't have to. He'd made his opinion perfectly clear.

"He doesn't have to stay the whole time." She flung the door open, shocked when Marsh twisted her in his arms and pushed her up against the front door, his hands in a vise-like grip on her arms.

"Why do you act like you don't even care?"

The hair on her nape rose. She kept her mouth closed.

"Why do you act like *nothing* ever bothers you?" Strain etched every muscle. His shoulders trembled and the skin around his mouth was deathly white. Her nerves hummed like a wasp. She'd pushed him too far.

"What would you do if he came after you?" He jerked away like he couldn't stand to touch her for a moment longer. "What would I do?"

Heart pounding, she started up the stairs.

"Josephine!" The anguish in his voice made her swing to face him. The light in his eyes vivid and bright, wringing out emotions she didn't know how to deal with.

"I can't do this, Marsh. I don't even know how to be in a relationship under normal circumstances." To her horror tears spilled out. "Right now I can't think of anything except getting through this alive."

Bolting up the stairs her footsteps rebounded through the stairwell. Her heartbeat raced faster and faster, her lungs bursting with the need for oxygen, but she couldn't take a breath.

She'd made it to the second floor before Marsh began to follow. She wasn't running away from him. She needed some space. *And you keep telling yourself that…*

At the top of the stairs she stopped so fast she skidded on the smooth floor.

The door to her apartment stood ajar. *Did I leave it open*? She slowed, uncertain. The wood was crushed beside the handle. It had been jimmied.

"Stand behind me." Marsh unclipped his weapon.

Waves of adrenaline caused blood to pulse through her ears. She grabbed the back of Marsh's jacket and held on for dear life.

Shit. Shit. Shit. Her heart hammered and sweat began to run down her forehead, dripping into her eyes.

Reaching behind his back with one hand, he pried her fingers loose and captured them in his. Bringing them to his lips he gave her a brief kiss and a tight smile before motioning her behind him as he hugged the wall. Never taking his eyes from the doorway, he took out his cell phone and speed-dialed a number, thrust the phone into Josie's hands.

"What now?" she whispered.

Marsh held his finger to his lips and mouthed, "We wait."

"For what?" she whispered back.

A door crashed open below and boots clattered up the stairs.

"Back up." Marsh smiled. The effect was terrifying.

Vince arrived at the top of the stairs with his pistol drawn, the sheen of sweat on his forehead and a deadly expression on his face.

Wordlessly the two men moved into position and swept into the apartment the way she'd seen a thousand times on the TV. Marsh dragged her inside, the grip on her wrist so tight it hurt, but she wasn't complaining. The last thing she wanted was to be left alone—a great moment for *that* epiphany. God, she was a stubborn fool.

The lounge looked undisturbed. Marsh and Vince tag-teamed every possible hiding place, checking the kitchen, bathrooms, closets.

Josie stood in the center of her studio stunned. He'd taken the painting...

Lightheaded, she allowed herself to be maneuvered into the guestroom as they checked under the bed and inside the built-ins. Nausea crept into her throat. He'd been here. A shiver of repulsion slid over her skin. She followed Marsh back into the living room. More footsteps echoed up the stairwell and voices shouted. Agents Dancer and Walker burst into the apartment, but Marsh and Vince never glanced up. They were focused on the last remaining possible hiding place for an intruder. Her bedroom.

Fear soured on her tongue as she followed them.

Vivid red splattered the white covers, dripped onto the hardwood floor. The stench of turpentine and paint curled up inside her nostrils; the tools of her trade used to terrorize. The message daubed on the wall sent a chill into her frozen heart.

U R DEAD.

"He has to get through me first." Marsh holstered his weapon.

She crossed her arms over her chest, fought to keep her teeth from chattering. "It's also the last thing he said to me the night he killed Angela Morelli."

"Funny how you forgot to mention that earlier," Special Agent Walker snapped.

"Funny?" Her voice rose shrilly. "I figured the message was clear enough that even the feds could figure it out."

"We need to search the whole building." Walker nodded to Dancer, and Vince followed them to the front door.

Her knees wobbled and Marsh swept her up in his arms and placed her gently on the couch.

Her teeth rattled. "He's telling me he can get to me anytime he wants."

"He's taunting you." Marsh rested his hands on his hips and stared down at her. "I won't let him get you, Josephine."

But there was a kernel of satisfaction in his voice. "You're glad about this?"

"No." He pressed his lips together, trying to control his temper. "But I'm glad you weren't here alone when the bastard broke in."

Point made.

"I was only gone half an hour." A sudden thought struck her. "How did he get in the building—did you see him?"

Marsh shook his head, glancing around the apartment as if looking for anything that might be missing. "He must have stolen a key from Angela Morelli's apartment but I thought your super was changing the locks?"

"Friday."

"I still don't know how he knew where you lived. Investigations can be slow processes but...*fuck*."

Agent Walker strolled back into the apartment. "We need to process the scene—"

"You don't really think he left anything behind, do you?" Marsh raised one quizzical brow at his fellow agent.

"Well, I'm not going to miss an opportunity to track this man, sir," Walker replied.

"You already have his DNA. Any hits?" Marsh asked.

She'd forgotten about the blood she'd drawn when she'd bitten him. The reminder turned her stomach.

Sam Walker's lips thinned. "He's not in the system."

Marsh frowned. "Did you finish checking the rest of the building?"

Walker nodded. "Got teams going through each apartment right now, but most of them are still empty following the first murder. And we're going to set up video surveillance back and front of the property ASAP."

Why hadn't they done that a few days ago?

She looked down and spotted the red paint encrusting her fingernails like fresh blood. "He took a painting."

"What painting?" the feds asked in unison.

Josie swallowed, feeling sick that she'd betrayed those women by painting an image of the torture they'd endured. It was abstract, but the Blade Hunter had known exactly what he'd been looking at.

"I painted it this morning." She scrubbed her eyes, feeling dizzy. "It's abstract, but it's about the murders. It's about blood and agony."

Marsh pressed her head between her knees

before she realized she was close to passing out. He knelt beside her on the rug. "You're coming with me, Josephine, and if you fight me I'm going to handcuff you and drag you there."

"There's always protective custody." Sam Walker spoke to Marsh not her. She gripped Marsh's hand and dug in her nails to tell him exactly what she thought of that idea.

"That's okay, Agent Walker." He rubbed her hand gently. "She's coming with me for a few days. After that we'll need to figure out some other arrangement until we can catch this guy."

"The whole city is on high alert. The media are going crazy so we should have more resources soon," said Walker.

"Can you walk?" Marsh asked her quietly.

"Of course." She hoped.

"Anything here you can't live without?" He held out his hand as if expecting her to say no.

Instead she shook him off and stumbled toward the closet near the front door. Her knapsack lay on the floor. She opened it and peeked inside. Marion's ashes were safe within the funky little urn Josie had painted.

"Just this." She clasped the knapsack in front of her and ignored his curious frown. "Nothing else matters."

***

Five hours later, Marsh watched the sway of Josephine's hips as he followed her and his mother along the upstairs hallway of the family home.

Alternate realities set on a collision course.

They glided like ghosts over the thick oriental

runner, footsteps silent as moth's wings. The subtle odor of beeswax teased his nostrils and brought with it a cascade of memories that faded inexorably with each passing year. Two boys sword-fighting along this hallway, sliding down the banister and clambering over furniture. He stuffed his hands in his pockets and forced away the memories.

His life was about to change. Again.

Whether they realized it or not, the two most important people in his life were sizing one another up. Josephine paused on the bedroom's threshold. It was the same room she'd stayed in six months ago, but his parents had been away at the time. Would Josephine recognize it? The décor had changed again.

His mother moved restlessly from one room to the next in their enormous Louisburg Square home, decorating in a forlorn effort to fill the void. Marsh worked his ass off and his father golfed. How else did you cope with the loss of a beloved son or revered brother?

Josephine lowered her knapsack carefully to the floor beside the bed where it landed with a hollow thud.

What the hell was in that thing?

The bed was made up with a lavish mixture of shiny mauve, cream and purple sheets, with enough covers and pillows to survive a Canadian winter.

"I can't believe what happened to poor Lynn." Beatrice Hayes stood inside the room, her hand resting on her heart. She gave a little shake of her head. "I called to leave my condolences, but Lydia wasn't receiving. She's under medication." Her eyes flicked nervously away.

Lydia—Lynn Richards' mother.

Josephine caught his eye and they exchanged a moment of guilt.

His mother folded and unfolded her hands across her chest, probably unsettled by the less than friendly expression on Josephine's face. This was the first time he'd ever brought a woman home, and she wasn't exactly the girl next door.

"Josephine has been attacked twice by this killer, once when she was only a small child." Marsh knew he'd go to hell for playing on his mother's sympathies, assuming Josephine didn't kill him first for sharing her secrets. His mom softened visibly, her maternal instincts staunch enough to overlook the fact Josephine was no longer a child, but a full grown woman that her son lusted after.

"I'll try and find you some clothes to wear, dear." Bea frowned as she assessed Josephine's tall slender frame. His mother was about seven inches shorter and four sizes wider. "Actually you'd better go out to the boutique at the end of the road, Marshall, and pick up some things. I can't believe he didn't give you time to change."

Yeah, because clothes were more important than getting Josephine away from danger.

She looked down at her paint spattered jeans and frowned, a bewildered light entering her eyes. "The FBI wanted to search my place and I didn't want to wear anything the guy might have touched…"

Bea's hand flew to her throat. "Oh, of course not. Please forgive me, dear. I don't know what I was thinking." She gave a delicate shudder, crossed over and hugged Josephine briefly, as if someone touching her underwear was the worst thing his mother could imagine. He hoped to God that never

186

changed.

Josephine's wild frantic eyes shot a pleading look in his direction. He shrugged.

This was what happened when two worlds collided.

"You redecorated in here?" He made an attempt at light conversation.

His mother released her and smiled, happy to be distracted from the baser side of life. "Yes, dear, though your father wasn't happy when I had the wood paneling painted white."

No kidding. Marsh coughed.

"Not that I told him until after it was finished." She squeezed his arm, her fingers soft on the sleeve of his jacket. He bet his father had gone ballistic when the antique wood had received a facelift, but then nobody really cared as long as Bea was happy. Except she was never really happy. Pain lingered in the corners of her eyes, in the lines around her soft mouth.

And that's why he'd gone on a date with a young woman who'd ended up dead.

"It brightens the room, don't you think?" Bea's anxious hazel eyes, so like his own, so like Robert's, appealed to him now.

He wanted to say *yes, it brightened the room,* but the lump in his throat blocked the words. *Who cared?* His mother's smile faltered.

"It's beautiful." Josephine hovered beside the bed as if afraid to sit down. She cleared her throat, walked to the casement window, peered into the dark square beyond. "Pretty fancy digs."

"And the security is top of the range." He squinted down at his mother. "You are still using the alarm system we installed, right?"

Bea flapped her hands at him. "Your father keeps setting the silly thing off with his midnight strolls to the kitchen." She smiled, the lines on her smooth cheeks creasing, "We keep the outside one turned on, of course, but inside…" Her voice trailed off.

"I'll talk to Dad—until we catch this killer we have to assume he might track Josephine here." He held his mother's gaze, read her silent query as to why he'd brought danger into their home. She was too polite to call him on it.

Josephine prowled the background like a tiger locked in a too-small cage. The sequins on her flip flops shimmered in the light from the ornate chandelier.

"So how long have you two known each other?" Bea asked, smiling at Josephine so guilelessly Marsh wanted to shout a warning, but she answered naively.

"We have a mutual friend who got into some trouble last April." Josephine shrugged a shoulder and missed his grimace. His mother didn't.

Bea turned back toward Josephine, assessing her for a full ten seconds with only the ticking carriage clock to fill the silence. The lighting made Josephine's hair glow white against the darkness of the window, all three of them reflected there like ghosts.

Conscious of possible onlookers, Marsh walked over and closed the drapes. Stood tall at Josephine's shoulder.

Eyes sharp, lips considering, Bea examined them both. Then she nodded. "You must be terrified, Josephine. Do you mind if I call you Josephine?"

"I prefer Josie." She swept a pale strand of hair behind one delicate shell of an ear.

Marsh released a deep breath.

"But Josephine is such a beautiful name." Approval shone from Bea's tone, but Josephine's eyebrows slammed together and her mouth turned down as she flicked him an irritated glance.

Marsh had always loved Josephine's name, refused to call her Josie…and yet she didn't like it. Maybe because it was old fashioned and formal, or maybe she'd been teased as a kid. He shoved his hands in his pockets and stared at a scratch that marred the otherwise perfect surface of his shoe.

His mother opened a white painted antique dresser and removed some sleepwear. She placed a pair of satin pajamas on the quilt and went to retrieve a matching dressing gown. They were deep damson, exactly the same color as the bedspread. Interior design had taken on new extremes.

What would Josephine think of a woman who spent all her time decorating walls and matching color swatches and why the hell did he care what Josephine thought of his mother?

Shame surged inside him. His mother appeared vapid, one of the idle rich, when she was so much more than that. Guilt mixed with self-disgust—what the hell gave him the right to judge the woman who'd given him life? Or the one he'd foolishly fallen for?

He should have stayed at a hotel. These two women never had to meet, and yet…

"You have a wonderful eye for color, Mrs. Hayes." Josephine stepped forward and slowly stroked the bedcover. "And for texture."

He turned away and willed his mother to leave

the room—he was anxious to get out of here, but didn't dare leave them alone.

"I can't claim much in that department either." His mother sighed, a fluttering, wrenching sound. "I have an interior designer who *guides* me." Her hand plumped a satin pillow. "But an old woman with no grandchildren needs some distractions to occupy her time, don't you think?"

With a pointed look between the pair of them, Beatrice Hayes swept out of the room.

There was a long silence where neither of them was breathing.

"She really *is* desperate for grandkids to contemplate letting my blood join the Hayes' family line." Josephine wiggled her eyebrows and gave him a strained smile. "Wanna do it now or later?" Shock tactics had always worked for her in the past—a defense mechanism to keep people away so she didn't get hurt. But he was smarter than that. Holding her gaze, he waited until she stopped fidgeting.

"My mother's adopted. She got lucky having wealthy parents, but she cares very little about blood and a whole lot more about family." His gaze slid down her frame, pissed with her continued charade and frustrated, not knowing how to break through the barriers that had protected her for so long. Maybe he'd never break through. Maybe she'd never really open up or let him close. "Don't judge her with your snobbery and prejudice. That's not who she is. And deep down, it's not who you are either."

He turned and walked out of the room, furious he couldn't control this situation. Frustrated he couldn't control his own emotions when it came to this woman. He had to get away from Josephine Maxwell.

***

Two hours later, Josie stroked a hand over the silk wall covering as she stole down the intricately carved staircase, her footsteps muted by the thick oriental runner. She was so nervous her stomach roiled. The desire to run was fierce. She'd never felt so out of her depth in her life.

She was also late for dinner.

She'd rather stay in her room and eat off a tray, or in the kitchen, or starve. But Marsh's mother had very politely invited her to join them and Josie was less able to deal with courtesy than antagonism. And that scared the hell out of her.

She self-consciously smoothed a palm over navy linen pants, absorbed the soft texture with a shiver of appreciation. It was teamed with a navy and white polka-dot cardigan with a red and white stripe running along the trim. She liked it. It was sexy and fun and she wouldn't have looked twice at it in any shop.

Not that Army Surplus stocked many polka dots.

Marsh had turned up twenty minutes ago with a large bag full of clothes, dumped them on her bed and left without saying a word. And she'd desperately wanted him to stay.

A laugh sounded from the dining room, followed by the gentle rumble of an amused male.

Reluctantly, she took that last step.

Marsh materialized soundlessly beside the balustrade. "Jesus H Christ!" She jumped an inch off the floor.

"Not quite." His eyes burned her up and down, and he nodded. "They fit?"

"Yeah, unlike me," she muttered.

He stared up at the ceiling and looked suspiciously like he was counting to ten.

Why was he *pissed?* Of course, they hadn't settled the fight they'd started earlier—but she was here, wasn't she? It took her a moment to admit she was being a bitch and it had more to do with her own insecurity than anything he'd done. She drew in a deep breath. "Thank you. For the clothes. And for helping me."

His expression softened but they were interrupted before he could speak.

"Ah, here she is..." A thinner, older version of Marsh appeared in the doorway and Josie steeled herself. Socializing was what other people did. She stayed home and watched TiVo or painted. She *hated* meeting new people. Felt the unexpected pressure of trying to impress Marsh's parents simply because they were Marsh's parents.

When is the last time anyone expected anything from me? Maybe never. Maybe that was the problem.

"Dad, let me introduce Josephine Maxwell. Josie, this is my father, General Jacob Hayes."

Her mouth dropped open. He'd called her Josie. She flicked him a shocked glance, but he'd already turned away as his father reached out a hand to her. It was hard to hold the general's bright green gaze, full of unspoken probing and silent appraisal. Jacob Hayes shot his son a sharp glance when he spotted her bare feet.

"Didn't you buy her any shoes?"

Marsh had bought her tons of footwear—shoes, runners, boots. Too many beautiful things for a few short nights away. She'd have to find a way to return them or spend the next ten years paying him back.

She wiggled her bare toes as everyone stared at her feet. "Actually, I figured if I wore shoes I might make a break for the front door. I decided not to chance it."

For what seemed like an eternity Marsh's father locked his gaze on hers.

"That nervous, huh?" He huffed out a laugh. "I'll be damned." He looked anxiously over his shoulder. "My one piece of advice is don't let Bea catch you cursing—thirty years in the Army and she still thinks *heck* is a suitable expletive to cover any and all occasions...including bloodshed."

Josie grinned—he seemed like a nice old guy. Marsh stood silently beside her and she knew her comment about running away had been noted and catalogued inside his efficient brain. She was escorted into the elegant sitting room and offered a chair beside the fire, feeling like she'd been transported into a Hallmark Happy Families card.

"Would you care for a drink?" the general asked her.

"I don't drink."

"Have a Pimms, dear." Looking slightly merry, Bea smiled and raised her brimming glass.

Avoiding Bea's hopeful gaze, Josie cleared the lump in her throat. "I don't drink alcohol, but I'll have water, please." She sent Marsh a forced smile, knowing she wasn't conforming to whatever the hell his family wanted, but unable to pretend to be something she wasn't.

Marsh went to get her some water. He'd been ominously quiet. His parents exchanged a look.

Josie took the glass from Marsh's grip, and thanked him with a smile. His expression didn't change. Guarded. Wary.

"What do you do, my dear?" The general asked.

"When I'm not being stalked by a serial killer, you mean?" Josie smiled over-brightly and the Hayeses swapped startled looks. There was no way she was pretending to be here as their son's date. Sure it was easier that way, but Josie had never gone with easy. There would be no happy ending for her and Marsh. It wasn't fair to pretend otherwise. What they had was hot and dangerous and would burn out the moment they caught the killer, or he caught them. "I'm an artist."

Bea's smile was delighted. The general took a swig of his scotch.

"And what about your family, Josephine? What do they do?" the general asked.

Vetting her...

She didn't want to hurt Marsh's parents, but they couldn't go on believing this was some family introduction to the future *Mrs.* Hayes. She knew they wanted him married but she wasn't that girl. The fact that a tiny portion of her brain wished she was pissed her off.

Marsh paced the floor near a window that faced onto the street. She had no idea what he was thinking. He certainly wasn't helping her out.

"My father was a factory worker who spent most of his life on disability and my mother was a school secretary who disappeared—now believed murdered—after having a fling with a visiting African missionary."

194

The fire crackled and Bea pressed a shocked hand to her mouth. Marsh turned to watch, but she could not read the light in his eyes. "The FBI thinks my mom was the first victim of this maniac who's after me now." The coldness of the water was soothing against the lining of her throat. "The only person who cared for me growing up was a woman named Marion. Because of my actions, she was tortured and killed last spring."

Appalled by the tears that grew hot in her eyes, she stared at Marsh in shocked realization that she'd never even remotely gotten over Marion's death. She hadn't even begun to forgive herself. "Her ashes are upstairs in my knapsack because I still can't bear the thought of losing her." She slipped the glass onto the nearest table afraid she'd drop it and it'd shatter, splintering into a thousand pieces like her composure. "I'd better go—"

"No." Bea rose and held both hands out toward her. Tears filled her eyes and Josie froze, unable to bear the empathy in the older woman's gaze. Marsh's mother should be turning her nose up about now—adopted or not, it was clear that Josie was totally unsuitable for their beloved son.

"Forgive us." Marsh's mother swallowed and blinked away the tears. "We should never have probed—it isn't as if our family hasn't experienced great loss, but I'm sure Marsh has told you all about it."

Josie swung overstretched eyes to Marsh who'd never told her a thing about his family. She'd never asked. He looked at the floor, mouth twisted before looking back with carefully shuttered eyes.

His mother stared off into the fire, sadness palpable as rain on the window. The general coughed. Marsh walked up beside her, took her hand, her fingers chilled against his heat of his skin. He led her across the room toward a photograph hanging on the wall between two casement windows. She'd thought it was a photograph of Marsh when she'd glanced at it earlier. Now she realized the uniform was different—Army, not Navy.

"My brother, Robert," Marsh spoke quietly. His voice was carefully level. "He died in Iraq."

Josie stared at the photograph of the blisteringly handsome young man, a man so like Marsh her heart gave a squeeze.

Beatrice Hayes began to cry, softly. Jacob handed her a handkerchief and the action made Josie's gaze flick to Marsh, who tightened his lips into what most people would think was a smile. She knew better. It was a flare of pain.

"Seems like yesterday," Bea sobbed gently. The general rubbed her back, the gesture both soothing and hopeless, as if he'd done it a million times before and finally realized it didn't help.

It *hurt*.

"The pain never really goes away does it?" Josie forced the words out through a throat rapidly closing with emotion, "Losing someone you love…"

Beatrice held her gaze, the emotional connection like tensile steel. Her eyes seemed to reach inside Josie and soothe her heart with tender hands. She hadn't felt this sort of comfort since Marion had died and wanted to weep.

Josie's head snapped up.

She'd been snared by a trap so complex she'd been blindsided. The woman had drawn her into their world, into Marsh's world and made her *care*, a feeling she assiduously avoided and yet it had slid into her body as effortlessly as a barbed hook.

Marsh leaned down, his breath warm against her cheek. "Welcome to my world."

***

Marsh hesitated as he opened the door to Josie's room. Shadows played across the walls, the smell of old wood overlaid by the sweet scent of a candle she'd lit beside the bed. He moved into the room. She sat fully dressed, leaning forward on a straight-back chair, elbows on knees, staring out into the empty street.

Noise was muted through the thick panes of century-old glass, sounds of downtown remote in this affluent citadel, just a murmur of wind rattling the frames.

Shocked by the fragility of her appearance, he reached for her hand, drew her carefully to her feet.

"I have to leave." Her voice quavered, too much strain born on too fine a wire.

He held her close, pressed her head to his chest. "Stay. Stay with me."

"I can't. I don't want to hurt anyone." Her body quivered against him. But despite the words she wrapped her arms around his neck, pressed her lips to his and he knew she wouldn't leave him yet.

Chapter Thirteen

They were eating at the breakfast bar in the kitchen by six a.m. Marsh couldn't believe how much he enjoyed such a mundane act. For a little while they were able to pretend they were ordinary people getting to know one another, and Josie wasn't being targeted by a killer. Then he saw the front page of the *NY News*. Tension stretched up his spine and across his shoulders like a crucifix. "Damn."

"Better watch your mouth. Your momma doesn't approve of bad language." Her sass dissolved when he turned the laptop toward her.

"Oh, no."

Bright lights glared down from the kitchen ceiling, highlighting her horror as her past was exposed for the world to see. Her hands curled into fists, knuckles gleaming white a hair's breadth beneath the surface of her skin. The *NY News* had gotten hold of the photograph taken after Josie's first knife attack. The bleak black and white image of a hollow-eyed child stared out at them next to the bold caption, 'The First Victim'. This case was about to blow wide open—a serial killer stalking NYC for the last twenty years. Front page news.

Marsh looked at the by-line. *Nelson fucking Landry.*

This was the reporter's revenge for Marsh putting the lid on his investigation into Elizabeth's disappearance last spring. Karma was a bitch. His cell rang. *Dancer.*

"Yo, boss."

"Yo?" Marsh pinched the bridge of his nose, "I'm a senior federal official and your boss, and all I get is *Yo*?"

"I'm channeling Donnie Brascoe. *Yo* is what you're getting today." Dancer whistled between sentences, clearly excited. Marsh recognized the theme tune to *The Godfather*. Please, God, don't let the mob be involved in any way, although there were rumors about the Gardner robbery.

"What have you got for me? And why are you channeling Joe Pistone?" Marsh forced a harsh tone to his voice, but knew he didn't fool his tech for a second.

"Because I'm going deep undercover in New York City, boss man."

Alarm bells jangled inside his mind. The pressure in his jaw started to give him a headache— these two cases were killing him. "What do you mean? I thought you were in Boston to help me interview the admiral?"

"I *was* going to be in Boston," Dancer corrected, sounding way too cheery.

Marsh ground his teeth, loosened his tie as his internal temperature exploded. He was getting a very bad feeling about this. Dancer was brilliant, but he could also be a royal pain in the ass when he wanted to be. A loose cannon—the nerdy kid left unattended for too long in the computer lab who ended up hacking NASA.

Marsh glanced at Josie. He seemed to attract wild sparks.

Maybe he was attracted to their fire, their disregard for the rules that bound him.

Josie met his gaze head on, crystal blue eyes

reflecting a soul-deep wound. He wanted to hold her, to wrap her up in safety. "Spill it, Steve, before I sign your transfer papers to Fargo."

"Fargo wouldn't be so bad—"

"D.C. then..." The thought of all those politicians would freak him out more than chainsaws and permafrost.

"Something about this case isn't adding up," Dancer said softly.

"Tell me something I don't know."

"So I figured I'd dig deeper—"

"What did you come up with?" Normally, patience was his strong suit, but right now...nothing was making sense. His focus was being pulled in a million different directions and the only thing he really wanted to do was put a smile on Josie's face and make it stay there.

"Nothing yet, but Pru Duvall phoned the office last night, just before I was supposed to catch my flight. She invited me to lunch today."

Marsh closed his eyes. "Do not get involved with that woman Dancer, I mean it—"

"So I agreed to have lunch with her—"

"For fuck's sake."

His mother came into the brightly lit kitchen. He turned his back on her astonished expression. There was a reason he didn't bring his work home.

"It's lunch, boss."

"I don't trust her, Steve. Do *not* meet her without back up—even for lunch." Marsh's fingers cramped from his death grip on the phone. Pain speared through his skull as his senses finally overloaded. Blindly, he stood up and reached for aspirin in the kitchen cupboard.

"I don't know why you do what you do,

Marshall," his mother whispered and shook her head as she stirred a silver spoon through milky tea in a porcelain mug.

Mentally Marsh counted to ten. In Latin.

"Come on, boss. She's a middle-aged politician's wife. What harm can she do to a razor-sharp, intelligent, specially trained, and armed, FBI agent?"

"I can think of a few things."

Dancer was silent for a moment. "Don't you trust me?"

Marsh sighed, tucked the phone into the crook of his neck as he filled a glass of water and swallowed two tablets. He needed to de-stress or work out. He needed to solve this damn case—which he was beginning to think was more a personal feud between two wealthy families—so he could get on with the job of finding the killer whose main aim in life was to slice and dice the woman he loved.

And wasn't that a hell of an epiphany to have while his brain pounded and his mother coaxed a smile out of Josie who was paler than skimmed milk.

"I trust you, Dancer. It's Mrs. D I don't trust." Marsh sighed, decision already made. They needed to get this off their desks. "I still want you to report in, before and after."

"Want me to order a SWAT team too, just in case? They could join us for lunch? Even SWAT guys gotta eat."

Remembering the feral look on Pru's face when she'd stared at Dancer the other morning, it wasn't such a bad idea.

"I'll be good. I promise." Dancer's cell

reception was breaking up.

"Watch your back."

He ended the call and threw the phone down onto the countertop where it landed with a clatter. Blowing out a harsh breath he walked around the counter and wrapped his arms around Josie's waist. Ignored his mother. Ignored the initial stiffness of Josie's frame, dipping his face into her hair as he waited for his headache to recede.

Nothing else really mattered anymore except keeping her safe.

***

They sat silently for some time. He was working. Josie was reading the news on his parents' laptop. His mother had left them to go supervise the lunch menu for a group of her cronies.

"Why *do* you do it?" The curiosity in Josie's tone cut through his concentration.

He looked up, met vibrant eyes and wondered what it would be like to look at her every single day of his life. He shook his head as though to shake the thought loose. Now wasn't the time to think about the future. They had to survive the present. "Why do I do what?"

"This." She waved a hand over the FBI badge that sat in its case on the kitchen counter. Gingerly, she picked up the smooth black leather case and flipped it open so the golden shield flashed. "You obviously don't need the money."

He studied her while she studied his badge—a badge he'd worked hard for despite his connections. She bit her lip and frowned, thinking too much as usual. In a floaty dress, teamed with tall brown suede boots and a long brown cardigan, she looked more feminine than he'd ever seen her. He'd grabbed the clothes from a nearby boutique. Just handed over her sizes and his credit card to the store clerk and asked for one of everything. Knew she'd look good regardless. The dress was casual—she wouldn't have worn it otherwise—mismatched fabric with a little tieback thing that emphasized her small breasts and tiny waist. Everything about her looks screamed pedigreed wealth and privilege. Appearances were deceptive, and he didn't give a shit.

His mouth went as dry as the Mohave Desert.

Realizing he was staring at her stupidly, he pressed his hand against the SIG-Sauer that rested beneath his arm. "What else am I going to do?" he ventured.

It was a non-answer and they both knew it. Marsh checked his wristwatch. Noticed Josie wore nothing on her wrists except a group of three pale freckles.

The gulf between their worlds couldn't be more noticeable and yet Marsh didn't give a damn about her lack of cash or family connections—it was Josie who cared, Josie who chose to carry the stigma of her upbringing and proclaim that she didn't fit in. He needed to figure out a way to make her understand what really mattered to him; who he was beneath the badge and the bloodline.

He had several hours before he had to meet the admiral. The guy lived in an Old Colonial in Charlestown. Not only was it the scene of the crime, it was where the old bugger felt most comfortable and hopefully off his guard. He climbed to his feet, pocketed his cell phone and badge. "C'mon. I'll show you."

"Show me what?" Twin lines formed between her brows as she peered up at him.

"Why I became a FBI agent." He picked up a dark brown velvet jacket, held it out for her to slip first one arm and then the other through the thick sleeves.

He led her through the house to the Georgian arch of the front door. Vince was meeting them here at eleven thirty. His secretary, Dora, had arranged a rental car because his Beemer was still in NYC and likely to stay there for the next few days. He glanced around the elegant cobbled street. Stared back at a minuscule Smart car that sat outside, next to the curb.

"What the hell is that?" he snarled.

Josie snorted loudly and put a hand against his chest. He felt the connection all the way to his heart.

"I told her I wanted inconspicuous. *That* is not inconspicuous."

"Now I wish I'd learned to drive." Josie was actually chortling as she stepped out the front door. "I bet it's a lot more environmentally friendly than that thing you drive."

Marsh scanned the area for reporters or killers, but Josie didn't seem to consider anyone might follow her here. They probably wouldn't, but they'd be hounding her when she got back to NYC, dammit.

He blinked. "What do you mean, 'learned to drive'?"

"Well, I can drive a little, but I don't have my license." Josie gave him a slow broad smile that was not a good sign.

"But you drove my BMW to the airport last

spring."

"It wasn't easy. Nearly crashed into a tree before I even got out of the drive and Logan Airport was a nightmare." Her shoulders trembled delicately. "I used the fake ID Elizabeth set me up with to hire a car in Montana."

His heart stopped. *Great.* He gritted his teeth. He was in love with the woman who broke the law without thought. She was nuts and he was about to try and explain why he'd become a FBI agent?

Maybe he was the crazy one.

It was only a couple of miles west on Huntington, past Northeastern University and along Louis Prang. The Gardner Museum. On game days you could hear the roar of the Red Sox fans less than a mile away.

"You ever heard of the Isabella Stewart Gardner Museum?" Marsh asked Josie as she climbed out of the tin can. The material of her dress clung to her body as she stretched her arms languidly to the sky. The longer he spent with her the more trouble he was in. The lust did not abate; the longing did not die.

"Yep." Josie wrapped her arms around herself. They strolled down the sidewalk, their footsteps ringing in perfect synchrony, ordinary lovers out for a day's outing.

It was too early to be open to the public yet, but he'd phoned ahead and spoken to the curator. As the lead FBI agent investigating the theft, it wasn't difficult for him to get inside. As the only son of a prominent Boston family who'd sponsored the museum since its inception in 1903, he'd have probably gotten in anyway.

A security guard Marsh knew checked them in.

Entering through a small doorway, both he and Josie squinted from the abrupt change in ambient light as they passed through dimly lit corridors.

As his vision adjusted Marsh watched Josie take in the Italian style Palazzo. Red brick archways ringed a courtyard, ancient carved stonework augmented by the natural beauty of grass and flowers.

Her eyes brightened, sharpened and a half smile of wonder played across her lips—lips he'd spent most of last night tasting. The centerpiece was a Roman mosaic tile floor picturing the Gorgon, Medusa, appropriately surrounded by statues. Nearly two thousand years old and the colors were still lucid.

It was quiet as a graveyard inside the cloisters.

"In March 1990, two thieves dressed as Boston PD officers strolled in here and stole eleven paintings and two artifacts valued at more than three-hundred million US dollars." He stuffed his hands into his pockets, stared at an ancient marble sarcophagus carved with beautiful women gathering grapes and thought of the plain wooden box in which his brother had come home.

"I'd just finished my BA in Art History at Harvard and was supposed to carry on the family tradition where the second son becomes a lawyer." A shudder ran through his body. "Jesus, can you imagine?"

Josie swept a gaze down to his highly polished shoes, touched the wool of his gray suit with one finger, and cocked one brow. "Yes."

He captured her hand and held it still. He wanted her to know who he was. Who he'd been. It had been a chilly day. Colder than usual. He still felt the bite of frost and the imbalance of ice, slick beneath the soles of his shoes. "I'd done a few months of law school and loathed every second of it."

Gently squeezing his hand, she turned to face him. "And you'd just lost your brother."

Clenching his teeth, he nodded. He didn't know how she'd linked that detail and didn't want to know. He'd come here that day because this had been Robert's favorite place, the spot where his brother had proposed to his girlfriend, Julianna, before he'd gone off to war.

The dean had pulled Marsh out of classes and told him the news. Marsh recalled the uncomfortable sensation of being cradled in a stranger's arms. Maybe that was why he'd never gone back. "Who's your favorite painter?" Marsh rapidly changed the subject.

Tugging her hand, he urged her along. He needed to get this right, needed to show her that they weren't so different. She let him guide her, a wonder in itself.

"Technically? Rembrandt. Use of light? Turner. Use of color? Vermeer. And for originality on top of amazing draftsmanship? Picasso." She bent forward to peer closer at the scrolled base of a ruined column. "Though I might give you different answers if you ask me tomorrow." Not that she was fickle…her smile assured him.

Their steps rang softly on the smooth stone floor.

"Close your eyes," he ordered.

"Why?" she questioned. But he slowed his pace when he realized she actually *had* closed her eyes, a subtle sign of trust that both gratified and spooked him.

Cautiously, he guided her down a couple of steps until they stood in a dark hallway. The air was cooler here. Above their heads, out of visual range, a surveillance camera guarded a masterpiece that hung in brilliant isolation.

Taking her by the shoulders, he turned her to face the far end of the corridor. They couldn't be seen or heard by the security system—he'd had a hand in all the updates they'd installed and knew all the weak spots.

He stood behind her, wrapped his arms around her waist and whispered softly in her ear. "This is my favorite painting." He bit gently into the cold fleshy lobe of her ear. Felt tense anticipation morph into dazed passion as she slowly shuddered out a breath.

"It's beautiful," she whispered, looking at the painting and absorbing the sensual bite all at the same time. Grasping onto his forearms, she gave a funny little quiver that vibrated through his flesh to his bones.

He held her tight against him, cupped her breast as she took in the artfully lit canvas painted by John Singer Sargent. *El Jaleo.*

It was more than three meters wide by two meters high. A flamenco dancer in a small town cantina.

With those clear blue eyes and loyal spirit, Josie was more stunning than any painting. Stroking her puckered nipple through the thin cotton of her dress while golden light reflected from the painting bathing the floor, the Moorish walls, the silhouette of Josie's profile in burnished fire.

"I love the way the light moves through the

picture." His other hand slipped lower, the coolness of her dress spilling over his wrist. Blonde hair trailed over his shoulder as she tilted her head to the side and he tasted the pulse hammering in her throat.

"I like the light too..." She gasped when he slipped his finger inside her. She was hot as Hades, as smooth as Chinese silk.

"I love the energy of the dancer, the intensity of the passion of the audience." Heat seared the palm of his hand. He could feel the strain of her muscles, taste the salt as sweat appeared on her skin.

"Oh god. I don't care about the painting. I want you, Marsh. Inside me. Right. Now." Her voice got low and then broke as he pressed his palm against her mound and stroked secret flesh.

"Can't do it, Josie." His voice was a low growl. "It's against the law." He sank his teeth into her shoulder as she came with an uncontrolled shudder. His own arousal pounded like a beast, but he breathed through the lust and held her gently as she came back to earth.

Slowly she turned in his arms, clasped her hands around his neck, gazed up, her eyes dark with desire.

"I bet I could make you forget your principles, Special Agent in Charge Hayes." Her lips were soft temptation.

"You already did." Gently he pulled away. He backed up a step, giving himself time for his breath to settle, his blood to cool. "But you wanted to know why I joined the FBI. What drove me into law enforcement." In an effort to restrain the emotions that always consumed him inside this building, he led her back through the courtyard and up some steps, past Italian masterpieces and priceless Japanese screens. Into the Dutch Room with its dark-paneled ceiling and heavy oak furniture.

***

Josie stood in the center of the room, awed to be in the presence of timeless masterpieces. Then she spotted it. "There are empty spaces on the wall." Iciness stole over her skin, made her scalp prickle despite the sun glaring through the big arched windows and the residual desire that made her limbs weak.

"Isabella Gardner left very clear instructions in her will about how this place was to be run." Marsh held his hands stiffly at his side. "The curator can't make changes to the permanent collection, so we're left with this..." Marsh strode over to one wall, pointed to the yawning space within an empty frame. "Rembrandt." He kept on walking, his voice getting fiercer as he circled the room, "Vermeer. Rembrandt. Flinck."

There was nothing but depressingly empty space, a sad testament to failed security and human greed.

"Isabella Gardner spent her life collecting art and left it for the American people to enjoy. My brother gave his *life* for those same Americans." His voice echoed loudly off the dark walls, sounding sacrilegious in the rarified atmosphere. "These fuckers didn't give a shit about any of it. So while my brother was willing to give up his life for his country, they just waltzed in and took what they wanted."

When he whirled to face her again, his eyes

were brighter than glass. "That is why I dropped out of law school and joined the military, to honor my brother. That…" he pointed his finger at the pillaged walls, "is why I joined the FBI and persuaded them to create a division devoted to art theft, which they didn't have back then. I wanted the satisfaction of tracking these bastards and shutting them down." Looking furious and isolated in the big empty room, he took a huge shuddering breath and held it, let it out slowly. Her own breath unfolded from her chest in a jagged wave.

"I want to catch these bastards and others who don't care about the rights of a nation. I want to lock them away if they think it is okay to steal what they want at the expense of everything my brother fought for."

He stared at her with an unholy glitter in his eyes, totally unlike the sensuous exchange they'd shared downstairs. And thinking about what they'd done in a public place made her cheeks burn. She didn't understand the justice system. It hadn't saved her. It hadn't even glanced in her direction.

But she understood art, and didn't think it should be a privilege of the wealthy. Tears pricked the backs of Josie's eyes. She'd always thought Marsh delusional, the way he believed in the law, and fought so hard for justice. She watched him from behind a veil of hair and thought about her own ideals and principles. It shamed her she had so few.

But she understood him now. He wasn't arrogant or conceited. He wasn't a rich boy playing at being a cop. He was driven and focused and determined to do the right thing for everyone. They couldn't be more different if she barked and wagged a tail. And here they were trapped, entwined together as intimately as oxygen and fire, as bound for tragedy as any manmade inferno.

The look in his eyes told her he'd die for her and she knew, deep down where she buried her secrets, she did not want to exist in a world without him.

No matter how ingrained escape was, she couldn't run. Not yet. He needed what comfort she could give, and she needed to offer it.

Life had been so much easier with her emotions locked away.

The distance between them was just a few yards, but stepping toward him felt like crossing the galaxy. Feeling his heat, running her hands up through his crisp dark hair, she drew his mouth down to hers. Kissed him with a fierceness that bordered on possession.

Chapter Fourteen

Dancer bent under the table to retrieve a fork Pru Duvall had dropped and received a totally unexpected flash of her Brazilian wax. *Holy mother.* He straightened sharply, banging his head on the edge of the table. The ruby-red claret in his crystal glass cost the same amount he and his mother had paid for a week's rent in Southie. He swallowed half the glass in one gulp. Three-and-a-half days rent in one mouthful.

"Is the wine all right?" Prudence reached for her glass and sniffed before taking a sip, smiling across at him. The information in her file put her at fifty-two years old; almost the same age his mother would have been had she lived. He'd have guessed thirty-five. On a bad day.

He'd secretly named her the Barracuda. It was a childish nickname, but it was childishness that got him through most days away from dark memories.

"It's lovely, ma'am, thank you." His cheeks continued to burn. *God.* He hated his complexion.

"Call me Prudence."

Call me stupid. Fifty-two years old.

Suddenly he was bombarded with memories. That tiny apartment. His mother's frail figure stumbling from one room to the next, using the walls to support her wasted limbs.

Tipping back the glass, he swallowed the rest of the wine. Wiping his mouth he tried to recapture the thrill of having lunch at the Ritz-Carlton hotel.

"So, I'm pretty curious as to why you wanted to meet up with me for lunch, Prudence." He gave her a shy smile, knew it made him look fifteen.

She raised one sharply defined eyebrow. "Do you really need to ask, Agent Dancer?"

"I'd rather not assume..." He let the question hang. Rather not assume a married woman would screw around on her husband? Rather not assume she would try to insinuate herself in an official investigation? Or that the wife of a potential nominee for the presidency would be so indiscreet?

Reaching across the table, she rested her hand next to his and stroked one fingernail along his freckled skin. The lines on her hand revealed her true age—no plastic surgery in the world could hide that reality.

Heat radiated from his cheeks like mini explosions. "I—I—I, I'm flattered, Mrs. Duvall." Yep, there was his stutter back, the icing on the cake of his humiliation. The Statue of Liberty saluted in the distance, and Dancer found himself grinning back at her. Before he could say anything Pru leaned forward, revealing cleavage as deep and firm as any twenty-year-old's.

Fifty-two years or not, she worked out and looked good. And it stirred not an atom of interest in any part of his body. Prudence Duvall was his mother's age and the idea of being with her repelled him so deeply he thought he might puke.

So hold it together, Joey. You don't believe she's really after your body, do you? She wants something and figures getting you in the sack would be the fastest route to the jackpot.

"Prudence." He smiled into her eyes and pretended not to see the unsheathed claws gleaming in her retinas. "I'm flattered, but you are a married woman."

The waiter arrived with their main course and Dancer breathed a sweet sigh of relief. Salivating at the aroma of prime sirloin he picked up his knife and fork then noticed a tear escaping Pru's eye. He knew it wasn't real, he knew she was putting it on, but the sight twisted his gut and had him placing a hand over hers.

"He beats me." Her voice dropped to a thick whisper.

"What?" Dancer didn't believe her for a second. "Who beats you, Prudence?"

Pursing her lips she shook her head, her ash-blonde hair coming down from one of its pins and making her look vulnerable for the first time ever.

Barracuda, he reminded himself.

"You don't believe me. I can tell." Her eyes were bright and she blinked rapidly at the wetness. Glancing around, she slowly inched back the sleeve of her jacket.

Indigo and green bruises encircled her wrists.

Shit.

Appetite wiped clean, Dancer leaned back in his chair and looked deep into her eyes. What the hell was going on? "You need to tell me everything."

She nodded frantically. "But not here. Someone might see me here."

Mentally rolling his eyes at himself, he rose and walked around to assist her from her chair. She pulled down the sleeves of her suit jacket and stood jerkily, spilling her wine with a crash. Red stained the white wool of her skirt like fresh blood.

"Come on." He took her arm, looked longingly at the steak on his plate. "Let's go somewhere quiet and talk." Maybe she'd tell him where she'd got that painting and why she'd lied about it.

***

"Well damn and blast, you finally found it." Admiral Chambers' brown eyes twinkled like Christmas lights as he examined the color photocopy Marsh held out to him.

"We got a tip off." Marsh followed the elderly naval officer into his oak-lined study. The golden wood of the desk shone brightly. The room smelled sweetly of polish.

"Your father will be proud."

Marsh had wondered how long it would take the man to bring up the family connection.

"When can I get it back?" The admiral moved with a stiff gait, like he was bothered by arthritis or maybe an old injury. But excitement propelled him eagerly to his desk and he was all but rubbing his hands together with glee. Chambers didn't know the painting had been reassessed in its absence and was considered by the few experts who knew of its existence to be a missing Vermeer.

Or did he?

Before Marsh could release it he needed to establish the rightful owner. He saw lawyers on the horizon. Lots of lawyers.

"Did you miss it that much or are you just anxious to sell?" Marsh wandered around the book-filled shelves, noting a thick layer of dust coating each volume.

Thick silver brows beetled together and the old man's jowls quivered with indignation. "None of your goddamned business."

"What if I wanted to buy it? As a present for someone?" Marsh examined his fingernails in a big show of nonchalance.

"You?" The admiral's eyes narrowed as if looking for a trap as he settled his bulk into a shiny brown leather chair, worn pale around the seams. It creaked with strain as he leaned against the backrest. "Jake said you'd finally brought a woman home. You kowtowing to the need for an heir or just screwing her?"

"None of *your* goddamned business." Marsh smiled at the old coot whom his father confided in during their twice-weekly golf games. If Marsh ever arrested the admiral, his father would probably disown him, whether the admiral was guilty or not.

The other man opened a drawer and hauled out a bottle of Jack Daniels and a shot glass.

"Want one?" Chambers' hand hovered over a second glass.

Deciding it was the best way of keeping the old termagant talking, Marsh nodded. "I didn't think you were allowed to drink anymore?"

Chambers grunted, slipped a nasty look toward the closed study door. "What Helen doesn't know won't kill her." His smile was small and bitter.

"After fifty years of marriage she must love you a hell of a lot to monitor your health so closely." Marsh kept a bland expression on his face. His private life wasn't the only one discussed among strangers. Helen Chambers had her husband by the proverbial balls and was slowly strangling him for past indiscretions.

He filled both shot glasses to the brim, passed one across the desk leaving a small streak of liquid marring the otherwise perfect surface.

"I'll give you one piece of advice, lad. Don't marry a woman who controls the purse strings. Hell, don't get married period."

Lad?

The admiral tossed back the bourbon and poured himself another. He held up the bottle, but Marsh declined. Chambers capped it and stuck it back in his drawer like a guilty secret.

What other secrets were locked up inside that devious old mind?

"So." Chambers breathed out slowly, the bourbon doing its job. "When do I get my painting back?"

"We need to establish provenance."

A flicker of unease entered the old man's eyes. As if aware he was giving himself away he turned and looked out of the window. "It was bought years ago. I don't have any proof of purchase."

"Prudence Duvall claims the painting was hers."

Chambers' head whipped around, his mouth drawn back in a snarl. "That woman is a lying bitch."

"She has evidence in the form of eyewitnesses who place the painting in her childhood home throughout her life."

A vein throbbed in Chambers' forehead, a vivid mark of temper. Suddenly he threw back his head and laughed. "She's lying, but she did promise to screw me one day." Suspicion entered his gaze as his fingers closed tighter on the shot glass. "Where'd you say you found it?"

"I didn't." Marsh didn't give out details to anyone during investigations. "So how do you two know each other?"

Annoyance puckered the man's brow as he

sipped his drink. "*Knew*. I haven't seen her in years and good riddance." He turned away again, stared at the velveteen green lawn sprinkled with this year's dead leaves. Sweat glistened on his brow. "She's evil."

Marsh ignored the bitter observation, wanting more information. "You slept together?"

"No." The admiral's tone grew dark as he glanced toward the oak paneled door of his study. "But I fucked her for a few weeks."

"Looks like she fucked you right back." Marsh rose to his feet, feeling nauseous that *this* was his father's best friend. He walked to the casement window, put his hand against the cold pane. "We figure that painting you two *both* claim to own could fetch as much as fifty million at auction today."

Chambers' face lost all color. Marsh wished he had the grace to feel sorry for the old fool, but he didn't. "I think it's time you told me the whole story and then maybe the FBI won't press charges about you falsifying the report of a crime and wasting police time."

***

The old church was boarded up, windows cracked and splintered, wire mesh enforcing the exclusion order. Grime coated each pane, blocking light until nothing but gray silt pervaded the empty nave. Echoes of an old life competed with the drums inside his head. The floor was smooth hardwood, worn down in places by the tread of long forgotten bodies, a lost congregation, a failed faith.

He lit three candles. One each.

God be with you...
And also with you.

Thick dust coated everything, spider webs shrouding the old pulpit where his father had once preached faith and charity. His mouth tightened with memories belonging to another lifetime. His family had been excited by their first trip to the US, away from their sanctimonious mud hut existence to the bright lights of America.

They'd never been the same again.

Darkness stirred. Hatred burned for the woman who'd started all this—a woman he'd already killed.

The man on the floor groaned, attempted to reach out a bound hand and ended up face down, writhing on the floor. A black nylon hood was strung over his head. Taking a small syringe he tapped it to get the air out and stuck the man with another dose of liquid codeine.

He didn't want to kill him.

Pru had gotten him into her car before he'd succumbed to the drug she'd put in his wine. He smiled. Everything was going perfectly, though Pru didn't fully appreciate the endgame yet.

"When are you going to kill him?" Her voice was breathy.

"After. You can do it."

A gleam of anticipation lit her eyes in the darkness. She'd never been involved this intimately before and was excited by it. They'd been sexual partners for years before she'd guessed his unusual sideline. Instead of turning him in, she'd been turned on by the fact he had a lethal hobby. So he hadn't killed her.

But she was high risk. Once Brook was

nominated as a presidential candidate, which looked more and more likely, the chances of being caught exploded exponentially. Pru lived for the thrill, didn't really care about getting caught.

She'd become a liability.

The candle flames fluttered like they'd been disturbed by a ghostly presence. A shiver ran along his forearms, tingled across his shoulders.

Pru's hands trembled and her breasts heaved like she'd run all the way here. She was aroused. Riding a sexual high. A kindred spirit who called to him—like a parched flower called for rain. The thought of doing it here, inside this church where his father had preached deceit, where he'd first seen Margo Maxwell and her anemic-looking daughter made him shake.

Perfect symmetry in an imperfect world. He touched his knife, painfully aware he needed to leave it behind this time.

"You know what to do." He kept his voice flat. Dampened the emotion because he needed the details to be perfect. She swept past him with a knowing look. The thought of blood brought the drums to full volume inside his skull. The desire to touch her was almost tangible, but he held himself in check and let his groin ache.

Sinking to her knees, she pressed her cheek to the grunt's stomach, lips pouting.

"Use your mouth." An experienced whore in the abandoned house of God, but she wasn't the only sinner here. "Let him go out with a bang."

Excitement curled along his nerves, unfurled like fire in his fists. Need clawed and bit and savaged his control like a wild animal half-starved and cornered. He reined it in. First she had a job to do because there were some things he didn't want to relive. Some actions he never wanted to repeat.

Drums thrummed along his veins, faster and faster.

God be with you...

And also with you.

Lying fucking assholes.

Walking up behind her, he handed her a plastic cup. Pity about the White House, but he had a greater goal now. Everything had shifted into place. He could finally see the big picture. Survival. Escape. A fresh start.

***

"So you don't even know if there *was* a crime?" Josie laughed so hard she forgot to breathe. Streetlights filtered through the open drapes to showcase pure masculine beauty, but left her enough darkness to be comfortable with her disfigured skin. Kneeling naked on the bed was pretty empowering for a woman who usually averted her eyes getting into the shower.

"It isn't funny." Marsh threw his arm over his forehead.

But it was and she saw a smile twitch the corner of his mouth.

"So, the she-devil gave the admiral her late daddy's very expensive painting when they were doing the dirty, but when the admiral broke it off because his wife was getting suspicious, she stole it back?"

"But the admiral never knew for sure it was Prudence who stole the picture, even though he suspected it was her, he still had to report the theft, or face an inquisition from Mrs. Chambers."

"That's pretty funny." She grinned.

"Not when you imagine them naked it isn't." He squeezed his eyes closed and grimaced. Then he opened his eyes and looked at *her*.

"Damn." His hot gaze slid over her body and the evidence of his arousal made her blush. Again.

"He must have been pretty good in the sack to warrant a 17th Century Dutch Master," Josie mused, trying to keep her distance because she wanted so desperately to touch him and didn't recognize herself.

"I'm thinking you're a Cezanne. Vibrant and unusual but perfect nevertheless." Dark eyes glittered at her, intense and unsettling. "So how'd you rate me?" The voice was teasing, but being an expert on the subject, she recognized basic insecurity.

"Hmmm…" She tapped her finger to her lip as if considering. "Maybe the grand master himself? Leonardo?"

"DiCaprio?" His chest shook as he laughed.

"No. DaVinci." She felt foolish and hid her unease by running her fingers over the satin covers, enjoyed the cool shiver that sparkled along her nerves. Wished she didn't prefer touching his warm sleek muscles. She was getting needy, and that suggested weakness she couldn't afford.

Marsh had arrived home an hour ago, but rather than sit down and eat, he'd wordlessly taken her hand and led her up the stairs, locked the door and jumped her.

It nagged at her that his parents were in the house and knew they were up here probably screwing each other's brains out. But the glitter in

Marsh's gaze had warned her not to question him and not to bow to convention the way she wanted to. She'd never cared about meeting other people's expectations before, and didn't like the guilt it wreaked on her conscience.

Role reversal with a twist of red-hot sex.

Marsh rolled away from her and she admired the carved planes of his back, rock solid columns flanking his spine and that tight ass she liked so much.

And it wasn't only lust that invaded her mind…

But their relationship was too fragile, her survival too uncertain to examine those growing feelings. Needing a distraction she ran her hand across his smooth skin, fascinated by the way his muscles bunched and played beneath her touch.

Grabbing his cell phone, he jabbed a speed dial number. "I wish I knew where the hell Dancer had disappeared to…"

"You're not really worried about him, are you?"

"Not really. Not anymore," Marsh admitted. "He's a smart guy, too smart to get tangled in any of Pru Duvall's schemes." But he frowned as he got bumped to voicemail yet again. "We could press charges against Pru and the admiral for wasting FBI time, but the powers that be would probably snuff them out before they even got to the AG's Office.

Lying down, her breasts pressed to his back, she slipped her hand around him, felt power shimmer through her as he groaned and dropped the phone. Tension and heat erupted from every pore of his body. Hot naked flesh pressed against hot naked flesh and she explored him in painstaking detail.

"Aren't you hungry?" she asked with a smile. "I'm hungry."

"Starving." His voice broke as Josie scraped teeth over smooth skin.

"You want to call him again?" she whispered.

"He'll be fine," Marsh muttered, jerking her to him and kissing the breath out of her.

***

Dancer felt sluggish, his arms heavy. For a moment, his worst nightmare rose inside his brain, dark and ugly—that the disease that had destroyed his mother had also taken control of his body. But he clenched his fists, felt the very solid connection of hard fingernails pressed into the palm of his hand and knew that wasn't the problem. A hood covered his head and panic gripped hard to his heart. Had he been abducted? He listened hard, trying to figure out whether or not he was alone. Couldn't hear anything except the creak of the wind against windows. Slowly he eased the hood off his head. There was something in his mouth—he spat out a rag covered in dirt and grime and tried to figure out where the hell he was. He lay on a filthy wooden floor. The boards were warped and rotten, mouse droppings scattered everywhere. Rusty nails wavered close to his face. Memory was hazy. He felt like he'd gotten shitfaced, but didn't remember going out. He squinted and vaguely remembered the Statue of Liberty raising her hand to him…

Rolling onto his back he realized his zipper was undone and he was exposed to the world.

Shit! *What the hell…?* Pulling his zipper closed, he rifled through his pant pockets frantically searching for his cell phone. *Where was it?*

Giving up, he staggered to his knees, relieved

when the giddy sensation receded and he was able to raise his head.

A strong scent hit him and he gagged. He knew the pungent odor of violent death. He might only be a glorified technician, but he'd been involved in some serious cases—not least Elizabeth being pursued by the mob last spring. And he'd been right there when scumbags Andrew DeLattio and Charlie Corelli had had their faces blown off.

Bracing himself he turned around. He wished he hadn't. He wished he hadn't woken up that morning. He wished he'd kept on sleeping like a baby, lids welded shut for as long as it took.

Prudence Duvall lay stretched across what would have been the sanctuary of the church, immediately beneath the altar. Duct tape covered her mouth. Handcuffs restrained her wrists above her head.

His handcuffs.

Sirens wailed in the distance, but they didn't pierce the fog of his brain.

Blood streaked her body, escaping from deep wounds that crossed her chest and abdomen. Her blouse was shredded and hung like a rag from one of her arms. Her skirt was bunched around her hips, leaving her completely, brutally exposed.

Blood dripped slowly down one side of her torso. In a daze, Dancer moved toward her.

Was she still alive?

How could she be?

He knelt by her side and checked her carotid. Noticed the knife lying beside her thigh one second before a voice called out, "Freeze!"

A flicker of something moved in her eyes, he was sure of it.

"I'm with the FBI, I think she might still be alive!" *Jesus.*

"Get away from the body, spread out on the floor and don't move a friggin' muscle." The voice boomed in his ear so loud he flinched. *Shit.*

Dancer eased away, his ears ringing, but repeated quietly, "I'm with the FBI." He lay on the floor, slowly. Tasted dust and shit in his mouth. "I think she's still alive."

"Shut your mouth, dickwad." One officer patted him down hard enough to hurt, but Dancer simply stared at Prudence and wondered what the hell had happened between the restaurant and here.

Another cop knelt beside her and put his fingers on her neck the same way Dancer had. "Nah, she's dead."

Dancer started to struggle as the cuffs snapped against his wrists, catching flesh. He didn't give a shit about the pain. "Give her CPR, you stupid prick! Get the EMTs in here! She's still alive—"

The first officer nailed him with a punch.

"Like to cut up women, do ya?" The beat cop blasted him again and pain shot through his skull as his nose split open and he collapsed to the floor.

As he lay face down in the dirt, blood dripping steadily from his broken nose, he knew he'd been set up and these bozos wouldn't listen to a word. "I need to make a phone call." He spat out dirt and blood and tried to breathe through his mouth. He was from South Boston; it wasn't the first time he'd taken a beating.

The police officer spat on him.

How can you be so fucking dumb?

"Give me a phone—"

The boot connecting with his kidney did what

the first two blows had failed to do. Blackness dragged him, pulled him under even as Marsh's name slipped past his lips.

Chapter Fifteen

Nelson Landry turned off the police scanner, laughing. He couldn't believe his good luck. He blew on his cold hands, wished he had time to make coffee before he wrote his piece, but he didn't. This was fate. This was God smiling and taking down the bastard who'd ruined his topnotch journalism career. They'd see how much weight all that FBI power got him today.

He could see the front page now. *The BLADE HUNTER—a knife-wielding G-man?*

It was better than TV.

Typing frantically, glancing at his watch, he used one finger to dial his editor.

"What?"

Either she had caller ID or she never gravitated from bitch mode.

"We need a second edition out ASAP," he said.

"What have you got?" The switch from pissed to hungry was palpable in those four little words.

"I'll email it," he glanced at his watch, "ten minutes. Tops." He cut the connection, cracked his knuckles. Christ, it felt good to be back at the top. Pleasure surged through him. He was about to get even with Marshall Hayes and he'd enjoy every second of the bastard's fall from grace.

***

"Say that again." Marsh couldn't believe what he

was hearing. He rubbed his temples as the information was rapidly repeated back to him.

"What is it?" asked Josie. Sitting up in bed, she looked like she'd spent a wild night having hot sex, all tangled hair, reddened lips and heavy eyes, which was exactly as it should be. But while they'd been trying to exorcise their demons and maybe forge a new relationship for themselves, the Blade Hunter had carefully set up his next move—orchestrating their lives as effortlessly as marionettes on a miniature stage.

Marsh turned away from her. Revulsion and shame burned him, blazing away the bubble of contentment that last night had wrapped around him. Sheets rustled behind him, then he heard Josie getting dressed.

"A broken nose?" This should not be happening in his country, damn it. Not to a good agent like Steve Dancer. Anger coalesced into something stronger, harder, meaner. "Contact Benedict Colavecchia." He named the best criminal defense attorney in NYC. "Tell him he has a new client and to get his ass to Brooklyn right now. And get me a flight to La Guardia." Marsh broke the connection to his secretary who'd called him even though it was four in the morning.

He needed to grab a shower and shave so that NYPD got the full force of his FBI status because this time he was using every ace up his sleeve, every favor he could pull in, every dollar at his disposal. Steve Dancer was not a killer. He'd stake his life on it.

Whatever Josie saw in his eyes made her swallow, but she narrowed her gaze, lifted her chin and stared him out. "What happened?" She'd dressed in dark cords and a roll-neck sweater that covered her almost entirely. She wrapped her arms tightly against herself, hunching slightly as if chilled.

He was cold to the bone.

"Someone murdered Prudence Duvall last night." His voice was gruff and he cleared his throat. Josie carried on staring at him as if somehow knowing that was only a small part of the story. "*The Blade Hunter* killed Prudence Duvall—or a copycat—and the NYPD found Special Agent Steve Dancer at the crime scene covered in blood."

"Is he hurt?" She picked up her knapsack and held it to her breast like a shield.

"It wasn't his blood."

Shit. He sat on the bed and cupped his face in his hands. He'd been too busy screwing Josephine to protect his team. *Fuck*! This was not how the law was supposed to work. Blind justice didn't have to be deaf, dumb and stupid, did it?

"Tell me exactly what's going on, Marsh." Her words were forceful and determined.

"The NYPD found Dancer inside an old church in Brooklyn after an anonymous tip was called in." Her eyes flashed, but he carried on, holding down a fury that was starting to feel cold and deadly inside him.

"Pru was stabbed and mutilated." God, he was going to puke and he hadn't even liked the woman. He braced his hands on his thighs. "Cops first on the scene arrested Dancer and beat the shit out of him—the stupid bastards thought they'd caught the Blade Hunter."

Josie slumped beside him, but he shifted away a fraction of an inch, unable to bear the thought of anyone touching him, anyone tapping into that valve that might make him explode.

"You're angry," she put her hands on her hips, "because we were together while Dancer was being set-up? Because we were busy banging each other when that bastard was cutting up his next victim?" She gave a harsh laugh that ended on a broken sob. "Welcome to my dark ugly world."

Swinging her knapsack over her shoulder, she jumped up and strode to the door.

"Where the hell do you think you're going?" Marsh's voice was little more than a growl in the darkness, but he couldn't soften it. Couldn't bring forth an ounce of empathy or sympathy to the surface.

"I'm going back to New York, so we can finish this thing—"

"You're not going anywhere."

"We're both going. You know that." She was undaunted by his anger. He'd forgotten that this was how she'd grown up; with anger and fear and pain. With shouting and violence and plain old-fashioned ugliness. He wanted to reach out and comfort her, but that part of himself was wrapped up tight by guilt and self-recrimination. If he let go now it would destroy him.

Her eyes were bright with tears, but it wasn't sadness in her eyes; it was rage every bit as powerful as his.

"It's *me* he wants, Marsh."

"Which is why you should stay here and let the law deal with it," he told her.

"They've done such a great job so far." She planted her hand on her waist, cocked her hip. "I'm not putting your family in danger as well as your

232

friends."

He started to rise to his feet. "Steve Dancer is a trained professional. You didn't put him in this situation—"

"Tell me you don't blame me, blame *us*," she pointed at the bed, "for getting him caught up in this mess—"

"I should have been paying more attention!" His voice bounced off the walls. *Shit.* He sank back onto the bed. Dropped his face into his hands. *Shit. Shit. Shit.*

Josie looked away, swallowed hard and nodded. "Exactly."

***

Marsh's FBI creds had got them seats on the first flight to NYC, but wedged between Vince and Marsh, she was squeezed tighter than a burger in a bun. They were in cattle class because these were the only seats available.

Josie knew Marsh was angry. She knew he felt guilty. But she was terrified of the feelings he'd evoked and he'd done nothing except ignore her for the last three hours—and that after a night of incredible mind-blowing sex and real honest intimacy.

"Can I get you anything to drink?" The stewardess asked Marsh. She was perfectly made up, white teeth dazzling and totally uncaring about anything except getting the job done. An automaton. Like Marsh.

Josie glanced at him, but he had his laptop open and was engrossed in work. He glanced up at the flight attendant's question and gave an infinitesimal shake of his head.

"How about you?" The woman lifted her coffee pot and smiled at Josie, vermillion lips clashing against pink gums.

Josie couldn't even remember if she'd brushed her hair. "No. Thanks." Couldn't even drum up a smile.

Marsh's fingers paused over the keyboard for one fraction of a second as if he'd just remembered she was there.

Vince's legs were too long to fit in the tiny space in front of his own seat and so he'd shoved them sideways, into her space as the trolley moved past. He accepted a black coffee and received the type of smile from the attendant that was banned in religious countries.

Josie *hated* flying. Her hands shook. That's why she said no to coffee. She'd spill it all over the place...maybe even over Marsh's spanking new laptop.

Tucking her hands beneath her backside, she closed her eyes and leaned against the headrest as the air pressure played havoc with her eardrums.

"You okay?" Vince asked her quietly.

She opened her eyes and he shifted his legs back out of her space. As if unable to help himself, he turned his head to appreciate the physical attributes of the flying waitress as she moved past them.

"Men." She rolled her eyes.

Marsh's fingers paused on the keyboard even though he was pretending to be absorbed in his work. A hiss escaped her lips. To think she'd nearly fallen for him.

Who was she trying to kid? She'd taken a running jump off the highest building and ended up splattered on the sidewalk.

It hurt.

He was treating her like she was a casual acquaintance, like someone he knew well enough that he couldn't ditch her there and then, but not intimately enough to actually work up an interest in how she was feeling.

Not enough to pretend he cared.

And so what if she was being stupid and bitchy? She hadn't wanted to get involved period. Now Pru Duvall was dead. Steve Dancer was in jail and it felt like Marsh was blaming her—blaming them—for what had happened, when she hadn't wanted to get involved anyway!

She understood the weight of guilt.

She carried it in her backpack on a daily basis.

And when she'd finally begun to work out what all the fuss was about with relationships and sex, wham bam! Shut out and isolated like the nobody she really was.

Dammit. Worse than before because she should have known better. People left. People died. People were murdered and she'd never been able to do a damn thing to stop it. But Marsh did. He spent his life trying to stop the darkness swallowing the world. He deserved a better person than her in his life and she knew exactly how to prove it.

"So are we through fucking each other or should I make myself available later?"

The woman in front of them twisted around, shock making her eyes wide before she remembered her manners and turned back to face the front.

Marsh's hands froze over the keyboard, but he didn't look up. Vince raised his table and tried to get the hell out. But an elderly woman with a stick made her way slowly past him and he was stuck.

"How'd I rate, Marsh? On a scale of say, Georgia O'Keefe to Rembrandt? Or am I more of a Jackson Pollock?"

"You want another rating?" His laughter was cruel, his tone tipped with biting sarcasm.

No, what she wanted was to get out of this mess and never see him again. She did much better alone.

"I always liked Jackson Pollock." He couldn't meet her gaze and that's when she really got it. He thought this was all her fault...

She sat in silence and used years of experience to remain dry-eyed and emotionless. She was not doing this. Pain was something she avoided assiduously. She wasn't having a relationship that would rip her to shreds. And maybe she was kidding herself about the relationship thing anyway, because right now he looked like he couldn't stand sharing the same airspace.

God knew her father had always told her she was trouble, had been from the day she was born. Looked like Marshall Hayes had finally figured it out.

***

The corridors heaved with cops, press and Department of Justice agents. The buzz around Marsh spiraled as a couple of the reporters recognized his face. Marsh pushed through to the building's atrium. A solid hand planted on his chest stopped him going any further. The cop's pale blue shirt stank of BO, his matching blue eyes dared him to push any further.

Marsh flicked the desk sergeant a glare and

flashed his badge. "Special Agent in Charge, Marshall Hayes."

The cynical glare came with a sneer. "Doesn't mean you can go back there."

Detective Cochrane, the bald cop from Angela Morelli's murder scene, tapped the big guy on the back, "Hey, Morris, we need this one." As if Brooklyn PD could keep him away. "Let him through."

Marsh nodded to Cochrane, caught a speculative gleam in the detective's gaze as he shoved past the big cop.

"Where's Special Agent Dancer?" Marsh asked. They were walking fast down bustling corridors filled with wall fliers, past excited uniforms, the air rank with the stale odor of under-washed, over-worked bodies.

"Back here." Cochrane held a door for him, twitched his moustache to indicate Marsh went first.

"You don't really think you've got the right guy, do you?"

"Your man was caught leaning over the still warm body of a senator's wife and the murder weapon was right there with his prints on it—"

"It's a set-up. Test his DNA and you'll know it's the wrong guy."

"We're running his DNA, but if it's a set-up it's a freaking elaborate one." Cochrane shook his head.

"The perp's trying to get to Josephine Maxwell—"

"Looks to me like he was trying to get to Mrs. Duvall, and succeeded…"

Shit. Another woman dead. In a city this big how the hell did he protect everyone? "How's Brook taking it?"

As if conjured, the steely-haired politician walked dazedly out of an interview room. Next to Steve Dancer, under normal circumstances, Brook Duvall would be the top suspect on the law enforcement radar. Marsh moved toward him, sympathy warring with an inbuilt suspicion. It had nothing to do with his dislike of the man, and everything to do with the statistics of murder.

Maybe this wasn't the Blade Hunter?

Maybe it was a copycat killer taking the opportunity to get rid of a liability. Both Brook Duvall and Admiral Chambers were right up there in Marsh's sights—the admiral had found out Pru had probably screwed him out of a painting worth millions—a painting that could change his miserable life.

Detective Cochrane put a restraining hand on his arm. "He might not appreciate chatting, right now."

Brook's face was ashen, his eyes bloodshot from tears still visible on his cheeks. He had a lost quality about him, of someone whose world had shattered without them seeing it coming.

"We're old friends." Marsh shook Cochrane's pudgy hand off his arm and walked over to the other man.

"I'm sorry for your loss, Brook." Marsh squeezed the guy's shoulder and studied him. Wearing jeans and a L.L. Bean sweater, he looked as if he'd been in the country.

"Were you out of town?" Marsh asked quietly.

Duvall nodded. "We have a house in the Hamptons." And then he started to cry. Threw himself on Marsh's shirtfront like they were brothers. "Pru hated the beach house, hated fishing and fresh air. Never wanted to come with us. Oh, God, oh, God..."

While Marsh had trouble believing the Duvalls had been faithful to each other, he had no doubt Brook was devastated by the murder—didn't mean he hadn't done it though, or hadn't set it up.

"What did she do when you were away?" Marsh probed, noted Detective Cochrane's interested gaze watching the senator carefully.

Brook drew himself upright, wiped his eyes. Marsh offered the man a handkerchief and had the weird thought that he'd have to get another one for Josie because he bet right now she was letting go of all the tears she'd bottled up since they'd woken to the phone ringing at four a.m. this morning.

And he'd behaved like a total asshole because everything he believed in was being challenged. The law. His personal code of ethics. And his views on marriage that he knew she wouldn't share. And how the hell did he deal with *that* when he was smack bang in the middle of a murder investigation and law enforcement snafu? How did he deal with that when a killer was putting every effort into making sure the woman he loved died viciously and soon?

Vince was protecting her... and more guilt ate at him because it should be him. But he couldn't leave Steve Dancer to face the wolves alone. Couldn't stand the guilt of knowing he hadn't been doing his job properly because he'd been too busy in bed with Josephine.

Dammit.

Brook looked away. "She had her own friends and social life. Geoffrey is getting her desk calendar from the apartment." Tears shone like varnish on his cheeks under the harsh glare of the strip lights. "I've told the police everything I know."

Pru had called Dancer to set up a lunch date and Marsh would bet she was somehow involved in the situation Dancer now found himself in. Pru Duvall was somehow involved in her own death.

Marsh grabbed Brook's arm, forced the man to meet his eyes. "I know this is painful for you, but did she have a boyfriend?"

Brook didn't bristle, didn't blink. "I don't know—we didn't…"

He started crying and Marsh felt like a bastard for pushing, but he pushed anyway. "You didn't have a sexual relationship with your wife?"

Brook shook his head. His lawyer came out of the room behind him followed by Special Agent Sam Walker, who looked like he'd spent the week in his clothes. Brook's lawyer hustled him away with a wary glare. Poor bastard.

Agent Walker lounged against the doorjamb in a white shirt, sleeves rolled up past his beefy elbows. They exchanged a look and Marsh wanted to grab the other fed by the throat and slam him through the wall. Walker looked about ready to do the same to him.

"What's going on?" Walker asked Cochrane, ignoring Marsh.

Marsh held his tongue. The detective shrugged and moved along the corridor. "Your man's through here, Agent Hayes—"

Walker blocked his path. "No way are you getting in to see the suspect."

Marsh was taller, but Walker was broader. Brawling was not in the FBI's Code of Conduct Handbook, but it wouldn't be the first time Marsh had broken that particular rule. He planted both hands on the other guy's chest and shoved him back a step. "Don't fuck with me, not today." He held the man's gaze, watched him bristle and raise his fists. *Come on. Give me an excuse...*

"Hey, Special Agent *in Charge,* this isn't a pissing contest." Detective Cochrane grabbed his arm. "Your guy's down here." Cochrane pulled him along and he went because Steve Dancer needed him.

Marsh followed him until they entered a viewing room. The Forgery and Fine Art team were as tight as family. They relied on each other. Supported each other, and steered clear of the competitive bullshit that invaded other divisions. Dancer was more than just another agent. He was his best friend.

Dancer sat with sagging shoulders in a hardback chair. Unfocused eyes registering nothing, dried blood caked his face, giving him a wretched appearance. Keeping hold of the rage that coursed through his veins, Marsh managed to sound casual.

"Has he seen a doctor?" he asked.

Cochrane nodded, rubbed his moustache. "Got a busted nose."

The flesh around one eye was red, swollen completely closed. Dancer's pallor shone white behind the dried brown blood.

"What evidence do you have?" Marsh asked. "Did he provide DNA? Have you run it yet?"

There was no way Dancer was the Blade Hunter.

"We've got semen on Mrs. Duvall's body, although we haven't run it yet." Cochrane smoothed his palm over the bald spot on top of his head.

"Your guy says his zipper was undone when he came to. Says he was drugged and doesn't remember a damned thing."

"The perp has never left semen behind before—"

"Yeah, that bothers me," Detective Cochrane admitted as he pulled at the tight collar of his shirt. "And he looks twenty, even though I see from his file he's thirty-three, but he still isn't old enough to have knifed Josephine Maxwell when she was a child—well, he is, but he'd have been a kid too..."

Kids did god-awful things every day. But neither figured a kid was into this type of sophisticated torture.

"And we're tracking the timeline and trying to place Agent Dancer at other scenes. But your guy has never traveled outside the US, so that fries the theory of this perp as an international killer."

Inside the square sterile room, Special Agent Nicholl leaned over Dancer and placed a photograph in front of him. Even from this distance Marsh could see the blood on the digital image.

Marsh stared through the glass, knowing Dancer couldn't see him but hoping to infuse the other man with some form of hope.

"He isn't the Blade Hunter."

Cochrane stroked his moustache. "So either he did Prudence Duvall and set it up as a copycat—a very obvious copycat—or he's being set up."

The unspoken question was *why* and *by whom*?

Cochrane was watching him closely, looking for what, Marsh didn't know. He no longer trusted these guys to get the job done. "What about the knife?" Marsh asked.

"At the lab with everything else." He shrugged,

scratched his head. "You know in the real world how long it takes for those results to come in."

"No CSI timeline for us, huh? Make sure it gets top priority." Marsh sent a grim look at the detective. "You got motive?"

The detective laughed with a smoker's rasp. "No motive."

Marsh stared at Agent Nicholl who was trying to push Dancer into a confession. Dancer shouted something at the other fed, fury firing up his one good eye. Nicholl was an excellent interviewer, but when you had the wrong guy…

"Does he fit the profile the FBI generated?" Marsh asked.

Detective Cochrane stared through the window beside Marsh, and Marsh watched him though the reflective surface—the same way Cochrane watched him back. Both looking for clues, for tells that someone knew more than they were letting on.

Unfortunately, Marsh didn't know a damned thing.

"Steve Dancer is a single white male who lives alone. Above average intelligence. Raised by his mother. Interested in law enforcement." Cochrane shrugged. "He fits some of the profile but not all."

Marsh looked through the glass at the best man he knew. "As a kid Dancer missed most of his formal education, but arranged his own home-schooling program so he could nurse his mother who suffered from MS. Then, after she died, he worked three jobs to pay his way through MIT—graduated top of his class at the age of twenty." A muscle ticked near his eye.

What the hell had Prudence Duvall been up to?

The scene through the one-way window twisted

his gut. Dancer had stopped talking and rested his forehead on clenched fists against the table. Nicholl left the room and Marsh heard footsteps along the corridor and the rattle of the doorknob as Nicholl entered the viewing room.

He stopped dead when he saw Marsh.

"Sir." He nodded his head, pursed his lips and seemed to make up his mind. "Special Agent Dancer refused counsel, but he's been asking for you."

Grinding his teeth, Marsh pulled out his cell phone and held up his hand for a moment's silence. "Dora, get Colavecchia back here immediately. Yeah, I don't care what he says and I don't care what Dancer says either. Colavecchia defends Dancer whether he wants it or not. Tell him I'm calling in all the chips this time."

Benedict Colavecchia, Brett Lovine and Marsh had been best friends for fifteen years growing up. He was going to talk to Lovine next and he was going to obtain Steve Dancer's exit visa from this shithole, whatever the cost to himself, his job, or his friendships. He knew things about the Director of the FBI that no one else knew. He pocketed the cell phone knowing he needed to make the second call in private. Steve Dancer was innocent and the Blade Hunter was out there, trying to get to Josie.

He wanted to play games? Game on.

***

"What. Are. You. Doing?" Each word boomed out like it was a whole sentence.

"What. Does. It. Look. Like?" Josie tried to imitate Vince's deep rumble but sounded more like a dog with parvo. She turned away, sick and tired of trying to pretend everything was all right when it was so far from all right she was ready to volunteer for a straitjacket and a padded cell.

Sitting on her knees in the closet, she was surrounded by shoes. After years of being a pack rat—grinding childhood poverty did that to a girl—she was finally having a clean out.

There was a pair of sparkly stilettos that Elizabeth had loaned her for some party her old roommate Pete had needed a date for. A straight date.

The heels had damn near crippled her and Pete had gone home with a blond named Dave.

She threw the stiletto at the bed, but it missed and thumped to the floor. Next came a pair of lime green Doc Martens that had seemed like a good idea at the time. She lobbed them out.

"Hey!" Vince yelped.

"Then get out of the way!" she snapped at the big man.

Vince rubbed his shin like she'd shot him. Then he picked up the sparkling high heels and checked the size.

"You want 'em, you can have 'em," she told him.

He laughed the way she knew he would. "Thought my girlfriend might look good in them, but they're two sizes too big."

Josie stretched her eyebrows high, though the effect was lost as he couldn't see her face beneath the rack of clothes. "I do not have big feet."

"I never said you did, but Laura has got the tiniest feet I ever saw." He'd never told her about his girlfriend before, it was like they'd crossed some barrier or threshold whereby she was suddenly to be trusted with classified information.

Maybe because she didn't have long to live…

"What exactly did you do to be a war hero?" She made her tone as dubious as possible because baiting Vince was a damn sight better than crying in the bottom of a smelly closet.

"I single handedly rescued thirty-six orphans from a refugee camp in Darfur that was under attack by rebel forces."

Suddenly very white teeth were smiling at her from a yard away. His diamond stud twinkled.

"You're making that up." Josie glared at him, chewing her lip.

"Why would I do that?" His tone suggested he was laughing at her. "That's what the press reported." He crouched lower. "That's what my military record says."

It was so obviously not the truth, but… if he could do that…

"Do you really think you can save me?" Josie swallowed and the tears started to flow. They were hot on her lashes and hotter still on her cheeks.

Big hands hauled her from the closet as if she were a rag doll.

"Josephine." He hugged her to the wall of his chest and wrapped her in his big strong arms and she wanted to believe Vincent would be enough to protect her from this man who dogged her life like a ghost. She told herself to be grateful it was Vince and not Marsh she was crying all over.

"I'll do for you what I did for those kids," he told her.

"What was that?" Her words were muffled and her nose was running. God, she hated tears.

246

Vince didn't answer and Josephine knew whatever it was, it wasn't in his file. She hoped it would be enough.

Chapter Sixteen

"You got anything from the tip called in?" Marsh walked fast. He'd parked a block east of the church the closest he could get even with a shiny gold badge.

Detective Cochrane had been sent to babysit him. Marsh didn't care as long as the veteran cop didn't get in his way.

"Disposable, bought in Manhattan last week." Cochrane was having a hard time keeping up with his stride, but Marsh didn't ease the pace. The little man huffed out deep breaths, clouds of water vapor condensing in the frigid air, his feet shuffling quickly through piles of fallen leaves. "The feds are checking it out. Maybe they'll get something off a surveillance camera or those financial records they're always pulling."

Marsh snorted. He wished the Blade Hunter was dumb enough to leave a trail. "You read all the files?" Marsh asked. He needed to know the detective was up to speed on this investigation.

"Sure, I read them and Special Agent Walker got a hit on what he thinks might be a Jane Doe who fits Margo Maxwell's description, but he's waiting for a court order to begin the exhumation—"

"And he never mentioned it to Josie?"

"You guys were out of town…"

Boston, right. A million miles away.

"And until they're certain…"

Walker hadn't informed him of any of this,

despite Marsh sharing the information on Admiral Chambers—who'd right now be Marsh's prime suspect for Pru Duvall's killing, except, the whole thing was *so* planned, so organized, so reeking of the Blade Hunter's insidious style.

So how the hell did Pru Duvall and Steve Dancer fit in? She didn't fit the profile of the other victims. And Dancer—he had to be a fall guy. Why him?

Marsh dodged a streetlight and kept moving. He checked his cell phone, made sure it was set to vibrate only. He was expecting the shit to hit the fan any minute when the admiral was hauled in for questioning. Unless the admiral was a damn sight smarter than he looked, Marsh doubted the guy had much to worry about except being caught in an extramarital affair. But his parents would go ape shit and the admiral's wife was going to freak. Brett Lovine had already gone ballistic.

Clenching his fingers, he knew he'd deal with the devil himself as long as Josephine was safe. He'd been an asshole, but he was going to make it up to her.

Keep her safe, Vince...I can fix anything but dead.

This was a nice part of Brooklyn. The sky was so blue it provided a deep backdrop for the bright-yellow Aspen leaves. They weren't far from Greenwood Cemetery and Marsh paused for a second, sure he heard the squawk of parrots. That nailed it on the head. He was going insane.

"Why would the perp set up Special Agent Dancer?" Cochrane asked.

That question bugged him constantly.

The UNSUB had targeted Josephine, then Lynn,

then Pru and Dancer—and the only link Marsh could see was...himself.

Do I know this fucker?

Or had that picture on the front page of *The NY News* been the catalyst the UNSUB needed to target his next set of victims? Had he been following Josie that day and seen Marsh talking to Pru Duvall in Washington Square? Did he have a source inside the investigative team? He shot the detective a look. The wrinkled suit and worn brown shoes screamed bad pay and crappy fashion sense. He didn't look dirty, but then they never did.

Cochrane remained silent, as watchful of him as he was of the NYPD detective. Thirty seconds later they were opposite a big old ruined church that was surrounded by acid yellow police tape. The walls of the limestone building looked solid, but the roof was buckled and the windows broken and boarded up. The cross on top of the old church tower was crooked and tilted to the north.

Why here?

A priest was talking to a beat cop and shaking his head with a worried expression on his face. A dead birch tree threw a shadow over the two men as they stood speaking too softly to overhear.

Marsh passed an old weathered sign and made out the faint shadow of a name. *St Mary's.* He took out his cell and dialed Agent Walker. "Did you figure out this was the same church Josephine Maxwell attended as a kid?"

The long pause told him the agent had already made the connection.

"You speak to the priest from back then?" Marsh asked, eyeing the gray-haired man talking to the uniformed officer.

"Priest from her day is dead." Walker sounded like he was talking through gritted teeth.

"Talk to anybody else from the parish?" asked Marsh.

"I've been chasing evidence and leads since Angela Morelli was murdered last week. I haven't slept in—"

"I'm not questioning your dedication, Agent Walker, just your results." He snapped the phone shut and flashed his badge to the cop, who looked all of twenty and puffed up with self-importance. The detective gave the beat cop a roll of his eyes, making the rookie grin as the kid backed away. Marsh didn't let his mood show. This was no good for law-enforcement relations—was that what the perp wanted? Cops divided and not sharing information? Purposely screwing up the investigation and slowing them all down?

Marsh held out his hand to the elderly gentleman in a tweed jacket and dog collar.

"SAC Marshall Hayes, and this is Detective Cochrane, NYPD." He indicated Cochrane with his right hand, realizing he didn't even know the guy's first name.

"Father Malcolm." The priest held out his hand to shake first Marsh's and then Cochrane's. "I'm the priest of this parish."

"Were you ever in charge of this church, Father?" Marsh asked, noticing the brisk wind that made both the priest and the detective shiver. Inside he felt as hot as a volcano on the verge of eruption. Every cell in his body was fueled with rage and focused on catching this killer. Nothing else mattered.

Father Malcolm had wiry gray whiskers and

nose hair that bordered on fluffy. "I was the priest here up until four years ago—"

"When did you start here, Father?" Marsh asked.

"March, 1998." The man crinkled a smile at him. Seemed to realize a murder scene wasn't the place for smiles and became somber again. "It was Father Mike before that—the best preacher and the best man I ever had the pleasure of working under."

"You knew him? You served with him here?" Excitement and hope started to trickle back inside Marsh's mind.

"I worked under him for four years. I thought he was odds on favorite to become Bishop." His mouth twisted with old regret. "He joined Our Lord in—"

"Sorry to cut in, Father," Detective Cochrane put in and Marsh could hear the same excitement in his tone that he felt rising up inside. "But do you remember any missionaries from Africa coming here about twenty years ago?"

"Well, yes." The priest recovered himself, hunched his shoulders up, crossing his arms as another gust of wind blasted down the street. "We've had lots of missionaries from Africa over the years—"

"It was about the time a woman called Margo Maxwell disappeared. Do you remember anyone in particular, Father Malcolm?" Marsh tried not to sound as desperate as he felt.

Thick wiry brows scrunched up into a bristled line. He shook his head. "I remember Margo—she was a beautiful woman and no one was surprised when she ran off. Her husband was a man...in need of counseling."

Marsh held the priest's gaze. "I met her

husband, Father Malcolm. I know what sort of man he was."

"Well, it is no excuse for going off with another man, especially when they left that poor little girl at the mercy of—"

"We don't believe Margo ran off. She was murdered, like the woman was murdered in that church last night." Marsh held the old man's stare, pissed at the judgmental attitude of a church that'd done nothing to help a small child. "Margo didn't abandon her daughter. She was stolen from her in the most brutal way imaginable."

And although it wasn't proven yet, he knew it was true.

"We think it might be connected to the visit of an African missionary around the same time she disappeared," Cochrane finished, sending Marsh a warning, *take it easy,* glance.

The old man had raised a hand to his chest as if feeling a pain there. "I don't remember the names…"

Marsh's hope deflated like a popping balloon.

"…but it'll be in the old church records."

Anticipation made him want to grab the clergyman by the collar and shake him, but Cochrane spoke first. "We need to see those records, Father."

***

The smell was a combination of fermented carpet and moldy mouse poop.

"I'll open a window." Father Malcolm walked over to the barred window and pulled it open.

"You have problems with theft, Father?" Marsh

eyed the steel bars.

"People'll steal anything that ain't nailed down." Cochrane stood at the door, looking at the row of filing cabinets. Sweat glistened on his face from the walk over.

Numbness had washed over Marsh. Calm. Purpose. Do the job. Find the name. Find the killer before he got Josie. He wanted to call her, wanted to tell her he loved her—because what if something did happen to her...? *Shit.* Why hadn't he already told her that? Because he was an idiot. Because right now she hated him? His cell phone weighed like a piece of lead in his pocket. Dancer was sitting in a cell with a broken nose. *I love you's* could wait.

"Where are the files?" Focus. Saving her life would give him time to make everything up to her, but if she died...

Father Malcolm coughed with embarrassment. "Well, we had a break-in about six months ago and—"

"Did you report it?" Marsh's gaze connected with Cochrane's with the unspoken question. *Could it be the killer?* This UNSUB wasn't omnipotent, but he was pretty damn thorough.

"We caught a couple of teenage boys in here, high on drugs. They'd emptied everything from the cabinets and were trying to break into the manse."

The priest nodded toward the white-painted doorway. He lived in a big old rambling house next door and ran a very modern looking square box of a church across the street. What the church lacked in character it probably made up for in central heating.

"They were looking for money," the priest offered.

Junkies. Maybe...

"So, what did the church do—give them ten Hail Mary's?" Cochrane raised a thick dark brow that matched his moustache and sauntered over to the nearest filing cabinet.

"We prosecuted them, Detective," the father's eyes had turned to stone. "You have to repent to deserve forgiveness."

Marsh didn't want to discuss theology and the law. "And this is pertinent because...?"

A metal drawer screamed along its runner as Cochrane opened it. Documents and files spilled out haphazardly.

Ah.

"Because we never got around to sorting it out. We just threw it all back in the filing cabinets and figured we'd do it another day." Father Malcolm shrugged and removed his jacket, showing off remarkably tanned forearms. "I'll get the deacons down here. We'll sort this out in no time."

They didn't have time. Marsh pressed his first finger into his temple and closed his eyes, concentrating on relieving the pressure building inside his skull. His cell vibrated in his pocket. He pulled it out and glanced at the display. There were so many people he didn't want to talk to right now, but maybe it was Josie... Yeah right, or a break in the case—

Philip Faraday? What the hell did he want?

Possibly his fifty-million dollar painting?

"Mr. Faraday, what can I do for you?" Marsh answered.

Now that the admiral had admitted what actually happened, as far as Marsh and the DA could tell, it was a case of he said/she said that they wouldn't pursue. They could sue each other until they were blue but there weren't going to be any criminal charges. As far as the DA was concerned Faraday owned the painting and could sell it as he saw fit. He might want to wait until it was authenticated but that wasn't Marsh's business.

"Special Agent in Charge." Faraday sounded like he was talking through a big smile. "I hear I can have my painting back. And I hear from one of your agents that you think the painting might really be a Vermeer." Excitement made his voice shake.

Aiden must have already called the guy. Marsh rolled his eyes. "Yeah, look." Marsh tried to keep the distaste out of his tone, but knew it wasn't working, "I'm in the middle of a really important investigation—"

"Mrs. Duvall's murder?" The man's voice was soft with sorrow. "I saw it on the news. Tragic."

"I'm not at liberty to discuss an ongoing—"

"You are such an arrogant ass, do you know that? You come into my gallery, take *my* painting and then don't even have the courtesy to apologize or return it? I'm filing a complaint."

Join the club.

"I expect my painting back *today* or else I'm going to the press," Faraday continued, but Marsh zoned him out. The press. *Going to the press...*

Damn it, why hadn't he thought of that before?

He rang off, ignoring the indignant ire spilling from Philip Faraday's mouth. Then he called information and got a number for Nelson Landry.

Time to reverse the flow of news. Time to start directing an operation.

***

Josie put the phone in the cradle and stood up, determined to feel energized instead of scared stupid. Weeping in a closet was not how she was going to live her life, but clearing out all the excess crap felt good.

The positive news was she had a new commission. The bad news was she had to go out and meet with the client this afternoon. She made a valiant attempt at a smile, but caught her grim reflection in the glass of a framed photograph on her mantel.

"What's going on?" Vince's bass rumble reached out from where he sat on the couch.

She glanced at the telephone, wondering if Marsh would call or if they were over. They didn't feel over, but they didn't feel together either.

"Are you in love with Laura?" The words got through the knot in her throat with difficulty.

His chuckle made her want to smile.

"Honey, can't you tell?" he said, raising a thick brow.

"The way you checked out that flight attendant's ass?" she shot back at him, wondering if she was way too uptight when it came to relationships.

He chuckled again, unperturbed. "Laura and I have a *look, don't touch* policy." He grinned up at her. "Although I'm not dumb enough to look when she's around, nor do I want to. To answer your question, yes, I'm in love with Laura."

Josie noted his happy expression. "So why does being in love suck so much for me?"

Taking his time, Vince started reassembling the gun he was cleaning. "I take it your little shot at Marsh on the plane this morning was an attempt to provoke some sort of a reaction?"

"Ya think?" Okay, so sarcasm wasn't something Vince deserved, not after he'd rocked her and wiped away her tears earlier. Not when he'd protect her with his life.

She slumped next to him on the sofa and pressed a cushion to her face. "He can't even look at me. Not since he got the call about Dancer."

Vince stayed quiet for so long Josie didn't think he was going to answer. Despite her sweater, cold trickled through her, stealing her earlier determination.

God, she hated the cold...

"In the teams, when we found out we were about to go on a mission, most of the guys would get very quiet and introspective." She heard a metallic snap as he finished with the Desert Eagle Pistol. Smelled the bittersweet scent of gun oil in the still air.

"Guys who are about to go into combat don't want sex. They don't want to jack off. They focus on the mission and on the job they need to do, so they can celebrate all that other shit when the job is done."

She frowned at him. "He was pissed because we were in bed together when that monster was killing that poor woman—"

"Of course." Vince nodded, tugged one corner of his lips up in a mirthless smile. "Marshall Hayes is a good man and was an excellent naval officer—a rare commodity, believe me. I'd imagine he's got a gutful of remorse that he allowed himself to be distracted during an important investigation." Vince raised his hand to stop her from interrupting. "And now he's trying to focus on getting the job done, rather than sitting around holding your hand, or any other part of your anatomy for that matter."

She smacked him with the cushion.

When he grinned his white teeth were luminous against his dark skin. "He's trying to keep you safe *and* get the job done."

Could it be that simple...?

"You told Marsh you love him yet?" Vince asked, stuffing the gun back into its holster and snapping the clasp closed. "Because that might go some way to easing the situation."

The bright afternoon light reflected off the walls and made her squint. She hugged her arms tightly around the cushion. "No."

"He ever say anything to you?" Vince asked.

The sigh deflated her chest. "No."

"So you've got into some pretty heavy shit with this guy, but you don't really know how you feel about one another?"

Swallowing back tears she nodded.

"Then why the fuck don't you pick up the phone and tell him?"

Josie laughed even as tears filled her eyes. It should be that simple. But it wasn't. Because she was terrified. She'd spent a lifetime erecting barricades around her heart and only letting a few people even touch the outer surface—not because she was tough—but because she was weak. Marsh had rammed his way through her defenses and left her completely vulnerable.

And it terrified her.

Because what if he didn't love her back? What if she took a chance on him but all he'd wanted was a quick fling? A lifetime of insecurity was hard to fight, but dammit she was going to try to be braver.

Try to be more worthy of a good man like Marshall Hayes.

***

The cop was a hot blonde with a *Playboy* figure, the top half of which was pressed against Marsh's shirt. "I didn't have this much trouble getting solicited in Vice." Detective Lanie Jenkins sank her fingers into his hair and dragged his mouth toward her, but still he resisted. Her Southern drawl reminded him too much of Prudence Duvall and his gut twisted. He couldn't do this.

He used both hands to hold her away from him. "Give me a minute, please."

She stood back and rolled her eyes.

These guys thought Dancer was good for the Duvall murder but he had airtight alibis, involving several FBI agents, for the previous two murders. Pretty much everyone had come to believe he couldn't be the Blade Hunter.

Marsh had taken his idea to the captain of the Brooklyn PD—whose acquaintance he'd made last spring when Walter Maxwell had been murdered—and convinced him that the killer seemed to have focused on him and maybe they should set a trap. The plan was to assume Marsh was some doomed Lothario and the real killer would turn his attention to this new target and the cops would be ready for him. He didn't have much to lose, but this cop was putting herself in the line of fire. He didn't think he could cope with being responsible for her death too. And if Josie ever found out he was kissing another woman it would destroy what little trust she had left in him.

"G-men really are duds." Jenkins scowled at him, then grabbed his hand and stuck it on her ass. He squeezed his eyes shut for a moment and gritted his teeth.

"Now look like you know what to do with a woman," she said.

Catcalls started from some of the uniforms standing at the end of the alley they'd cordoned off near the Precinct for this particular photo-shoot. Marsh bet most of the guys standing there would beg to fill this role. Meanwhile he'd rather be anywhere else.

Nelson Landry stood at the end of the alley taking shots as if he was spying on Marsh.

Marsh had made more deals in the last half hour than he'd made in his entire life and the last one promised an exclusive to a reporter he might have wronged six months ago. Not that he could have let the story about Elizabeth run, but there might have been a better way to deal with the situation.

He was eating crow, with humble pie for dessert.

Jenkins rubbed against him. "I won't tell anybody about your little problem, feeb—"

Josie being angry with him was better than Josie being murdered in cold blood. So he pressed the detective up against the wall, knee thrust high between her thighs, and kissed her deep and hard, keeping her pinned against the wall.

Not that she tried to get away.

The lady was the hottest cop he'd ever met. She was sexy as hell and she kissed him back, tongues tangling as she tried to close the gap. A hell of an actress too.

Satisfied Nelson had all the material he'd ever

need, Marsh stepped back and held her gaze which was a little less derisive. "Thank you for your help, Detective Jenkins, and please be very cautious until we catch this killer."

After a moment she grinned. "Let's hope we can draw this guy out before he attacks your girlfriend again."

Their eyes met, guilt and gratitude making him feel like the biggest prick ever, even as she grinned up at him and ran a finger down his chest. "And if she dumps your ass, you know where to come for some mind-blowing rebound sex."

She winked at him and strode away, every inch of her lush figure squeezed back into cop mode. One of the uniforms dropped to his knees and begged to be next, but she flipped him off.

Marsh raised his face to the slice of bright blue sky that glowed above him. *God help him,* he hoped he never had rebound sex.

Chapter Seventeen

Thirty minutes later Marsh skimmed his eyes over the crowded squad room at the Brooklyn Precinct. The feds were in the corner of the room, as far removed from eavesdroppers as they could get. Walker sat on a table, one foot planted on the floor, the other dangling in the air, swinging backwards and forwards.

The lieutenant was outlining the plan to the next shift. They'd let the press believe they'd caught the Blade Hunter, but the FBI, Brooklyn PD and NYPD knew better. Not that they'd released Dancer, yet.

Detective Jenkins would work her day shift and tonight, after the evening edition of *the NY News* came out, she would go back to her lonely apartment in Bay Ridge. Except tonight she wouldn't be lonely. They'd have officers all over her apartment building.

Setting the trap and baiting the hook.

"You really think this is going to work?" The skin under Agent Walker's eyes looked sunken and heavy. Red veins formed a delta across the whites of his eyes and the stubble on his chin was almost enough to be classified as a beard.

Marsh shrugged. Maybe not tonight, but given time the Blade Hunter would go after the pretty cop—he was too egotistical not to.

"You have a better idea?" Marsh countered.

Walker gave a small laugh that sounded anything but amused. "No."

"Dancer is innocent." Marsh walked over to the vending machine and got black coffee that tasted so bitter he gagged, but it fired up some neurons and he seriously needed something fired up somewhere.

His brain ached.

"He was leaning over the body of a dead woman with the murder weapon next to him." Walker shot him a look full of warning, so Marsh held his silence. "And Special Agent Dancer knew enough about the murders to arrange a copycat killing—if he wanted to."

"So why the fuck get caught?" They didn't get how smart the other agent was. NASA smart. Bill Gates smart.

"I'm not finished." Controlled anger battled the threadbare patience in Walker's tone. "Dancer's tox screen came back positive for narcotics, but a smart perp could plan that himself. We don't know exactly how or when he received the drug. Might have taken just enough to be found during a routine screen if he was caught, giving himself an alibi. You said your boy was smart?" Walker's eyes held his.

Marsh finished the lousy coffee, crushed the paper cup in a tight fist. "But he's not a killer. Dancer loves women."

"Yeah, so did Bundy."

Fury rose in Marsh's chest with each particle of oxygen he drew in. He got in Walker's face. He used to be able to control his temper but in the last six months his control had evaporated.

"Hey, no fighting unless we all get to play." Cochrane cut it. "Preliminary DNA evidence is in." The expression on Cochrane's face made Marsh's heart freeze. "DNA from the semen matched

Special Agent Steve Dancer."

Everyone in the squad room had turned to face them.

This couldn't be happening...

Turning away Marsh placed both hands against the opaque glass of the precinct's window, spread out his fingers. He ground his teeth and felt the pressure build behind his eyes. "This UNSUB is a pro. He's been doing this all over the world for twenty years and who knows how many people he's set up to take the fall for him." Marsh turned back to face Walker and Cochrane, ignoring other prying eyes. "We have got to catch this man before he kills again."

"You really don't believe your guy did it?" Cochrane lowered his face. "Not even Prudence Duvall?"

"You think I couldn't get your semen if I wanted it?" Marsh held the detective's gaze and watched him lose all color.

"Jeez, there's a visual I didn't need," Cochrane rubbed his bald spot and backed away a step.

Prudence Duvall had invited Steve Dancer to lunch. If she hadn't ended up dead he'd have suspected her of setting him up. Something inside Marsh's mind clicked and suddenly it started to make sense. To understand the crime, you had to know the victim.

"Dammit."

"What?"

"Maybe Pru Duvall knew this guy."

Cochrane paled. "Oh, shit. I can tell I'm not going to like our next move."

Marsh grinned at him. Walker looked on, watchful but impassive.

Grieving or not, future president of the US or not, he needed to talk to Brook Duvall.

***

About to knock on the huge double doors to the Duvall's Gramercy Park apartment, Marsh heard raised voices inside and stilled his hand.

"I want that damn painting!"

"I don't know anything about your painting you selfish bastard. My wife just died!"

He exchanged a glance with Cochrane. Did they stay and listen and maybe learn something, or knock on the door and reveal their presence?

The scrape of furniture and the crash of something fragile against an unyielding wall forced them into action. Marsh unclipped his holster and Cochrane pulled his weapon as he stood to one side. Ignoring the gleaming polished brass knocker, Marsh hammered hard against the solid wood with the base of his fist.

"FBI, NYPD. Open up." He upped the volume, repeated, "FBI, NYPD. Senator Duvall, open up, please. We know you're in there."

There was quiet, broken by the sound of footsteps slowly approaching the door, the indiscernible sound of whispered instructions.

"You too, Admiral, don't bother hiding. We need to talk." How screwed up was their investigation about to become with so many politicians and bigwigs watching their own backs?

The lock clicked and the door swung open to reveal a disheveled Brook Duvall, wearing the same clothes he'd had on earlier. Iron-gray hair stood on end and a puffy red mark cruised one cheekbone.

Eyes were bloodshot from both tears and alcohol. Marsh smelled the whisky on his breath.

Although if ever there was a day when a man deserved to drown his sorrows, the day of his wife's murder would be it.

"May we come in?" Marsh asked.

Brook nodded, rubbed his throat.

Admiral Chambers had two decades on Duvall. He hovered beside an overturned table, fists clenched, murderous rage glittering in his eyes. He took an unsteady step, crunched fine porcelain beneath his Rockport shoes.

"Admiral Chambers, so nice to see you again." Marsh felt anything but amused.

The admiral grunted.

"The admiral happens to be my father's best friend." Marsh gave Detective Cochrane his most plastic smile and was pleased that the detective grinned at him as they holstered their weapons.

"So you're up shit creek with everyone, huh?" Cochrane laughed, a deep cynical sound that said he'd been there, done that.

"Never a dull moment." Marsh turned to the senator. "Is there somewhere we can discuss things like civilized gentlemen?"

The senator's PA barged through the door behind them and glanced at the shattered vase on the dark hardwood floor. "What happened?"

"Geoffrey, can you get the gentlemen a drink please, and clear up this mess?" Senator Duvall patted the other man's arm and looked up at Marsh. "I gave the housekeeper the night off. She was devastated." Tears welled up in his eyes again and he looked away, stumbled toward his office.

Marsh followed, doubting the senator would get

to the White House now, but who knew? If Duvall wasn't implicated in the murder of his wife, the sympathy vote alone might rocket him into the Presidency. Now there was an angle to investigate—if he wanted to get strung up by his balls.

The admiral followed, tailed by Cochrane.

Cochrane was his new best friend because the rest of his team was busy going through the church records and NYPD wanted him under the microscope. He needed to find the killer and get Dancer out. Then he'd deal with Josephine.

In the office, Brook poured himself a tumbler of single malt and Marsh wished to God he could have one too.

"I need to know what's going on," Marsh said quietly.

Duvall sank slowly into a wingback chair as if his body was so weary he might collapse. Admiral Chambers helped himself to a shot of whisky and then leaned against the oak mantle, warming himself before the fire.

"Nothing's going on," the admiral sneered.

Miserable old goat.

"Try again, Admiral."

Cochrane was wandering around the study, selecting and examining books from the dark bookshelves.

"Want me to arrest him for assault, Senator Duvall?" Marsh asked the bereaved man.

"You wouldn't dare…"

"Try me."

The admiral's mouth dropped open as he stared at Marsh, the crimson in his cheeks fading to reveal parchment-like white skin.

"But it's up to the senator," said Marsh.

The admiral glanced down at Brook Duvall who stared sightlessly into the flames. "Can't prove a damn thing."

"The same way you can't prove Prudence stole any painting from you. Do you know about this painting?" Brook looked up at Marsh. "He says my wife stole it from him years ago and he picks *today* to come and claim it." His head swung round to face Chambers. "Did you kill her for it?"

Brook leapt out of his chair and tackled the admiral to the floor, the whisky glass crashing into the fire with a shattering hiss of flame. Both men landed with a hard thud, but Brook had the advantage of surprise and age on his side and straddled Chambers, gripping the old man's throat. "Did you kill her?"

Marsh looked on. If it looked like Duvall was going to do serious damage he'd step in.

"I haven't even seen her in years." Chambers' hands fought for purchase on Brook Duvall's fingers, but the senator wasn't giving up easily.

"You're lying!" Tears started to flow again and Brook looked up and seemed to realize what he was doing, or maybe who his audience was. He stumbled off the older man and crawled onto his chair, wrapped his arms over his head and wept.

Chambers sat up, loosened his tie, undid his top shirt button and wheezed out a breath before he could speak. "You'd know all about lying, wouldn't you, you fucking queer."

Oookay.

Marsh scraped his fingers over his eye sockets as he stared at the broken figure of the next would-be president. There had never been a hint of scandal. "You're gay?"

Duvall said nothing, sat with his face hidden against his knees, shoulders shaking.

"Did you *ever* do her?" The admiral asked with a leer. "Because she was rabid by the time she got to me."

"She'd need to be," Cochrane muttered under his breath.

Chambers climbed to his feet, wobbling unsteadily. Duvall sobbed harder and Marsh noted the PA stood at the door, directing a vicious look at Chambers.

"So Pru was a beard?" asked Detective Cochrane.

Duvall sat up straight, his gaze going to Geoffrey in the doorway and Marsh put the final piece of the puzzle together.

"It was her idea." Duvall palmed the tears off his cheeks. "We met in Savannah when her father was still alive." He glanced up and caught Marsh's gaze. "I think he abused her, but she never talked about it. She never talked about much." He gave a bitter laugh, "She caught me with Geoffrey in a compromising situation at some house party the Huntingfords threw." Brook closed his eyes.

"Geoffrey and Pru are...*were* second cousins. She knew I had political aspirations, and as she found me," he glanced at his PA, "*us,* literally in the closet, it didn't take long to convince us that we could actually make a marriage of convenience work. Plus, I was in the Navy..." He looked away from Marsh into the flames. "You know how the military loves homosexuals."

"So lying to the American people is an ethical way to start your political career and an okay way to win the Presidency?" Marsh questioned.

Cochrane snorted while Admiral Chambers sank stiffly into the second chair with a smirk.

Geoffrey came over and poured himself a large one. "All those years..." He turned and looked at his boss, his lover, shaking his head as if they'd lost everything. "I never thought it would end this way."

"Did you kill your wife?" Detective Cochrane asked, a hard expression closing down his features.

The senator looked surprised. "Me?"

"Yeah, *you*. She get fed up of the arrangement? Threaten to spill the beans?" Cochrane had a viable suspect in his sights, and leverage to make a powerful man talk. "Spouses are always top of the pile when it comes to murder."

"But I thought a serial killer murdered her?" He didn't know they'd ruled Dancer out as the Blade Hunter. Duvall's eyes ricocheted violently, a pinball gone crazy. They came to rest on Geoffrey and he held out a shaking hand that the other man took.

"You lovebirds got an alibi for last night that doesn't involve each other?" Cochrane's New York accent got thicker with each word.

The senator and his PA looked at each other frowning. "We were in the Hamptons."

The admiral laughed, a nasty ugly sound.

"What about you, Admiral? Got an alibi?" Marsh's words stopped him cold.

"Me?" The old goat had the gall to look affronted.

"Yesterday, you find out Prudence took a painting that might be worth as much as fifty million dollars." Marsh watched the old man's faded brown eyes grow cold. "You have an alibi for last night?"

"I wouldn't have killed the bitch until after she'd told me where the painting was." His lips twisted as he looked into the fire.

"But *the bitch*, as you so politely put it, *is* dead," Marsh said quietly. "And I think she knew her killer."

Everyone spoke at once.

"What?"

"Oh my God…"

"It wasn't me."

"Hey! One at a time!" Cochrane pointed at Geoffrey. "You said, *oh my God*, like you knew something?"

Geoffrey sat on the arm of Brook's chair, stiff as cardboard. "It's just…"

"Spit it out," Detective Cochrane ordered. Marsh let him lead.

Geoffrey glanced uncertainly at Brook. "Pru was heavily into S&M and I know she was seeing someone, but I don't know who it was."

The admiral snorted. "She was a sick bitch. Wanted me to whip her. If she was still alive I'd be happy to oblige."

"Shut up! That's my wife you're talking about and no matter what kind of marriage we had, I loved her." Brook sat up in his seat, vibrating like he was about to go for Chambers' throat again.

"Where'd she keep her stuff?" They might have a solid lead.

"Stuff?" Brook was oblivious, but Geoffrey knew exactly what Marsh was talking about.

"In her room." Geoffrey stood up and walked to the door, visibly shaking. "I'll show you."

The PA led them down a corridor, to a bedroom dressed in deep crimson and gold. Opulent drapes, a king-size four-poster bed with a painting of a naked woman curled up against a red backdrop on the wall above it. An ornately carved trunk sat behind the door, sporting a big fat padlock.

"I could shoot out the lock." Cochrane started to unclip his weapon.

"I think someone might know where the key is?" Marsh tilted his gaze to Geoffrey.

The man squeezed his eyes shut. "She wanted me to try it on. That was all. She wanted to tell me what she was into."

"She tell you a name?"

He shook his head. "We were friends even as children but lately she'd drifted away…"

"Just get us the damn key." Cochrane looked nervously around the bedroom. Marsh felt it too; a creepy sensation trickling through his bones as if Pru's ghost lay curled on that bed purring, beneath the painting that shared an uncanny likeness with her.

Geoffrey left and quickly returned, lowered his voice to a whisper and glanced at the door to make sure the admiral and the senator were out of earshot. Neither man had followed them and Marsh hoped they didn't kill each other while they were gone. He inserted the key and the mechanism opened easily.

"She tried to get me to dress up in this stuff." He looked up, eyes wide. "I was curious, you know? Not about the sex." He shrugged. "About the gear."

He opened the lid and inside was a black leather whip, crops, paddles, masks and leathers.

Geoffrey reached out as if to touch something and Cochrane slapped his hand. "That's all the S&M I've got in me. Touch anything else and I'll shoot you."

Geoffrey backed away. "But, oh my God, my DNA is on that stuff." Geoffrey started to cry and Marsh felt like growling in frustration. Because the Blade Hunter was still out there and had given them more evidence than they could process in a week.

Unless it was good old Geoffrey, which wasn't impossible but didn't seem likely. Although the women weren't raped, merely tortured.

He closed the lid, careful not to touch anything with his bare hands. "We need to get this to the lab."

Cochrane nodded.

"We need Pru's telephone records and address book." Marsh frowned. "What about email?"

Geoffrey's shoulders drooped and he swept a quick look around the room. "She had a laptop, but I don't see it here."

"Are we going to need a warrant to get this information?" Marsh asked.

Geoffrey shook his head. "No. Brook might not have loved Prudence in the traditional sense, but it doesn't mean he doesn't want to find the bastard who killed her. And so do I."

***

"How far we gotta walk and why can't we take a cab?"

"I walk everywhere. It's good exercise." Josephine smiled up at Vince, glad to be out in the fresh air. Being protected was stifling. Living in fear was crippling. This guy wasn't going to attack her in broad daylight. There was no reason not to pretend some things were normal.

The streets were full of dead leaves. An overfull

274

trashcan rolled and littered the street. Metal fire escapes snaked up walls, parked cars lined the streets, and tall trees competed with concrete lampposts for the sun. Manhattan at its finest.

"I guess you were too poor to take cabs when you were younger, huh? And now even with a psycho after you, you're too tight?" said Vince.

"Ha." She liked the fact Vince didn't baby her. She'd rather be baited than coddled. But what she really needed was movement and space. She needed endorphins and she needed a physical release. They were walking down Sullivan Street in SoHo. Not far from where she was meeting her client. She wasn't ashamed of her poor roots, took pride in having actually made something of herself with a little help from her friends.

"After my mother left, even food was a luxury in our house," she told him. Then she remembered the kindness of Marsh's parents, and their generosity. It was nothing to do with how much money they had—although that helped—it was to do with a goodness of spirit.

Being poor wasn't anything to be proud of. Surviving her childhood was.

Her mood dropped. Before they'd left the apartment, Walker had phoned her to ask for a DNA sample. They'd exhumed a body that might be her mother and needed to compare her DNA.

"I feel sick." She needed to catch her breath. She sagged against the wall of a drycleaners, but the smell of chemicals coming from the vent was strong enough for a glue-sniffer to get high. Gagging, she moved on, leaned against a corner convenience store that carried everything except fossil fuel.

"You pregnant?" Vince grabbed her arm and

swung her around to face him.

She shook her head. "I got my period this morning."

"That explains a few things." He raised his eyes to the heavens.

"Like what?"

"Like the tears. Like the bitchiness—"

"I wasn't bitchy." Tears welled in her eyes again. *Shit.*

"That's right, and you're not moody either. Come on, sunshine." Vince hauled her along the street, stopped at the intersection waiting for the lights. She moved automatically, putting one foot in front of the other. What would it be like to be pregnant? To have a child to love and care for? To have a relationship with a man she loved, a family.

"I feel like this is my last chance..." The words popped out of her mouth.

"Did you phone him? Did you tell him?" Vince peered down at her, eyes darker than coal, full of compassionate irritation.

She looked away. "No."

"Do it. Do it right now." Vince stalked back from the edge of the curb and heaved out a massive pissed off male sigh.

Fine. She could do this. She faced her reflection in the dirty streaked window of the corner store. Her heart hammered against her ribcage in distinct beats as she dialed Marsh's number. It rang four times before she got bumped. "Damn." Looking over her shoulder, she caught Vince's eye. "Voicemail."

"Just tell him you love him!" Vince dragged massive fingers through his close-cropped hair and looked like he wanted to crush something. Probably her.

"Marsh. I called to say…" Her voice was rough and sounded more angry than loving. She tried to clear her throat. "To apologize for everything. I'm sorry Dancer got arrested, sorry I got in the way of you doing your job." The words *I love you* stuck on her tongue. She did love him. She didn't want to but apparently this wasn't something she got to decide. She licked her lips but words dried up. Maybe if they were face to face, she could squeeze them out, but talking to a cell phone?

She couldn't do it.

A car engine revved down the street.

Pissed, Vince threw his hands wide and began crossing the junction as the lights changed.

Tires squealed and a horn honked as a vehicle peeled away from where it was double parked and raced toward the intersection. Josie didn't even have time to scream as the SUV plowed straight into Vince and threw him high into the air. The car braked sharply and he slid off the hood.

Time stopped.

Her body was in motion though her mind was still screaming back on the sidewalk. She dialed 911 as she ran toward him. "I need an ambulance. Someone's been hit by a car on the corner of Sullivan and—"

Someone was pulling her shoulders. She tried to shake them off, tried to give the operator exact details about where they were and Vince's condition. His leg was bent awkwardly beneath him. Blood poured from his thigh and a head wound. She touched his face, careful not to move him. He was unconscious.

Hands grabbed her but she pulled away. "Get *off* me!" She turned to shake off whoever the hell was manhandling her, but froze when she recognized him.

Red hot anger surged through her veins. "You hit him with a car!"

He grabbed her but she fought him. He wrapped both arms around her waist, trapping her arms to her sides and holding her to him, walking backwards to his SUV.

"You should be grateful." A hate-filled whisper seared her ear as she kicked wildly. "I was going to shoot the moron, but he was standing right there."

She started to scream and someone shouted at him to stop. But they were too late. He threw her in the car. Stabbed a needle into her ass. It hurt as he slammed down the plunger.

He ran around the hood, flashing a gun to keep passersby back. Josie grappled with the door handle but her fingers felt spongy and couldn't grasp anything. Vince lay in an ever-increasing pool of blood. Her vision wavered in and out and then started fading at the edges and she knew she was about to pass out. He'd got her. The man who'd killed her mother. He finally had her exactly where he wanted her. She was as good as dead.

Chapter Eighteen

"Just tell him you love him!" Vince's voice was distinct against a background of traffic noise.

Marsh and Sam Walker were back at St. Mary's Church going through records. All of a sudden this investigation had so much freaking evidence it was going to take weeks to process and something told him this wasn't a coincidence. They didn't have weeks.

He listened to Josie's message, knew she was struggling. Apologies were not her strong point. Revealing emotions was not part of her persona. The heaviness around his chest lightened because he'd been about to phone her.

Just tell him you love him.

But instead, after a long silence, she hung up.

Shit. Groaning, Marsh ran his hands over his face. The woman was tearing his heart to pieces. Goddamn her for not saying the words he was desperate to hear. Needed to hear. But who was he to talk when he hadn't been upfront either?

He hit call return and didn't know whether to be relieved or frustrated when it was busy.

"I love you. We are not done talking about this." He hung up and saw Walker staring at him strangely.

"She dump you?" Walker asked.

"Not for the first time." Marsh met his gaze head on. "Make a move on her and I'll re-arrange your face." He'd turned into a jealous ass.

279

Walker shrugged. "It's her call."

Yeah, didn't he know it.

He looked across the small room at the agents carefully laying the church papers three deep on two tables. Anything with a date on it was being filed by the year. Anything without a date was being read and separated into an African pile, missionary pile, charity organizations, personal correspondence, etcetera.

They were all doing everything to catch this asshole and get their fellow agent released. Aiden glanced up. "I think I've got something."

Marsh strode to his side. "What is it?"

"Receipts for an apartment rental in Queens the year Josephine was attacked."

Walker hovered behind them. "Local PD checked with the building's owners, but it was prior to computerization and they didn't keep records that far back."

There was no name associated with the document aside from that of the church. Marsh picked up a sheaf of papers, handed a stack to Walker. "We need to find this guy fast. I have a sick feeling Pru Duvall was the appetizer."

They worked as quickly as possible. Scanning documents as the cold air blasted them from the street through the open window.

And then he saw it. The name that pulled it all together.

Joshua Faraday.

"Father Malcolm." His voice cut through the din of the small room crowded with federal agents and cops.

"Yes?" The father squeezed past two agents and stood beside Marsh, peering over his elbow.

"Joshua Faraday?" Marsh watched the man's face as his memories bloomed. Excitement lifted his mouth. "Yes, yes, that's the man. I'd forgotten his name, but now you've said it, it was definitely him."

Aiden stilled beside him. He got it.

"How old was he?" Marsh asked.

"He wasn't a young man, maybe late forties?" The priest seemed hesitant.

It was a little older than the profile estimated, but that could be wrong. Or... "Did he have any family?"

The priest scowled down at the stained carpet, his mouth tight. "I do believe his whole family came with him—wife and children."

"Philip and Gloria?" Aiden asked from Marsh's side.

A smile spread over the priest's face. "Why, yes, and I believe his wife was Nancy, lovely lady."

Philip Faraday fit the profile *exactly*. A quiet rage filled Marsh. The asshole had been under his nose the whole time. Worse, Aiden had handed him back the painting a few short hours ago. Faraday might not get the full fifty million but he had the connections to get enough to disappear.

He looked at Walker, "Find out where Joshua Faraday is today. If he's still alive. We need an arrest warrant for Philip Faraday, and bring his sister in for questioning." The agent turned away to make the call.

Cochrane held a phone to his ear and barked out, "Senator Duvall just reported that his wife cleared out her bank accounts before she died."

"It's the bastard's getaway money." Marsh's mouth went dry. The killer—all indications pointed to it being Philip Faraday who also fit the general description of the attacker—had probably been Prudence's lover and had somehow convinced her they were going to run away together. She'd met Steve Dancer for lunch because the bastard had wanted to set Dancer up, maybe punish the FBI agent for his involvement in confiscating the painting, or to screw with Marsh as he was protecting Josie. And the bastard had killed her as easily as he'd murdered all those other women. The guy had no conscience, no empathy, not even for a woman who was willing to give up everything for him.

Facts were starting to come together. How the killer accessed Josie's address even though it wasn't in the public domain. If he had access to people in the NY art world it was merely a question of bribing the right person for the information.

Marsh took out his cell phone and dialed Vince. Sweat broke out along his brow. If they could keep Josie away from Faraday until he was picked up, this whole thing would be over.

"So you think Joshua Faraday was fucking Margo Maxwell and the son found out?" Walker was also on his cell, obviously waiting for information. He winced as he glanced up at the priest's face. "Sorry, Father."

Marsh held up his hand as the call to Vince went through. "Who the hell is this?"

"EMT on the way to Downtown Hospital. I'm afraid the person you're calling was involved in a hit and run—"

Sweet Jesus. "What about the woman with him?" Marsh's voice cracked, his breath so tight in his chest he thought he might be having a heart attack.

"I'm sorry sir. There wasn't anybody with him when we arrived."

Shit, shit, shit. He held the phone down as he pressed his hands against the surface of the table, every muscle in his body screaming with tension, papers scattering around him as he struggled to breathe. He put the phone back to his ear. "Is Vincent going to make it?"

"We don't know. He's pretty badly injured and needs surgery—we need to get in touch with next of kin…"

"I'll deal with that." Marsh rang off and noticed the silence.

Everyone in the room was staring at him expectantly. The smell of rot and decay crawled around inside his senses and made him feel sick. *Do not think about Josephine. Do your job.*

How could he not think about Josephine being at the mercy of a killer? He knew the guy had her. "Vince was involved in a hit and run and is seriously injured." He swallowed to get the words out. He tried Josie's number again. "Josie isn't answering her cell and wasn't with him when the paramedics arrived."

He stared at Walker. "Get a trace on her cell. We need to pick up Philip and Gloria ASAP." Saying the words made him want to puke—why hadn't they found that clue ten minutes earlier? "I need Steve Dancer out of jail now, helping me get Josephine back." His nerves twanged, strung so tight it would take one small push to make him snap.

He needed to hold it together. The law had to be enough to get Josie out of this alive. And Vince…

Please God.

"Aiden." He worked through his cell phone address book, pulled out one for Vince's girlfriend, Laura. "Get in touch with Vince's girlfriend and get her to the Downtown ER." He held the man's gaze. "Stay with her and with him. We need to know if he saw anything, or heard anything or..." *In case he dies...*

Aiden was dialing his cell as he grabbed his jacket and disappeared.

"This doesn't let Dancer off the hook—" Walker started.

"We know who the Blade Hunter is." Marsh shrugged into his tailored jacket. "I bet with a little detective work we can place Philip Faraday at all the locations of the murders and I *know* he knew Pru Duvall, even though she lied about the fact."

"How do you know that?" Walker asked.

"Because the day he tried to kill Josephine, Pru Duvall was at the same gallery opening as Lynn Richards and Steve Dancer. *His* gallery opening." Marsh was running out of patience. "The same gallery opening where I confiscated his fifty million dollar insurance policy."

That painting had never been for sale for eighty thousand dollars no matter what the price tag said— it had been on display to some of the most powerful art connoisseurs in the world.

Why the hell hadn't his brain been working? Marsh shouldered past Walker, stood outside and inhaled huge lungfuls of fresh fall air.

God. Please, let him find Josephine alive. *Don't hurt her.* Don't fucking hurt her.

Marsh needed a cigarette even though he'd given them up months ago. Walker followed him out onto the street and they stood looking at each other as Walker held his phone to his ear and repeated whatever he was being told.

"Joshua Faraday died in Africa in 1996, no details. Nancy Faraday died in England a couple of years later."

Walker stared up at the bare branches of the silver birch. "Officially I cannot get Steve Dancer released…" He put his hands on his hips, determination obvious in his stance.

"Wait." Marsh held up his hand. "I know what you're going to suggest, but before we get everybody's ass screwed to the wall, let's see if I can do something."

Marsh dialed Brett Lovine, the Director of the FBI, on his private cell.

Lovine didn't bother with small talk. "I've fielded calls from a senator, a retired admiral and a retired general this morning. The latter two want you sacked immediately, one of whom is your own father."

"Brett—"

"Marsh—"

"Shut up and listen! None of it matters." Silence on the end of the phone told him he finally had his friend's full attention. "We know who the Blade Hunter is. We know he set up Agent Dancer to take the fall for Mrs. Duvall's death and we know he has taken Josephine Maxwell hostage."

Walker's eyes bulged because they didn't have proof of any of it, but Marsh *knew*. Marsh was silently praying. Praying the guy he'd grown up with trusted him. Praying the woman he loved survived long enough so that he could actually say the words to her.

"What do you need?" Brett said. The quiet tone and somber pitch told him he had his friend's attention.

"I need Special Agent Steve Dancer released immediately. Drop the charges and give me my best man back, so we can find Josephine."

Silence. The hesitation was killing him. Doubt booming inside his chest with each beat of his heart.

"If it turns out Agent Dancer was involved in *any* way I'll have your badge."

"If Dancer was involved you can have any damn thing you want, Brett."

"Dangerous promise to make to a politician, Marshall. I thought you'd have figured that out a long time ago." Brett laughed, but it was a hollow bitter sound.

"Some things are worth selling your soul for."

***

The knife was sharp. Not as familiar in his hand as the last one, but it slid through the outer layer of his skin like he had no more substance than water. He sucked in a breath. Watched the blood slide over his wrist and drip onto Josephine's olive green t-shirt in ugly dark blotches.

Her chest rose steadily, fell gently on a silent exhale. He'd thought he'd have had more trouble getting her away from her FBI handlers, but one fake call and a little fast thinking and it had been brutally simple. He'd intended to lure them both inside one of his friend's galleries and kill the bodyguard and anyone else who got in his way. He'd set up in position to watch them and make sure it was just the two of them and then WHAM!

Literally.

Placing a finger against the soft skin that covered her carotid, he felt the calm settled beat of her heart. Her skin was warm to the touch.

She was still unconscious.

Good. He didn't want to rush this.

Breakers crashed on the beach. A seagull screamed and he looked out of the darkened window, feeling the energy of an incoming storm, excitement and poignancy competing inside him because this would be the final chapter of this part of his life.

He had money to aid his escape and transform into someone new. He'd stop killing for a while and see if he could tame the beast that raged within him in other ways.

He had the painting back.

Since the gallery showing he'd had several offers from people who wouldn't care how bloody his hands were. Their greed had fewer morals than his bloodlust.

He felt an unexpected ache of loneliness in his chest. He missed Pru.

When they'd met there had been that sexual spark. He'd always been attracted to things he wasn't supposed to have, and to doing things he wasn't supposed to do. He'd sensed a kindred spirit and their affair had crossed continents without anyone ever suspecting. Poor Pru.

She was still serving him well.

Pru had first brought him here to the senator's North Fork hideaway one weekend not long ago when Brook had been in D.C. It was secluded, nestled between two vineyards. This was where the big butch senator came to relax with his gay lover.

No neighbors close enough to spy and no staff except for the woman who cleaned once a week.

She was going to get a bit of a shock this week.

It was isolated but less than two hours drive from NYC. The perfect kill zone. Pity he couldn't stay longer.

Light from the hallway sparkled in Josephine's pale hair, made it translucent beside her fair skin. So beautiful. He'd killed her once. The bitch who'd seduced his devout father and destroyed his family.

She had been dead for a long time.

He'd enjoyed that day. The shock on her face when his father had left and he'd found her still in the apartment across the hall from where they were staying. They'd used the place to fuck, not twenty feet from where his mother was cooking dinner. He'd killed her and then spotted the shadowy figure on the fire escape. She'd been asleep. He'd planned to kill her too, but when he'd grabbed her she'd been so frail and thin. So miserably unloved. He'd let her go and always wondered why he'd been so weak. Now he knew. It wasn't weakness, it was some divine plan.

He'd never been able to recapture the pure adrenaline rush of that first time, but now… Now he was going to get his revenge, close the circle and finally be free.

Philip picked up the knife again and ran it along his flesh, sucking his teeth as he sliced his skin.

He walked over and picked up the canvas. The one he'd taken from her apartment in Greenwich. The color shone with vivid light. Intensity, passion and hatred visible to the blindest onlooker. It was unsigned. He propped it against the bed and took up a hammer, standing over the woman's limp body.

His shadow fell across her as he felt the weight and brought it down hard against the nail on the wall.

Josephine had painted blood and pain as if she was intimately acquainted with it. But those memories were old. Time for a refresher course.

***

Special Agent Steve Dancer stumbled out of the back door of the Brooklyn PD and climbed into Marsh's Beemer, his face as white as china clay.

"You okay?" Marsh asked, cataloguing the lines of strain around the other man's mouth. He'd been patched up, but still looked like shit.

Dancer nodded, clearly unable to speak. Closed his eyes and leaned back against the headrest. The only light was the blotchy liquid reflection of yellow streetlights on the rain-splattered windshield.

Christ. Marsh couldn't begin to think what Dancer had gone through, but right now they needed to concentrate on finding Josephine. There was no time for healing, no time for acceptance, or recovery. No time for the man suffering by his side.

"I didn't think I was ever going to get out of there, boss." Dancer twisted his face toward him and peered through the dark interior. "Thanks."

If it hadn't been for Marsh pulling strings, he wouldn't have for a long time.

So much for law and order.

Marsh tightened his hands on the leather steering wheel. The rule of law wasn't enough to deal with an SOB who twisted the rules and sacrificed people like a chess player sacrificed pawns. Fear crawled up his belly and landed in his throat. Rain lashed down from a moonless night, battering the glass and tempered steel that encased them.

"He's got her, Steve." His voice vibrated. No matter how hard he gripped that wheel he couldn't stop his fear from leaking out.

"What?" The expression of defeat on Dancer's face morphed into alarm, then anger. "What about Vince?"

Marsh ground his teeth together and bit down on his emotions. Sweat gathered on his skin despite the autumn chill. He turned on the wipers, the dull rhythmic whoosh steadying his heart.

"Ran him over with an SUV." Marsh turned to the backseat, grabbed Dancer's laptop that he'd retrieved from Special Agent Walker—who hadn't been able to crack the passwords anyway—and maneuvered it awkwardly through the gap between the seats. "The Blade Hunter is none other than Philip Faraday—"

"The art dealer?" Snarling, Steve banged his head against the headrest. "That puny shit killed all those women?"

"And set you up." Marsh finished, "Yeah. Smarter than he looks." He buried the acid terror beneath professional impatience. "We've got to find him, before Josie ends up like Prudence Duvall."

Blood leeched from Dancer's face.

"She was still alive when the cops got there, you know that? They could maybe have saved her." Dancer frowned, still concentrating on the past when Marsh needed him to think about the future.

"Steve, I need you. We've got to find Josie before he kills her too." His voice broke.

Dancer gave him a blank look, which suddenly cleared. "The transmitter?" He swiped his unruly hair out of his face as he began to unzip the laptop from its case. "I'd forgotten about it."

Marsh had implanted the transmitter into Josephine without her knowledge last April when they'd been hoping she'd lead them to Elizabeth. Right now that little bit of moral impropriety was the only thing keeping an infinitesimal speck of hope alive in his heart.

Dancer booted up, battered through a whole series of passwords to access encrypted files, fierce concentration on his face. "Those transmitters may only last a couple of months. It could be dead by now," Dancer warned.

Marsh knew there was little hope, but without that signal, Josephine was on her own with a vicious serial killer. Gloria Faraday was telling them squat. Maybe she didn't know anything, but Walker had her in custody and Marsh hadn't been able to get near her.

The need for air forced a breath into his lungs as Dancer clicked on the tracking program.

Please God. Please God...

Dread and uncertainty ravaged his nerves. Even if they found Josephine this second it might already be too late. She might be dead. The SOB had had her for one-hundred and fifty-six minutes. The terror was unbearable, crippling, and Marsh shoved the feelings away. Concentrated on the need to *find* her. He needed to find her. She was going to be OK. They were going to have a life together.

Beep. Beep. Beep.

Thank God.

"Where is she?" Grim determination filled him. This bastard wasn't getting away this time. Whatever he'd done to Josephine Marsh was going

291

to reap ten-fold on the twisted fucker's body.

Dancer looked up. And Marsh knew he was thinking the exact same thing.

"Signal is stationary. North Fork of Long Island, but we don't have an address yet. Should we alert the locals?"

Sticking the car in gear, Marsh shook his head and checked his watch. "I don't fancy their chances against this guy. They'll spook him and if Josephine isn't already dead, she will be when they arrive all sirens blazing."

Steve stared intently at the screen of the computer. "It might be better that way," he said quietly.

"Goddamn it, Dancer, don't quit on me now."

"How the hell are we going to get there before he—" Dancer cut himself off, unable to say the words neither of them wanted to hear.

"Call Walker and tell him to get HRT ready." Marsh scrambled in his pocket and lobbed his cell phone at Steve. "First call Dora. I want a chopper and a pilot ready to fly at La Guardia in fifteen minutes."

"Ah fuck." Dancer was terrified of helicopters, but he dialed the number and got through to Dora straight away.

Marsh shot him a glance, but didn't say a word, just pressed his foot to the floor and headed for the Brooklyn-Queens Expressway, turning on the siren and driving hard.

Chapter Nineteen

Lightning flared and thunder vibrated through the air, waking her. Shivers wracked her body as she registered the icy temperature.

Where am I?

Waves crashed, the scent of brine pervading the air, so thick it filled her nostrils. *Mystic? Visiting Elizabeth?* Her tongue felt swollen and parched; she tried to swallow but there was no moisture in her mouth to ease the dryness. She went to sit up, but had to lie back down as she reeled, breathing hard. Her brain was slow. The light hurt. She turned away from it.

"Oh, good. You're awake."

A bolt of terror shot straight through her. She tried to swallow, but the muscles bunched and clenched in her dry throat, constricting her airway, choking her. She squinted, though her eyes didn't like it. She needed to see.

A man stood in front of her. Lean, not overly tall; the cold steel of his eyes matching the knife that glinted in the lamplight. Her oldest foe. The man who'd killed her mother and shaped her life. Her arms and legs jerked instinctively, only to be brought up short by a rope on each limb. She glanced upward and saw the painting she'd done of blood and death hanging on the wall like the promise of a sacrifice.

The lights flickered as he watched her.

"Why?" her voice cracked. The more she

strained, the tighter the bindings became, cutting off her blood supply, making her hands and feet go numb. *Not good. Not good at all.* She forced herself to relax.

"Why what?" His voice was as cold and flat as his eyes.

Vague bits of memory floated along her consciousness like fish darting in a pond.

The screech of car tires then the muffled thump of a body hitting the asphalt.

"Is Vince okay?" she asked slowly.

He shrugged. "I doubt it. I hit him pretty hard." He smiled, but no light reached his eyes.

The horror of Vince being hurt made her stomach wrench. And, oh god. *Marsh.* He was gonna freak and figure this was all his fault—as if he could keep everyone he cared about safe when this man was hell bent on destruction. Tears filled her eyes. The love she felt for him was so strong, his dedication to the law so convincing, she'd almost believed they had a chance of something normal. But this wasn't normal, and if the guy with the knife had his way she'd be dead soon. She didn't want to be dead. She didn't want to miss her chance of something normal, something wonderful.

She was fully clothed. He'd taken her boots, but thankfully not her clothes. *Yet.* There was blood on her t-shirt and she frowned.

"Why?" she asked again. She narrowed her eyes at him, glared with every ounce of hatred she held in her heart. "Why are you doing this?"

He slapped her cheek. He stood breathing heavily beside the bed, the knife gripped between whitened fingers. And then she recognized him from a vague childhood memory.

"You're the missionary's son."

Shadows flickered in the depths of his eyes.

"I saw them together, you know."

His eyes flashed.

"You don't think their actions hurt me just as much as they hurt you? You selfish miserable asshole." Anger gave her voice strength. "You killed her, didn't you? You killed my mother."

"Your mother was a whore." Teeth flashed as he bared them, leaning close. "She dragged my father into hell and he burned!"

"He looked like he was in Heaven the last time I saw him—"

Blood exploded on her tongue as he backhanded her.

"*He* was a good man."

"What the hell happened to you then?" she yelled.

It was foolish. The knife was at her throat, stinging her flesh as he held her down, hand so tight to her scalp her eyes stung. They stared at one another for a long moment. The strength in his body incredible, the light in his eyes pure evil.

"When I found you on that fire escape I was going to kill you." His breath touched her lip, the tiniest bit of spittle hitting her. Revulsion was ice cold on her skin. "But you were so pathetic, the look on your face. Sorrow. Heartbreak. Anguish.

"Maybe that's why I didn't kill you—all that little girl innocence destroyed right in front of my eyes by adults who should have known better." He laughed and she flinched. "I felt *sorry* for you. Then when I looked for you again all these years later, and heard you were an artist in NYC—I knew. You were waiting for me." He glanced toward the painting then looked back and caught her gaze. "It's a circle of death and it closes tonight."

The light in his eyes was crazed…and yet he seemed incredibly controlled as his fingers gripped her hair and the knife, already slick with blood, pressed against her flesh. Fear was growing inside her, the need to scream out her terror all consuming. He'd admitted killing her mom without an ounce of compassion. The sonofabitch made it sound like it had been her mother's own fault.

"Did you kill *him* too?" God, she hated him, with every atom of her being. "Your father? Did you kill that cheating bastard?"

Breathing hard, he blinked, released her and heaved himself away from the bed.

"*She* killed him." He turned to face the window as lightning illuminated everything in cold blue before thunder shook the house again. "We'd been in Africa for ten years and the trip to America was supposed to be special. My father offered to look after someone's plants while they were away on a week's vacation." He shrugged and walked closer. "It was the sort of thing he did all the time. We never gave it any thought, until I spotted the secretary from church walking along the sidewalk, and I saw her go into that apartment. I knew what was going on then." His eyes grew hard again. "He committed suicide when we got back to Africa— condemned himself to purgatory. Because of her.

"She was beautiful, your mother." He leaned over the bed, closer, and she held absolutely still as he nicked her earlobe with the point of the knife. It hurt like hell, but she kept her mouth shut. *I won't kill you if you don't make a sound.* "Just like you. She cried so hard when I put my knife inside her."

His smile was evil incarnate. "She screamed out my name."

All these years she'd strived only to survive; not to live, to survive. Suddenly, it wasn't enough. "There's something wrong with you. You're twisted and warped—"

He lunged at her, but she jerked to the side, the knife sinking into the pillow beside her head. *Shit.* Why the hell couldn't she keep her mouth shut?

Because fear wasn't enough. Survival wasn't enough.

But death didn't look so great either.

She froze as he lay sprawled on top of her. She could feel his heartbeat thumping through his black sweater, through her t-shirt and into her body. This was not a good time to discover she needed help.

Marsh. Damn you. Save me. Please, save me.

He moved until he sat astride her, the fury in his eyes making her wish for their previous flatness.

The knife tore through her t-shirt as if it were silk. Severed her bra with the same stroke and there she was, exposed from the waist up, the indelible scars on her flesh catching the light in a series of crosses.

"You like your handiwork?" The bitterness was ripe on her tongue, but his mood had changed. The anger gone. Calm back in its place. He slammed his fist into her jaw and the world tilted on its axis as her eyes rolled back.

***

Riding through an electrical storm in a helicopter was not a way to deal with someone's phobia. But right now he and Dancer were both facing their worst nightmares.

Marsh wore a dark t-shirt from the gym bag he kept stowed in the trunk of his car. He'd left on the tailored slacks because they were deep navy but swapped his shoes for dark-colored trainers. Both he and Dancer had on bulletproof vests.

Walker had called them en route with the news that Senator Duvall had a beach house in the vicinity of the signal coming from Josie, and Marsh had to believe this was the right place. He forced the image of her blood-soaked corpse from his mind.

Lightning flashed across the heavens, making the froth of the breakers glow in the blackness of the night. The pilot placed the chopper gently on the beach, sand whipping in every direction. Trees struggled against the wind and rain blotted out the landscape.

Marsh could barely hear the chopper over the storm. Dancer was deathly pale but had a determined look in his eyes Marsh hadn't seen before. This was personal. For both of them.

Marsh jogged up the sand, the footing heavy, debris stinging his cheeks and making him squint. There it was, up ahead—a rambling old beach house on the North Fork.

Marsh's heart kicked up a gear as he spotted a light on in one of the upstairs rooms.

Josie.

He ran, not caring if Dancer could keep up or not, desperate to get to Josie before Philip Faraday hurt her.

And still the loose sand slowed him down, filled his running shoes and made his legs move agonizingly slowly. There was grit in his mouth that he spat out.

It had come down to this.

With most law enforcement agencies in the world looking for Faraday, it had come down to Marsh and Dancer running along a sandy beach, racing to beat the clock.

Fuck.

There was a path up through the dunes and Marsh took off, immediately hitting a boardwalk and picking up speed. Dancer was right behind him, the thunder and wind drowning out any noise they made.

Marsh crashed to a halt. There were outdoor security lights.

Shit.

Marsh didn't know if they worked or not. He looked up at the window and saw a shadow cross in front of it. And then over the howl of the wind, over the boom of a storm-crazed sky, he was sure he heard Josie screaming his name.

Chapter Twenty

She screamed as he cut off her pants and left her lying naked on the bed like a damn pig waiting for butchery. She trembled with fear. Her carefully choreographed fate was spelled out in the monster's eyes.

He smiled.

Fury blinded her.

Without him seeing, she'd managed to loosen one wrist from the bindings. The monster with the knife paced a few feet from where she lay, muttering. And she'd loosened one lousy wrist.

She was going to be sick.

Lightning flashed and held for a few seconds before thunder rolled and the night went black.

She watched the knife. Him constantly squeezing and stroking it. Revulsion and terror warred inside, but mainly she was pissed.

The mattress sank as he climbed over the end of the bed and she wished to God she'd freed a leg so she could kick him in the face.

Her friend Elizabeth had been raped.

That idea terrified her even though he hadn't raped the other victims. Ugh, her stomach roiled. Finally she had to accept she was a victim. Josephine squeezed her eyes shut and tried to keep her knees close together, remembering her shattered friend the night after Andrew DeLattio had finished with her. Well, Andrew DeLattio had gotten his and this bastard would get his too.

What had Elizabeth said?

Fingers gripped her knees and yanked them roughly apart. She flinched as cold metal pressed against her leg. Bit her lip, knowing begging wouldn't help. Rape was about domination. That's all she remembered and right now it didn't take a rocket scientist to figure he was dominating her in every way.

The knife moved up her body, scratched her soft skin in a scoured line along her abdomen. Blood welled where the blade occasionally sank deeper. Death by a thousand cuts.

She gritted her teeth on a flinch. "Why does it turn you on so much?"

His eyes glittered, his voice hoarse. "It's the only thing that turns me on."

"Not sex itself?"

He flinched.

"Have you ever had sex?"

"Shut the fuck up."

"Do you even have a dick?"

His lips pulled back, madness in his eyes. "Is that what you want? Me to fuck you? Are you nothing but a dirty whore like your bitch of a mother?"

She slammed the base of her palm into his nose the way Elizabeth had taught her. He screamed and reared back. She tried to free her other wrist but he was back, lunging at her. She grabbed for his knife hand, desperate to keep it away from her body. Knowing she wasn't strong enough. Knowing he would kill her but unwilling to lie silent like a doll as he hurt her. Not this time.

He reached over and transferred the knife to his other hand, blood pouring into his mouth and dripping onto her bare skin. Revulsion turned her stomach but she saw excitement stir in his expression. His hands shook.

"I wonder how long it'll take you to die if I stab you here?" Pain exploded like a firework as he plunged the knife deep into her shoulder. She arched off the bed as agony flashed through her body, tore through her brain.

It hurt so freakin' bad she was definitely going to die. Blood flowed from her body in a hot wet rush. Thoughts of Marsh invaded her, calmed her. She loved him. And he loved her. She'd gotten one thing right. She knew that now.

Now that it was too late.

She felt herself zoning out into a much better place. Maybe one day Marsh would get over her and meet someone else. Someone to give his mother those grandchildren she craved. It was a pity it couldn't be her.

He slapped her cheek. "You're not slipping away that easily."

She spat at him and it landed smack on his lips.

Fury burned in his eyes and he raised the knife as if to finish this thing once and for all. Finally.

An explosion jerked him away from her. A warm spray of blood hit her face before he dropped onto the hard wooden floor.

Relief was so profound she almost stopped breathing.

"FBI. Put down your weapon or I'll shoot." Marsh walked across the room, his gun in a two-fisted grip. He didn't look at her as he walked around the end of the bed to the monster bleeding out on the floor.

A sound gurgled in the monster's throat. It

sounded a lot like '*Help*.'

"Is he still alive?" Josie whispered.

"Not for long." Marsh told her, ignoring the injured man as he undid her bonds. "Are you okay?"

Josie remembered she was stark naked, her shoulder bleeding like crazy. The naked part didn't matter right now. Her voice was high pitched and frightened. "He drugged me with something, but the only damage is the cuts you see."

Marsh's eyes flicked nervously over the stab wound in her shoulder. It was a little bit more than a cut, but she wasn't going to think about it that way. She did not intend to die. Not now. The guy on the floor groaned again. Her gaze flashed to the edge of the bed.

Dancer cuffed him. "He's going to bleed out long before the ambulance gets here." The grim satisfaction on his face told its own story. So many people had suffered so much at this man's hands.

"I hope so." She wanted him dead.

"Even if he lives he'll never hurt you again," Marsh told her, freeing her other wrist. For once she believed him. "I, for one, wouldn't mind him paying for his crimes."

Finally she was free but too weak to lift her arms. Everything already hurt. "How did you find me?"

"I'll tell you later."

"How's Vince?"

Marsh touched her hair and kissed her brow. "He'll live. You will too." He ripped off his t-shirt and padded it hard against her shoulder. *Crap!* She wanted to touch his face but didn't have the strength. He tugged the sheet around her and lifted her in his arms. "Let's go."

"I'll watch him until the locals turn up," said Dancer. His eyes looked tired and bleak. Whatever he saw in Marsh's expression made him say, "Don't worry, I won't do anything stupid. I'm happy to watch him suffer."

Marsh gathered her against his chest and she felt safe and secure, but her shoulder screamed with pain, and her head felt like it was floating two feet away. "I've got you. We need to get to a hospital." He strode out of the room and down the stairs, each step jarring and making her grit her teeth against the pain.

Love and tenderness mixed with stark fear in his eyes.

"I'm not going to die, Marsh. I've got too much to live for." She'd survived. She was bleeding and battered, but she'd left that dark ugly place and gone instead to a place filled with hope. "I love you," she admitted, free of the fear that had stalked her life. Not just the killer who lay upstairs bleeding, but the fear of getting close, getting hurt.

She needed to *live*.

He squeezed her harder. "I love you too."

She could hear the sound of the surf, and something else. A deep thrum. And a fierce blast of wind and sand. She pressed her face into his chest. Marsh tucked the sheet tightly around her body and then hugged her hard against him. "Ever been in a helicopter before?"

"No, and I hate flying," she admitted through gritted teeth. Pain radiated through her body in a single throbbing pulse. Shivers raced over her as a cold wind pierced the thin shroud covering her.

She was jostled and jarred and then laid flat

across two seats. She felt that weightless sensation as they took off but she couldn't enjoy it. Strong warm fingers gripped her hand, then pressed hard against the wound in her shoulder. At first it was agony before slowly easing into numbness. She clung to those fingers, clung to the pain. She wasn't losing the battle now. Marsh had beaten the Blade Hunter and she'd faced her demon and survived. She drifted into unconsciousness as the loud throb of rotors pounded through her blood.

***

She woke up in the hospital, her shoulder tightly bandaged and a dull ache radiating all the way up to her neck and down her back. Marsh gripped her hand so firmly her fingers tingled, but she liked it.

"Hey." Her voice cracked. "Can I get a drink, please?"

Marsh leaned over and poured her a glass of water from a jug beside the bed. He raised her up with the automatic control and kissed her gently.

Placing the straw between her lips she took a sip of water and relished the cold freshness that cooled her throat. His hazel eyes locked onto hers. "How do you feel?"

"Alive?" She laughed and almost sobbed as she remembered her ordeal. "Did he make it?"

He shook his head. Relief swept through her in a massive wave. *Good.* He was dead and that was good.

Marsh was smudged with dirt and blood, and wearing running shoes with dress pants and a dark green scrub top.

Not the smart, dapper Marshall Hayes she was

used to.

"Where's Dancer?"

"Checking on Vince."

"Is he going to be all right?"

Marsh nodded and took the cup from her.

She closed her eyes in relief and sagged against the pillow. "I thought Vince was dead when that car hit him." Tears ran down her cheeks and unable to stop them she drew up her knees and sank her face into the pillow. The bed sagged as Marsh gathered her in his arms. He pulled a handkerchief out of nowhere and she laughed, but then sobered at his expression.

"What is it?" she asked.

"There's something I never told you and you're not going to like it…"

Everything inside her froze. Maybe he didn't really care for her. Maybe he'd fed her a line as part of the job.

Lines of tension radiated around his eyes and mouth. "You asked me how I found you, at the beach house?"

"It doesn't matter—"

"Yeah, it does." He scrubbed a hand over his hair then looked her in the eye. "First of all I need you to know that I do love you. Nothing will ever change that. God knows, I tried."

"Okay, I think." She laughed nervously. Movement hurt but he loved her and nothing could be as terrible as losing Marsh again. Whatever he had to say couldn't be that bad.

"When I tracked you down back in April and drugged you, I, er, did something else." He stood and started pacing, not at all the self-assured man she'd come to know. "I implanted a tiny transmitter into your shoulder. It's still active and that's how we were able to pin down your location so quickly."

"What?" She sat up a little straighter, frowned. *Why would he do that?* It explained the itch she sometimes felt there. Then she got it. *No way.* "You always planned for me to get away from your cabin in Vermont so I could lead you to Elizabeth." His eyes told her she was right. Her jaw dropped. "All that time I felt guilty for drugging and deceiving you, and yet my escaping was part of the plan all along." Anger started to build, hot and furious in her gut.

"Yes and no." He held up his hand, palm out. "You drugging me and us having sex were never part of the plan. Me waking up naked, handcuffed to a bedpost was never part of the plan. Leaving you unprotected for any length of time was *never* part of the plan." His voice rose, words vehement.

Memories of being grabbed out of her rental car in Montana bombarded her. Andrew DeLattio's hands stroking her skin as if he could do with her as he pleased. She'd thought he was going to murder her. A bullet in the head after he'd finished using her body for his own gratification.

Marsh's hazel eyes were shockingly dark against pale skin. "If I'd have known DeLattio was going to escape custody and get hold of you, I'd never have let you leave." He was trembling. Hands fisted as if he tried to hold everything inside.

All the emotion of the past days and months swirled in her mind, but the biggest feeling that overtook her was relief and gratitude that Marsh was here with her now. That they'd found their way back to one another despite everything they'd gone through. Sure she was angry but she'd get over it,

307

especially if it stopped her feeling guilty about what she'd done to him six months ago.

"Is it still in there?" She looked toward her shoulder but it throbbed too painfully to examine.

He shook his head, pulled something miniscule out of his pocket and handed it to her. "I asked the surgeon to remove it." He swallowed audibly. "Can you forgive me?"

She examined the tiny capsule in her palm. "Considering it ended up saving my life I think I can forgive you. But next time you want to stalk me just track the cell phone, okay?"

He leaned over and kissed her, stroking her hair off her cheek. "There better not be a next time. You took a decade off my life last night; I want to spend all the days I have left being with you."

"Did I remember to thank you? For saving me?"

He leaned his forehead against hers. "All part of the service." He kissed her and she wished she wasn't lying in a hospital bed. After a moment he pulled away. "I better go see how Vince is doing."

She struggled out of his grip, swung her legs over the side of the bed.

"Where do you think you're going?" His voice was a growl that told her not to push it.

She stood and wobbled. "I'm fine, Marsh. Get me some clothes. I'm going to see Vince too."

"No." His raised voice had the nurses looking over and then striding toward them.

She planted her fist on her hip. "I need to do this. Please, don't try to stop me." The nurses bustled around her, clucking and trying to make her sit while they checked her vitals. "Go find something to wear." She flapped her hospital gown at him, revealing a lot of flesh. "Scrubs, pants, anything. I'm going to visit Vince if I have to walk naked through the halls."

"Fetch her a wheelchair from behind the desk, too," a dark-haired nurse told him with a grin. "What are you waiting for? Go do what the lady asks."

Epilogue

It had been a long hard week. They IDed Josephine's mother through dental records and Marsh was arranging a proper burial. Prudence was being buried today—as a victim rather than an accessory—a concession to Brook Duvall's position and Director Lovine's wishes. Steve Dancer was on enforced leave, until Marsh and the departmental shrink deemed him well enough to return to work.

Gloria Faraday had been released from custody, with no proof of her involvement in the crimes. Marsh didn't know what to make of that. The painting that had been the catalyst behind the whole thing had been reluctantly donated to the National Gallery by all the parties involved. It wasn't much consolation but it gave him some satisfaction that no one person would walk away rich from such a terrible situation.

Josephine was slowly regaining movement in her shoulder, but she was not a woman who took immobility gracefully. Thankfully, Vince was recovering well enough to have left the hospital yesterday with only a broken leg and the rapidly healing scar from an emergency splenectomy to show for his near death adventure.

They'd all survived and right now that was all that mattered.

"What are you doing?" Marsh watched Josie sling the rucksack over her good shoulder. "I can carry that for you." But she shook him off.

She looked up at him, blue eyes bright and alive. He'd been so certain he was going to lose her when he'd raced into that damned beach house.

"I need to say goodbye," Josie said quietly, making his pulse pound.

"Goodbye?" he asked her warily.

"Not to you." She pulled a face. "I'm moving out of NYC."

Did this mean...? His heart stopped beating. "Where exactly are you going?"

Fingering the strap of her rucksack, she rocked back on the heels of her Doc Marten boots. "I'm moving to Boston to live in sin with a hot FBI agent, though *not* with his parents."

"Oh, yeah?" He took a step until his body brushed up against hers and caused all sorts of short circuits to his brain. "Who said I wanted to live in sin?"

Her smile was wicked. "Trust me, you want to live in sin."

"No, I don't." He took her hand and leaned down, parting her lips for a deep kiss.

She wrapped her good arm around his neck. "What do you want then?" She planted a kiss on him that stopped his breath, not the kiss itself, but this newfound confidence to treat him like he was hers. Because he was hers.

"I want to take a cab up 5th Avenue to Tiffany's and pick out the biggest diamond ring you've ever seen."

She laughed, but he caught a glimmer of happiness lurking in her eyes.

"Diamonds are so cliché." She faked a yawn.

"How about the tab off a can of soda?" He interlinked their fingers and grinned. She hadn't said no.

"Not *that* cliché."

"So where are we going to first?" he asked as they got down to the lobby.

"We're going to say goodbye to somebody very special." She lifted the flap on her bag and showed him the urn for Marion's ashes.

Ah.

He bent to pick up an old newspaper that had dropped out of someone's recycling box.

"Hey! What is that?" Josie's tone turned icy as she pointed at the paper.

He looked down and there he was on the front page of the *NY News* with his tongue down Detective Jenkin's throat.

"That was Plan A, before you were kidnapped." He looked at her furiously jealous face and suddenly everything in his world righted itself. Even when she drove him nuts, she was what he'd been searching for his whole life.

Then he kissed her, dragged her back up the stairs to her apartment and even though she bitched at him the whole way, he knew that this was going to work. They'd go scatter ashes and buy rings later. Right now he finally had her where he wanted her. In his life. In his heart.

*Want to know more about how Marsh and Josie
first met? Read the opening scenes of...*

HER SANCTUARY
©Toni Anderson

New York City, March 31st

Elizabeth Ward eased back the blinds and peered
into the quiet street that ran alongside the apartment
building. Rain streaked the windowpanes, drops
running together and fracturing in the orange glow
of the streetlights. A dark-colored Lincoln crouched
like a shadow next to a squat, black and silver
hydrant. Her former colleagues from the FBI's
Organized Crime Unit sat in that car. Watching.
Waiting. Her so-called protection.

Betrayal burned the edges of her mind like
battery acid.

The grandfather clock in the hallway chimed
five times, making her jump.

Five a.m.

Nearly time.

Her fingers gripped the edge of the window
frame. Night's gloom clung to the red brick of the
Victorian tenements opposite, its weak edges and
cold breath eating into what should have been
springtime.

A drunk wove his shopping cart down the back
alley, searching for a safe spot out of the killer
wind. Even Midtown's exclusive neighborhoods
were scattered with down-and-outs, hunched behind
dumpsters, curled up between parked cars. A

community of desperate souls, listless, gaunt, and stinking like the dead.

She envied them.

She wanted to be that invisible.

Swallowing past the wedge in her throat, she counted to ten and slowly inhaled a lungful of air. She'd done her job, and done it well, but it was time to get the hell out of Dodge.

She sat at her computer in the darkened room and signed in to an anonymous email account. Wrote two messages.

The first one read, *Terms of contract agreed. Proceed.*

There was more than one way to skin a cat.

Her teeth chattered, but not from cold. A rolling shake began in her fingertips and moved up through her wrists—whether from rage or fear she didn't know. She clenched her hands together into a hard fist, massaged the knuckles with her interlocked fingers, grateful for the unyielding gold of her signet ring that bit into her flesh.

Pain was a good reminder.

She pulled her shoulders back, typed carefully, *Beware the fury of a patient man.*

Baiting the tiger, or the devil himself.

Bastard.

A tear slipped down her cheek, cold and wet. She let it fall, blanked the searing memories from her mind.

Elizabeth logged off. Reformatted her hard-drive, erasing every command she'd ever received, every report she'd ever sent. Letting the computer run, she headed into the stylish bathroom of the apartment the FBI had leased for her undercover alter ego and prepared for the final chapter of her

New York life. She leaned close to the mirror and put in a colored contact lens.

One eye stared back, frosted iced-blue, the other looked eerily exposed, its pale green depths shining with fear. With shaky fingers she put in the second lens and made up her face. Heavy foundation hid the dark circles under her eyes and translucent powder covered her rampant freckles. Blood-red lipstick and thick black eyeliner dominated her face, making her look harder, bolder.

"Hello, Juliette." She knew the old fraud better than she knew herself.

Blush emphasized cheekbones sharp enough to cut, and mascara elongated her thick lashes. She pinned her hair back into a neat bun, tight to the nape of her neck. Pulled on a wig that was similar to her own dyed, red hair, but cut shorter into a bob that swung just beneath her chin.

She was ready to die now.

Her lips curved upward. Her cheeks moved, her eyes crinkled, but there was not an ounce of happy to buoy it up. The façade held, despite the escalating internal pressure.

FBI Special Agent Elizabeth Ward had sat quietly when the Assistant DA had informed her that mobster Andrew DeLattio was being allowed to turn state's evidence. Then she'd excused herself and thrown up in the restroom.

Lines of strain etched her eyes and mouth. Her pulse fluttered.

Truth was she didn't mind dying, but she wasn't going to stand on the sidewalk with a bulls-eye tattooed to her ass. Juliette Morgan was a target for every organized-crime family in the US and Elizabeth intended to make her disappear.

Permanently.

She walked through to the main bedroom, pulled out a scarlet Versace pantsuit and a tangerine silk blouse and walked back into the bedroom.

Can I really do this?

Yes! The answer screamed inside her head. How else could she reclaim her life? And if she died trying? So be it.

She dressed. The red and orange clashing violently in an eye-catching display of high fashion—exactly the effect she was going for.

Satisfied, Elizabeth walked through to the lounge and took one last look at the stylish Manhattan apartment. She was done with it, burned out, wasted, with no future to speak of and a past full of regrets. Time hadn't diminished her fury; if anything it burned brighter and stronger every day. DeLattio owed her and Witness Protection or not, she was going to get her revenge.

Forcing herself to move she stopped before she'd gone two paces. Her eyes caught and held an old sepia photograph staring at her from the hall table. A young couple grinned at her from their perch, affectionately hugging two tiny figures between them.

It knocked her sideways, the lifetime of grief locked up in that treasured photograph. She swallowed three times before she could catch her breath.

Ah, God.

Elizabeth blinked to kill the tears and slid the photograph into her purse, next to her Glock. Hiding behind dark sunglasses, she picked up her keys and left without a backward glance.

***

Triple H Ranch, Montana, April 3rd

In the open doorway of the ranch house with his old dog pressed against his side, Nat Sullivan gazed up into the inky depths of the night sky. No moon shone tonight, though stars glittered like tiny diamonds against the blackest coal.

It was two a.m. and his eyes hurt.

A thin layer of fresh snow covered the ground, gleaming like exposed bone. The storm had been a quick blast of fury, totally unpredicted, but not unexpected, not this high in the mountains. Trees popped like firecrackers deep in the heart of the forest.

A dull throbbing poked at his skull like a hangover. Not that he'd had the time or luxury to get drunk. The headache was the lingering aftereffect of a difference of opinion he'd had with a couple of repo men that afternoon. They thought they had the right to come to the ranch and steal his property. He figured they'd be better off dead.

Stroking the silky fur that covered the old dog's skull, tension seeped from his stiff neck as his muscles gradually relaxed. He let out a breath and his stance tempered, shoulders lowered as the tightness slowly eased.

Peace, finally, after a day of almighty hell.

The Sullivans had been granted a temporary reprieve when his mother suffered a heart attack. A life-and-death version of the silver-lined cloud.

Nat tried to force a smile, found the effort too great, his jaw too damn sore to do it justice. Last time he'd seen his mother she'd been pasty gray, her hair standing on end, lying flat on her back in a hospital bed.

Still giving out orders.

Old. Weak. *Cantankerous.* His mother would go to her grave fighting for this land. He could do no less.

Absently, he played with the silky fur of Blue's ears. The Triple H was nestled in the foothills of the Rocky Mountains, a lush valley butted up close to the Bob Marshall Wilderness. Settled by his great, great grandparents, it was as much a part of his heritage as his DNA. A few hundred acres of prime grazing land, carved over millennia by the friction of ice over rock.

Nat had had his adventures, traveled the world, seen more than his fair share of beautiful country, but now he was back to stay. Montana was in his bones, the backdrop to every thought and the oxygen of every breath. He leaned against the doorframe, looked out at the mountains and welcomed the fresh clean air pressed close against his cheeks.

It was sacrilege to think the ranch could be taken from them.

A shooting star plunged across the night sky, falling to its death in a brilliant display. Nat drew in a sharp breath at the flash of beauty. The dog stiffened beneath his palm, a low growl vibrating from its belly all the way to its teeth. Nat cocked his head, ears tuned in, attention focused. A low humming sound grew louder, like the buzz of a honeybee getting closer.

A car.

Heading this way.

"Quiet, Blue. Go lie down." He didn't want the

dog making a racket and waking his niece. Pulling the baby monitor from his pocket, he checked it against his ear to make sure it was still working, and turned back to the open door.

Could be nothing.

Could be Ryan driving home drunk even though he knew better. But Ryan didn't always show good judgment after a bad day. Didn't sound like Ryan's truck though. Nat flicked off the baby monitor.

Hidden Hollow Hideaway was remote and secluded, with mountains surrounding and enclosing the ranch on all four sides. Miles off the beaten track it was hard to find even in daylight. At night it was damn near impossible. People did not just pass by and they weren't expecting any paying guests for at least another week. Troy Strange was their only neighbor for miles and he was more likely to visit smallpox victims.

Trouble was coming—Nat smelled it, almost tasted it at the back of his throat.

Cursing, he grabbed his rifle and ammo off the gun-rack above the kitchen door and loaded it, chambering a round. He moved quickly outside to stand in the deep shadows besides the big Dutch barn. Cattle lowed behind him and a wolf's howl echoed through the hills to the east.

Prickles crept up Nat's spine. Were the repo men coming back for another shot at his horses? Despite all his attorney's fine words?

The car was cresting the rise a hundred yards from the main house. It sure as hell wasn't Ryan's truck. Nat's heart thumped hard against his ribcage and adrenaline banished tiredness. He hugged the side of the barn as headlights cut deep into shadow. The rig, a Jeep Cherokee, pulled into the yard in front of the main house, cut the lights, cut the engine.

Silence resonated around the granite peaks like a boom in his ears. Nat breathed in and out. He smelled the exhaust fumes tainting the pure mountain air, listened as silence combed the darkness, as if nothing existed except the colorless wasteland of night. Just time and universe, cold and rock.

Anticipation sharpened every sense as he waited, balanced on the balls of his feet. Nobody moved. Nobody crept out of the Jeep. Nobody sneaked into his stable to steal his prize-winning Arabian horses.

Nat's breathing leveled off, his heart rate slowed. He relaxed his stance and adjusted his grip. Waited.

The repo men had brought a truck this morning.

Nat waited another minute, then another. His eyes grew gritty with fatigue and he fought back a yawn. This wasn't the repo men. He didn't know who it was, but it wasn't them. Cold seeped into his hands from the frigid metal of the gun; his trigger finger was freezing up.

"Damn it all to hell."

He wasn't about to leave some stranger hanging around his property in the middle of the night.

Though it was pitch-black, Nat's eyesight was sharp and well-adjusted. He knew every inch of ground, every stone, fence, and broken-down piece of machinery on his land. Picking out shades of gray, he moved toward the car. Flicked off the rifle's safety and peered in through the frosted-up glass. It was like trying to see to the bottom of a riverbed in the middle of winter. He couldn't make out a damned thing.

With one finger, he lifted the handle of the driver's side door. It clicked open, but no interior light came on. Nat took a step back and peered inside, made out a bundled up figure in the back seat, curled up, unmoving.

Gripping his rifle he felt the tension crackle like static on a dry day. The fine hairs at his nape sprang up, tensile and erect.

"Drop the rifle, mister." The voice was softly feminine.

"Now why would I want to do that?" he asked.

She was silent. He could feel her apprehension; almost see her weighing her choices in the concealment of the Jeep.

His teeth locked together. "I don't think so, ma'am." He might have been raised to be polite to women, but he wasn't dumb. "Not 'til you tell me why you're sneaking onto my property in the middle of the night."

She shifted slightly. He heard the rustle as she pushed aside the blankets.

"What's your name?" she asked. There was a lilt, some sort of accent in her voice that sounded both warm and aggressive at the same time. It undid some of his irritation and sparked a glimmer of curiosity.

"Well, ma'am." Pitched low, Nat's voice was steely with courteousness. "A better question would be what the hell's yours?"

Read the start of Chapter One of Toni Anderson's Romantic Spy Thriller...

THE KILLING GAME
©Toni Anderson

It looked and felt like the dominion of Gods.

Special Air Service trooper Ty Dempsey had been catapulted from a rural English market town into the heart of a colossal mountain range full of pristine snow-capped peaks which glowed against a glassy blue sky. Many of the summits in the Hindu Kush were over five miles high. The utter peace and tranquility of this region was an illusion that hid death, danger and uncertainty beneath every elegant precipice. No place on earth was more treacherous or more beautiful than the high mountains.

He was an anomaly here.

Life was an anomaly here.

Thin sharp needles pierced his lungs every time he took a breath. But his prey was as hampered by the landscape as they were, and Ty Dempsey wasn't going to let a former Russian Special Forces operative-turned-terrorist get the better of an elite modern-day military force. Especially a man who'd shockingly betrayed not only his country, but humanity itself.

They needed to find him. They needed to stop the bastard from killing again.

The only noise in this arena was boots punching through the crust of frozen snow, and the harshness of puny human lungs struggling to draw oxygen out of the fragile atmosphere. The shriek of a golden eagle pierced the vastness overhead, warning the world that there were strangers here and to beware. Dempsey raised his sunglasses to peer back over his shoulder at the snaking trail he and his squad had laid down. Any fool could follow that trail, but only a real fool would track them across the Roof of the World to a place so remote not even war lingered.

But the world was full of fools.

As part of the British SAS's Sabre Squadron A's Mountain Troop, Dempsey was familiar with the terrain. He knew the perils of mountains and altitude, understood the raw omnipotent power of nature. This was what he trained for. This was his job. This was his life. He'd climbed Everest and K2, though the latter had nearly killed him. He understood that there were places on earth that were blisteringly hostile, that could obliterate you in a split second, but they held no malice, no evil. Unlike people...

He relaxed his grip on his carbine and adjusted the weight of his bergen. None of the men said a word as they climbed ever higher, one by one disappearing over the crest of the ridge and dropping down into the snowy wilderness beyond. With an icy breath Dempsey followed his men on the next impossible mission. Hunting a ghost.

***

The small plane taxied down the runway at Kurut in the Wakhan Corridor, a tiny panhandle of land in the far northeast of Afghanistan. Thankfully the runway was clear of snow—a miracle in itself.

Dr. Axelle Dehn stared out of the plane window and tried to relax her grip on the seat in front of her.

She'd been traveling for thirty hours straight, leveraging every contact she'd ever made to get flights and temporary visas for her and her graduate student. Something was going on with her leopards and she was determined to find out what.

Last fall, they'd attached satellite radio collars to ten highly-endangered snow leopards here in the Wakhan. This past week, in the space of a few days, they'd lost one signal completely, and another signal was now coming from a talus-riddled slope where no shelter existed. This latter signal was from a collar that had been attached to a leopard called Sheba, one of only two female snow leopards they'd caught. Just ten days ago, for the first time ever, they'd captured photos from one of their remote camera traps of the same leopard moving two newborn cubs. If Sheba had been killed, the cubs were out there, hungry and defenseless. Emotion tried to crowd her mind but she thrust it aside.

The cats might be fine.

The collar might have malfunctioned and dropped off before it was programmed to. Or maybe she hadn't fastened it tight enough when they'd trapped Sheba, and the leopard had somehow slipped it off.

But two collars in two days…?

The plane came to a stop and the pilot turned off the propellers. The glacier-fed river gushed silkily down the wide, flat valley. Goats grazed beside a couple of rough adobe houses where smoke drifted through the holes in the roof. Bactrian camels and small, sturdy horses were corralled nearby. A line of yaks packed with supplies waited patiently in a row. Yaks were the backbone of survival in this remote

324

valley, especially once you headed east beyond the so-called *road*. People used them for everything from milk, food, transportation and even fuel in this frigid treeless moonscape.

It was early spring—the fields were being tilled in preparation to plant barley in the short but vital growing season. A group of children ran toward the plane, the girls dressed in red dresses with pink headscarves, the boys wearing jewel-bright green and blue sweaters over dusty pants. Hospitality was legendary in this savagely poor region, but with the possibility of only a few hundred snow leopards left in Afghanistan's wilderness, Axelle didn't have time to squander.

Her assistant, a Dane called Josef Vidler, gathered his things beside her. She adjusted her hat and scarf to cover her hair. The type of Islam practiced here was moderate and respectful.

"Hello, Dr. Dehn," the children chimed as the pilot opened the door. A mix of different colored irises and features reflected the diverse genetic makeup of this ancient spit of land.

"*As-Salaam Alaikum.*" She gave them a tired smile. The children's faces were gaunt but wreathed in happiness. Malnourishment was common in the Wakhan, and after a brutal winter most families were only a goat short of starvation.

Despite the worry for her cats, it humbled her. These people, who struggled with survival every single day, were doing their best to live in harmony with the snow leopard. And a large part of this change in attitude toward one of the region's top predators was due to the work of the Conservation Trust. It was a privilege to work for them, a privilege she didn't intend to screw up. She dug into her day pack and pulled out two canisters of children's multi-vitamins she'd found in Frankfurt Airport. She rattled one of the canisters and they all jumped back in surprise. She pointed to Keeta, a teenage girl whose eyes were as blue as Josef's and whose English was excellent thanks to some recent schooling. "These are *not* candy so only eat one a day." She held up a single finger. Then handed them over and the children chorused a thank you before running back to their homes.

Anji Waheed, their local guide and wildlife ranger-in-training, rattled toward them in their sturdy Russian van.

"*As-Salaam Alaikum*, Mr. Josef, Doctor Axelle," Anji called out as he pulled up beside them. The relief in the Wakhi man's deep brown eyes reinforced the seriousness of the situation.

"*Wa-Alaikum Salaam.*" They could all do with a little peace. The men patted each other on the back, and they began hauling their belongings out of the plane and into the van.

Axelle took a deep breath. "Did you find any sign of the cubs?"

Anji shook his head. "No, but as soon as I heard you were on your way, I took some men up to base camp to set up the yurts, then came back to get you." Although only a few miles up the side valley, it was two bone-rattling hours of travel on a barely-there gravel road to their encampment. During winter, they did their tracking online from back home at Montana State University. In summer, they took a more hands-on approach.

"Thanks." Axelle stowed her frustration and smiled her gratitude. From their tracking data she had a good idea where Sheba might have denned up. Barring accidents or breakdowns they might get there before nightfall.

She was praying for a collar malfunction even though that would put their million-dollar project way behind schedule. The alternative meant the cubs and their mother were probably dead. Her instinct told her losing two cats in a couple of days wasn't coincidence, nor was it a local herder protecting livestock. A professional poacher was going after her animals for their fur and bones to feed China's ravenous appetite for traditional medicine. It was imperative to find out exactly what was going on, and with the continuing conflict in Afghanistan it wasn't going to be easy.

"Do the elders know anything about what might be happening?" she asked. Only twelve miles wide in places, the Wakhan Valley was a tiny finger of flat fertile ground separating some of the tallest mountains in the world—the magnificent and treacherous Hindu Kush to the south and the impenetrable Pamir Range to the north. Harsh winters trapped locals inside for seven months of the year. Wildlife was scarce and the region mercilessly inaccessible, but these people knew the land better than a visitor ever could.

"No." His eyes shot between her and Josef. "They are scared that if the snow leopards are dead, you will blame them and they will lose their clinic."

The Trust not only had an anti-poaching scheme, they also vaccinated local livestock once a year against common diseases, *gratis*. The program promoted healthier livestock and reduced the losses herders suffered to sickness, which in turn compensated for the occasional snow leopard kill. So far the scheme was working, except now they had two missing, possibly dead leopards and two tiny cubs unaccounted for.

The weight of responsibility sat like an elephant on her chest.

"Josef, run over and reassure them while Anji and I finish loading." She held his gaze when he looked like he'd argue. The village elders sometimes struggled to deal with a woman. She didn't mind because she loathed politics. "Be quick. We don't have time for tea—you'll have to make your excuses."

It wasn't how things were done here and she didn't want to offend these people, but the survival of a species trumped social niceties today. Ten more minutes and they were finished packing. Anji tied the spare gasoline canisters onto the roof and made sure both big gas tanks were full. They honked and Josef jogged over and jumped into the van.

"Everything be okay." Lines creased Anji's leathery skin. "*Inshallah.*"

God willing, indeed.

She and Josef exchanged a look as Anji gunned the engine over the rough road marked only by a line of pale stones. Dust flew, stirred up by the tires, the land still soft from the thaw. They bounced over rivers, ruts and alluvial fans. Axelle craned her neck to stare at the imposing mountains.

"If the collars *are* working"—Josef spoke from the backseat—"there could be some crackpot in these hills picking off critically endangered animals for money. Anyone that desperate isn't going to care if a couple of foreigners end up as collateral damage."

They'd left some weapons with their other belongings last fall. Her father had insisted she have some sort of protection when he'd heard she was conducting her research in Afghanistan. Now she was grateful.

She glanced at Josef sharply. "Do you want to go home?"

"I'm just saying this could be dangerous." His hands gripped the back of the seat as they bounced over a rickety bridge.

"If you want to go back you should say so now. The pilot can fly you out in the morning." She kept her voice soft. They were almost the same age but he was her responsibility and she had no right to place him in danger. "I don't want you thinking you don't have a choice. I can handle this." He had a life. He had a future. She only had her passion for saving things that needed saving.

"Ya, I run away and leave you alone in the wilderness." Josef sat back and crossed his arms, muttering angrily.

She held back an instinctive retort. She didn't care about being alone in the wilderness, but with this amount of ground to cover, she needed all the help she could get. "I have Anji," she said instead. "We can get more men from the village."

The Wakhi man grinned a gap-toothed smile, his eyes dancing. After generations of war and decades of being ignored by the government in Kabul, a few missing teeth were the least of anyone's problems. A few dead leopards might not rank high in the concerns of government either, not with the resurgence of the Taliban, not with the constant threat of assassination, insurgents and death.

"If we find sign of a poacher we will gather men from the village and hunt him down," the smaller man said.

Axelle nodded, but she was worried. This would be Anji's responsibility when he finished training and was appointed the wildlife officer for this region. He needed to be confident enough to take charge of dangerous situations like this. She bit her lip. He was such a sweet little guy she didn't know how he'd confront armed poachers. The idea of him hurt didn't sit well. He had a family. People who cared.

Isolation pressed down on her shoulders. All she had was an estranged father and a grandfather she hadn't visited in two long years.

Energetic clouds boiled over the top of the mountains. A spring storm was building, but it was nothing to the growing sense of unease that filled her when she thought of someone lining up her cats in the crosshairs of a hunting scope.

AUTHOR'S NOTE & ACKNOWLEDGMENTS

I wrote *Her Last Chance* (originally titled *Blade Hunter*) as a follow-up to *Her Sanctuary*, but it languished on a virtual shelf for years because the publisher went bust before it was released. In response to reader pressure I finally managed to find the time this summer to edit the manuscript and get it ready for publication. I hope you enjoy the conclusion to Marsh and Josie's story. I feel like I've come a long way as a writer since I started my publishing journey but I hope you enjoy these two related stories. I want to thank my editor, Ally Robertson, for doing such a wonderful job and helping me improve both manuscripts.

Thanks always to my critique partner, Kathy Altman, who is not just my sounding board—she's my sanity. And to Loreth Anne White for always being on-call for emergency tea breaks and brainstorming sessions.

The biggest shout-out of appreciation goes to my husband and children who put up with the day-to-day minutiae of me being a writer. And to readers who have made my dreams come true!

DEAR READER

Thank you for reading *Her Last Chance*. I hope you enjoyed it. If you did, please:

1. Help other people find this book by writing an online review. Thanks!

2. Sign up for my "Very Infrequent Newsletter" to hear about new releases and contests. The link is on my website: www.toniandersonauthor.com

3. Come "like" my Facebook Fan Page at: www.facebook.com/pages/Toni-Anderson-Author-Page.

ABOUT THE AUTHOR

Toni Anderson is a *New York Times* & *USA Today* best-selling author of Romantic Suspense. A former marine biologist, Anderson traveled the world with her work. After living in six different countries, she finally settled in the Canadian prairies with her husband and two children. Combining her love of travel with her love of romantic suspense, Anderson writes stories based in some of the places she has been fortunate enough to visit.

Toni donates 15% of her royalties from *Edge of Survival* to diabetes research—to find out why, read the book!

She is the author of several novels including *Dark Waters*, *The Killing Game*, and *A Cold Dark Place*. Her novels have been nominated for the prestigious Romance Writers of America® RITA® Award, Daphne du Maurier Awards, and National Readers' Choice Awards in Romantic Suspense.

Find out more on her website and sign up for her newsletter to keep up-to-date with releases.

www.toniandersonauthor.com

REVIEWS
A COLD DARK PLACE
(Cold Justice Book #1)

"Toni magically blends sizzling chemistry between Alex and Mallory with lots of suspenseful action in *A Cold Dark Place*. At times I wanted to hide my eyes, not knowing if I could face what might or might not happen! The edge of your seat suspense is riveting!" —Harlequin Junkies.

"Recommended for fans of Toni Anderson and fans of dark romantic suspense. You'd definitely love this one!" —Maldivian Book Reviewer's Realm of Romance.

THE KILLING GAME
(2014 RITA® Finalist and National Readers' Choice Award finalist in Romantic Suspense)

"I'd recommend this to any romantic suspense reader looking for a unique, intricately woven story that will really touch you." —Peaces of Me (5 Stars)

"Realistic scene descriptions, endangered species, and plenty of spies made this a sure fire hit in my reading collection." —SnS Reviews (5 Stars)

DARK WATERS
(International bestseller and 2014 National Readers' Choice Award finalist in Romantic Suspense)

"In this action-packed contemporary, Anderson (*Dangerous Waters*) weaves together a tapestry of

powerful suspense and sizzling romance." —
Publishers Weekly.

"The pacing in this book is superb. The tension really never lets up ... I never felt there was a good 'stopping point' in this book, which is probably why I was reading all night." —Smart Bitches, Trashy Books.

DANGEROUS WATERS
(International bestseller and 2013 Daphne du Maurier finalist)

"With a haunting setting and a captivating cast of characters, Anderson has crafted a multifaceted mystery rife with secrets. Readers will have to focus, as red herrings abound, but the result is a compulsively engrossing page-turner." —*Romantic Times* (4 Stars)

"A captivating mix of suspense and romance, *Dangerous Waters* will pull you under." —Laura Griffin, *New York Times* and *USA Today* best-selling author

"With vibrant writing, a cast of damaged, captivating characters and a plot that's deliciously diabolical, *Dangerous Waters* will have you mesmerized from page one." —HEA USA Today

EDGE OF SURVIVAL

"... more substance than one would expect from a romantic thriller." —*Library Journal Reviews*

"*Edge of Survival* is without a doubt, one of the most exciting, romantic, sexy stories I've had the pleasure of reading this year and I will definitely be looking for more by Toni Anderson." —Blithely Bookish (5 Stars)

"Sensual, different; romance with a bit of angst, just how I like them; *Edge of Survival* is a romantic suspense not to be missed." —Maldivian Book Reviewer's Realm of Romance (5 Stars)

"Whoever thinks a story concerning a woman who does fish research would be boring hasn't read *Edge of Survival*!" —Book Lovers Inc. (5 Bookies)

STORM WARNING
(Best Book of 2010 Nominee —The Romance Reviews)

"*Storm Warning* is an intense, provocative paranormal romance with a suspenseful twist...This is a book that I am unquestionably adding to my keeper collection." —Night Owl Reviews (TOP PICK)

"It is exactly the way I like my romantic suspense novels to be." —The Romance Reviews

"The plot is full of suspense and some pretty incredible plot twists. ... will have you on the edge of your seat." —Coffee Time Romance & More

SEA OF SUSPICION
(Best Book of 2010 Nominee —The Romance Reviews)

"Deeply atmospheric and filled with twists and turns, *Sea of Suspicion* kept me flying eagerly through the pages." —All About Romance

"Set along the coast of Scotland, *Sea of Suspicion* is a riveting story of suspense and the depths and heights of human character." —The Romance Reviews

HER SANCTUARY
(National bestseller)

"*Her Sanctuary* is a riveting fast-paced suspense story, filled with twists, turns, and danger. As the story flows seamlessly between the protagonists and antagonists, the tension rises to fever pitch. Just when you think you know the good guys from the bad, Anderson provides a surprising twist, or two." —Night Owl Romance (TOP PICK)

"Suspenseful, riveting and explosive, this reader absolutely loved this story." —Fallen Angel Reviews (5 Angels)

"Ms. Anderson presents us with one fantastic story that has me wanting more." —Romance Junkies (4.5 Blue Ribbons)

"For a fast paced, enjoyable read filled with secrets and surprises, *Her Sanctuary* will fill all your expectations." —Romance Reviews Today

Made in the USA
Coppell, TX
07 July 2020